I0677920

The Quest for Inez

Other books by Kitty Burns Florey

Nonfiction
Script and Scribble: The Rise and Fall of Handwriting
Sister Bernadette's Barking Dog: The Quirky History and Lost Art of Diagramming Sentences

Fiction
The Writing Master
The Sleep Specialist
Solos
Souvenir of Cold Springs
Five Questions
Vigil for a Stranger
Duet
Real Life
The Garden Path
Chez Cordelia
Family Matters

The Quest for Inez

Two Ways to Find a Grandmother

Kitty Burns Florey

Genealogy House
Amherst, Massachusetts

The Quest for Inez: Two Ways to Find a Grandmother

Copyright 2015 by Kitty Burns Florey

Genealogy House, a division of White River Press
PO Box 3561
Amherst, Massachusetts 01004
Genealogyhouse.net

ISBN: 978-1-887043-15-1

The disclaimer attached to works of fiction usually reads something like: "This is a work of fiction. The characters and events are solely the products of the author's imagination."

This book consists of both fiction and nonfiction sections. The fictional parts describe events lived by characters who actually existed, but they have been modified and enhanced according to my own conception of what kinds of people they might have been and what might have happened to them.

In fairness to the originals, I add this disclaimer: The characters and events portrayed in this book are sometimes—but not always—the products of the author's imagination.

All photographs are from the author's collection.

Library of Congress Cataloging-in-Publication Data:

Florey, Kitty Burns.
The Quest for Inez / Kitty Burns Florey.
    pages cm
ISBN 970-1-007013-15-1 (pbk. : alk. paper)
1. Families--Fiction. I. Title.
PS3556.L588Q47 2015
813'.54--dc23
                            2014041604

FOR KATHERINE,
AND IN MEMORY OF MY MOTHER

AUTHOR'S NOTE

Truth is stranger than fiction,
but it is because Fiction is obliged
to stick to possibilities; Truth isn't.
~Mark Twain, *Following the Equator*

This is a book of family history unlike any other—at least, unlike any other that I've come across.

It begins as a straightforward account of the search for my mother's lost mother—my grandmother, Inez Willick—in which I organized the facts as I found them. Over the course of a year or so, I went from almost nothing to an abundance, complete with shocks and surprises that included a lost cousin, a box of old photographs, and encounters with forebears both famous and infamous. This was very satisfying. It was also very frustrating.

In the course of my explorations, I found such a vast cavern of wonders that I naively assumed everything I wanted—the whole story—was there to be found if I just kept digging. So dig I did, until my shovel became bent and rusty. I sent increasingly desperate queries to a succession of kind and helpful librarians. I fired up search engines in endless courthouses and bureaus of vital statistics. I combed through records of mind-bending obscurity (the dinner menu of a long-gone Toledo hotel is just one example). I talked on the phone to possible relatives who either knew nothing or weren't telling.

Eventually, as genealogical research often does, mine came up against the proverbial brick wall. No matter how much battering and knocking I did, the wall remained intact.

Some of the crucial facts of my grandmother's life—and therefore of my mother's, and of mine—refused to be found.

Throughout this process I did plenty of speculating, as I'm sure we all do. We look up from the database where we've been burrowing and think up a scenario, then try to make the facts fit. Sometimes this helps; it can inspire us to burrow in new places. More often it's an exercise in futility (entertaining or exasperating) that comes down to a reluctant conclusion, the words that every family historian dreads: *We'll never know.*

But I've been a fiction writer all my life, so I went one step further. Alongside the "real" story, I constructed an alternate universe, starring Inez Willick's alter ego, Agnes Miller. Like Inez, Agnes comes from a tiny Ohio town; her out-of-wedlock child is born at a foundling hospital in Syracuse, New York; she works as a waitress; she has curly brown hair and worries about getting fat; she has a scandalous wedding that is even more scandalously dissolved. I made Agnes's story as factual as I could, but when a "true fact" was missing, I concocted a "fact" of my own.

The definition of fiction as "a lie that tells the truth" has been attributed to various writers, from La Fontaine to E.M. Forster. The fact-based fiction I've created here may or may not be *the* truth. But it is *a* truth. It makes sense to me. It explains my grandmother, and it makes her real. And isn't that the goal of genealogy?

I know the ghost of Inez is here somewhere, hovering around my laptop in her big hat and her excruciating corsets. I hope she approves of not only her own story but also the story of Agnes. Only she could know if, and where, the two intersect.

CONTENTS

ILLUSTRATIONS

FAMILY OF INEZ WILLICK

Jacob Kiel Willick—Inez's father

Margaret (Maggie) Strawbridge Willick—Inez's mother

Lucinda Frick Willick—her paternal grandmother

Lewis Willick—Jacob's brother, Inez's uncle

Doris Willick—Inez's first daughter

Geraldine (Jerry) Goodson Burns—Inez's second daughter, adopted by Cora and Horace Goodson

Maud, Mabel, Mary Fay, Ralph Willick—Inez's siblings who lived to adulthood

Charlie, Raleigh, Hester, Lucy—Inez's siblings who died in childhood

Emery Balliet—Inez's half-brother, Maggie's son

Willick Family Tree

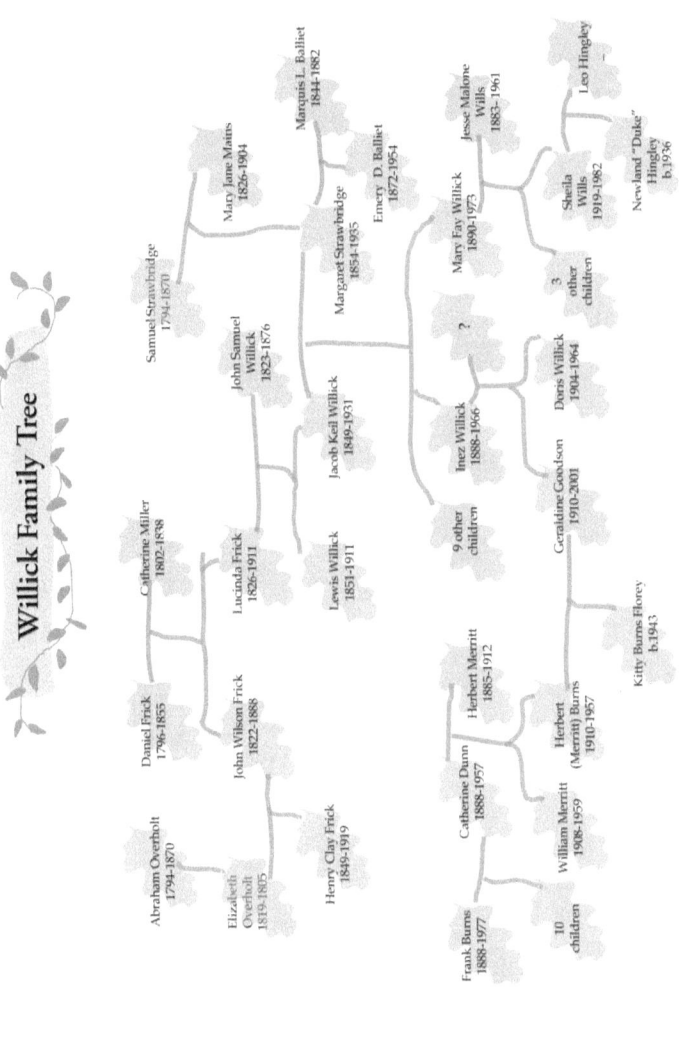

Samuel Strawbridge
1794-1870

Mary Jane Mairs
1826-1904

Marquis L. Balliet
1844-1882

Emery D. Balliet
1872-1954

Margaret Strawbridge
1854-1935

John Samuel Willick
1823-1876

Jacob Keil Willick
1849-1931

Lewis Willick
1851-1911

Catherine Miller
1802-1858

Lucinda Frick
1826-1911

Daniel Frick
1794-1855

John Wilson Frick
1822-1888

Henry Clay Frick
1849-1919

Abraham Overholt
1784-1870

Elizabeth Overholt
1819-1905

Mary Fay Willick
1890-1973

Jesse Malone Wills
1883-1961

Sheila Wills
1919-1982

Leo Hingley

Newland "Duke" Hingley
b.1936

3 other children

Inez Willick
1888-1966

?

Doris Willick
1904-1964

9 other children

Geraldine Goodson
1910-2001

Kitty Burns Florey
b.1943

Herbert Merritt
1885-1912

Herbert (Merritt) Burns
1910-1957

Catherine Dunn
1888-1957

William Merritt
1908-1959

Frank Burns
1888-1977

10 children

CAST OF FICTIONAL CHARACTERS

Agnes Miller
Gilbert Miller and Bessie Trowbridge Miller—Agnes's parents
Sally—her younger sister
Robert and Sam—Agnes's younger brothers
Helen—Agnes's older sister, mother of twins, and married to Roger
Hazel—Helen's twin, married and living in California
Uncle Clement Miller—Gilbert's brother
Grandma Lu (Lucinda) Miller—Gilbert's mother
Doris (Doritt) Miller—Agnes's first daughter
Anna—her second daughter
Emery Trowbridge—Agnes's half-brother, Bessie's son

Jesse Zorn—Agnes's beau
Rudy Killian—her other beau
Olive Webster—Agnes's friend
Clarence Webster—Olive's husband
Sister Josephine—head of St. Mary's Foundling Hospital
Sister Marie-Angèle and Sister Elberta—nuns at the hospital
Mr. Carmody—the dining room manager and maître d' at the Yates Hotel
Mr. Dumont—an actor, Mr. Carmody's friend
Frances and Stanley Clury—Mr. Dumont's sister and her husband
Michael Devlin—Agnes's husband, briefly
Tim Devlin—Michael's father

Miller Family Tree

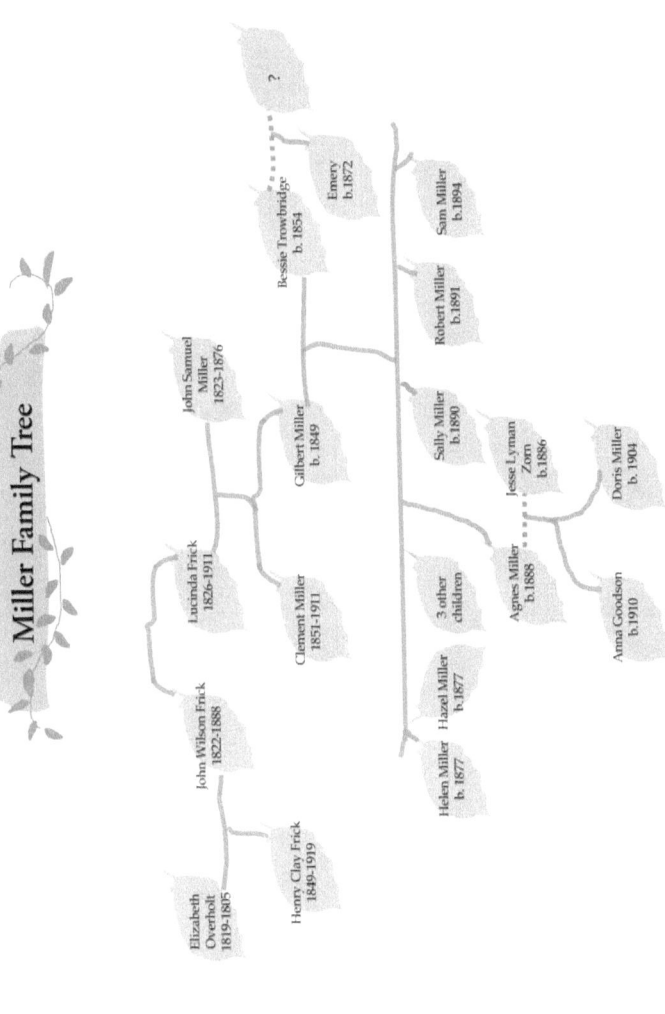

Elizabeth Overholt 1819-1805

John Wilson Frick 1822-1888

Henry Clay Frick 1849-1919

Lucinda Frick 1826-1911

John Samuel Miller 1823-1876

Bessie Trowbridge b. 1854

?

Emery b.1872

Clement Miller 1851-1911

Gilbert Miller b. 1849

Helen Miller b. 1877

Hazel Miller b.1877

3 other children

Agnes Miller b.1888

Jesse Lyman Zorn b.1886

Sally Miller b.1890

Robert Miller b.1891

Sam Miller b.1894

Anna Goodson b.1910

Doris Miller b.1904

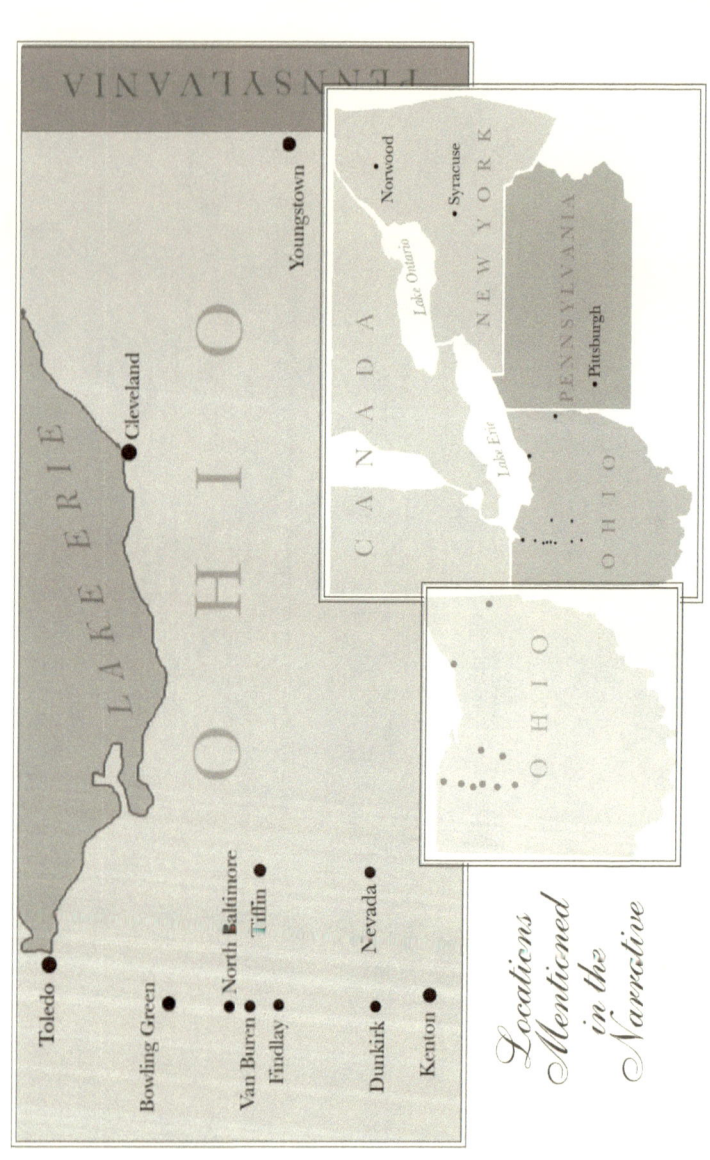

Locations
Mentioned
in the
Narrative

PROLOGUE

A WOMAN WEARING GLASSES

On a spring day in Syracuse, New York, in 1928, my mother, Geraldine Goodson, age eighteen, was working at a department store, selling hats. She glanced up to the mezzanine and saw her mother and another woman watching her. She waved. They waved back.

Not long after that, her grandmother, the famously no-nonsense Nana Woodruff, took Geraldine aside and told her it was high time she knew the truth: that Geraldine had been adopted as an infant, that she had been illegitimate, that Cora and Horace Goodson were not her parents, and that her real mother was Inez Willick, who lived in Toledo, Ohio.

"Remember that woman you saw up on the mezzanine with Mom? That was her. That was Inez Willick."

When my mother told me this story forty-odd years later, she said, not without bitterness, "I hardly looked at her. All I noticed was that she wore glasses."

One vague sighting, and then—like a rare bird glimpsed in a forest far outside its natural habitat—Inez Willick vanished back into the mists of Toledo.

PART I

SOME CHARACTERS

*The complexity of things—the things within
things—just seems to be endless…. Nothing is easy,
nothing is simple.*
~Alice Munro

INEZ

My mother never stopped being ashamed of having been born out of wedlock, never stopped wondering why her mother had given her up. It wasn't until she was well into her sixties that she told me—reluctantly, her voice shaking—about her "illegitimacy," her adoption, and the mysterious woman on the mezzanine.

It took a lot to make my stoical mother show such strong emotion. Her pain was eye-opening: this was something she had struggled with all her life, but she'd buried it deep, as if she were the one who had done something shameful, unforgivable.

I don't recall why she told me then, but I do remember very well that what distressed my mother fascinated me. I immediately seized on this stunning bit of family history, the revelation that, suddenly, I wasn't actually related to hordes of aunts, uncles, and cousins. Certain things suddenly made sense, like my mother's 5'3" daintiness amid a family of tall men and strapping women, and my lack of a feeling of kinship with most of my cousins, which I no longer had to attribute to my own weirdness. Here was a plausible out.

My first thought—or second, maybe—was that we had to investigate. My Nancy Drew instincts kicked in: *The Secret of the Missing Grandmother*. It was the mid-'70s. Inez Willick was probably born around 1890. I was determined to find the trail of this elusive, nearsighted Ohio granny. Everyone leaves traces. People can't just disappear. She might even still be alive.

As I knew she would, Mom cheered up at the idea of a search—*a quest*, I called it, which made her smile. We began brainstorming about how to track her down. This was in the innocent, helpless pre-Google era, when nobody knew how to find anything. A nearsighted woman named Inez Willick with some connection to Toledo, Ohio, had produced baby Geraldine in Syracuse in 1910. Nana Woodruff had also revealed that my mother was born at St. Mary's, the foundling hospital there. That was absolutely all we knew.

I've tried to put together a timeline of when I learned what. I have racked my memory, pawed through years of haphazard notes in my INEZ INFO folder, even skimmed decades of handwritten diaries[1] for references to the quest. Too many years have passed, though, and my memory is unreliable. But I do recall that, like any good quest, mine began with a journey—not a spectacular one, just a long drive from New Haven, where I lived then, to the seat of Wood County, where Toledo was located: Bowling Green, Ohio, where I hoped to excavate some relatives at the court house.

Floods, fires, and mice had combined forces to eradicate many of the records I sought, but I managed to locate the Willick family in the 1900 census, living on South Second Street in the tiny town of North Baltimore in north-central Ohio. Inez was twelve. I also discovered that her father, Jacob, had served three terms (1889–1896) as the town clerk, that her mother was Margaret

---

[1] In a large storage bin in the back of my closet are notebooks covering most of my life until 1996, when I began keeping the diary in a Word document, which now approaches a million words. Tallulah Bankhead once said (supposedly), "Only good girls keep diaries, bad girls don't have the time." Sometimes I'm good and sometimes I'm bad, but I'm a committed diarist, and I find the time.

Strawbridge, and that Jacob's widowed mother, Lucinda, lived with the family.

Here was the first proof of my grandmother's existence outside Nana Woodruff's head. It gave her a family, a town—a context. It was thrilling.

North Baltimore is less than twenty miles south of Bowling Green. I should have taken the time to drive down there and poke around. But I had a five-year-old, a husband, and a pride of cats waiting for me at home, and so I didn't.

I did, however, find a local genealogist, and Mom and I hired her to do research. She located the earlier and later censuses that I hadn't been able to dig out and finally provided us with a list of, among other things, Inez's siblings. We learned that her brother Charlie had drowned at the age of ten; two other Willick children (Hester and Raleigh) had died of diphtheria; and a last child, Doris, had been born in 1904, when Margaret Strawbridge was in her early fifties—improbable but not impossible, especially in those fecund days when large families were the norm, birth control was not a given, and a woman's work was never done.

But it turned out that Doris was, in fact, not Maggie's daughter at all. Doris was my grandmother's first child.

Inez L. Willick[2] was born in 1888, to Jacob Willick and Margaret Strawbridge. Inez's sisters were named Mabel, Maud, Mary, Hester, and Lucy. The name *Inez* sticks out like a flamenco dancer at a hoedown.[3]

---

[2] I'm guessing the L. was for Lucinda, her grandmother's name; the first Lucy died in infancy before Inez's birth.

[3] In the 1880s, Inez—the Spanish form of Agnes—was a surprisingly popular name for baby girls, not far behind Maria and Evelyn and well ahead of Louisa and Sophie.

The earliest thing I know about her is that in 1904, when she was sixteen, Inez gave birth to her first out-of-wedlock child, a girl with the prosaic handle Doris.

I didn't find out the truth about Doris until, in 2012, I received an email from Margaret Dube, a genealogist in Kittery, Maine, who had become intrigued by a blog post I'd written about Inez.[4] Margaret had done some specialized digging and discovered Doris's marriage record (1928) and her obituary (1964), both of which listed Inez Willick as her mother.

Suddenly I knew something about Inez that went beyond cold facts: she was the kind of girl who could get "in trouble," once as a teenager and again six years later when she was twenty-one.

But what kind of girl was that?

Inez lived much of her adult life in Toledo; when she died she was living in Springfield, a couple of hours south. But she was born and grew up in North Baltimore, Ohio, where her family had close ties and where both her parents died.

Jacob Kiel Willick, Inez's father, came from Pennsylvania. He fought for three years in the Indian Wars in Colorado. By the time he returned home in 1870, his parents had moved from a small town near Pittsburgh to the newly incorporated town of Van Buren, Ohio, 250 miles west, perhaps because they had family there: Jacob's Uncle Daniel Frick, Lucinda's younger brother, had been elected Van Buren's first mayor. When Jacob finished his army stint in Colorado, he moved there too and lived with his parents.

---

[4] For less than a year, needing to be writing something—anything—I wrote a blog; eventually, this history began to grow out of it and I abandoned blog for book.

In 1876, when he was twenty-seven, Jacob married Margaret (always called Maggie) Strawbridge, who was born on the Fourth of July in 1854. She had a *Mayflower* ancestor—Abraham Pierson, one of the founders of both South Hampton, on Long Island, and Branford, Connecticut; his son, Abraham Pierson Jr., was one of the founders of Yale College.

I've traced the family back to a man named Edward Church, born in 1490 in the county of Essex, England. His daughter Elizabeth married a Pearson, a Pearson married a Miller,[5] a Miller married a Strawbridge, and a Strawbridge married a Willick: my grandmother's maternal lineage in a nutshell. The line is so long and complicated (and, unlike other parts of my family, so minutely documented) that I lost interest after a while. Does it really matter that Inez's who-knows-how-many-greats-grandfather graduated from Trinity College, Cambridge, in 1629 and ended up a Congregational minister in Boston? That another far-off ancestor founded Newark (originally New Ark), New Jersey? Or that the Strawbridges and George Washington share a common descent from Robert de Washington, born in England in 1230?[6]

What I like best are the odd bits. The tombstone of Maggie's great-great-great-grandmother, Jane Miller Strawbridge (1715-99), reads: *Life so short, eternity so long.* Maggie's father, Samuel, was wounded in the Civil

---

[5] Maggie's maternal six-greats-grandfather, John ("the Dutchman") Miller—he's always referred to that way, though I can't find out why—married Mary Pierson, first cousin of the first Abraham, and emigrated from Ireland in 1634.

[6] It's estimated that there are 40,000 Washington descendants in this country, including General George S. Patton and the late actor Lee Marvin. There's even a National Society of Washington Family Descendants. I do not plan to seek membership, and I doubt they admit relatives from the wrong side of the coverlet.

War; his brother, her uncle Emanuel, died in January 1863, from wounds suffered in the battle at Murfreesboro, Tennessee. She had a cousin with the amazing name Wilberforce Lavender Strawbridge.[7] And there's a statue of Abraham Pierson on the Yale campus: I probably walked past it dozens of times when I lived in New Haven, unaware that he's my great-great-great-great-great-great-something-or-other.

After their marriage, Jacob and Maggie Willick settled in North Baltimore, five miles north of Van Buren and thirty miles north of Dunkirk, Maggie's hometown.

North Baltimore was part of Henry Township, whose first settler, Henry Shaw, named the township after himself—giving it his first name, as if it were a son instead of a swamp: the Great Black Swamp, in fact. Despite its muddy, mosquito-ridden intractability, the place drew settlers—once they got over the idea that, as one contemporary historian put it, "there was nothing there which the Caucasian might covet." But after the swamp was drained, what it had was good, fertile soil.

The Ottawa Indians had lived on the fringes of the swamp for a hundred years, after having been pushed out of their ancestral grounds further north. They had learned to live with the mosquitoes (long sleeves, insect repellent made of goldenseal and bear fat, and the judicious use of smoke). They tried to get along with the new settlers (the Ottawa were traders, not fighters), but in time—this is a story that scarcely needs telling again—they became an inconvenience: their settlement turned out to be in the way of a proposed canal, and they were evicted, sent off to Kansas.

---

[7] The family name was also spelled Trowbridge.

Purged of swamp and Indians, North Baltimore thrived, a tiny dot on the map. The place was originally known as Peter's Crossroads after the general store that opened on Main Street. In 1873, the Baltimore & Ohio Railroad chugged through the town for the first time, giving it a proper name and a few decades of prosperity. When Jacob and Maggie arrived, the population was about 600; in fifteen years it had grown to 2,857,[8] a number that included an alarming number of Willicks, all under one roof in a house on South Second Street: Jacob and Maggie, the six remaining kids (out of a total of eleven), Grandma Lucinda, and, for a while, Jacob's younger brother, Lewis, who never married, didn't work much, and seems to have spent his life shuttling between Van Buren and North Baltimore.

Jacob's maternal great-grandfather, Johann Nicholas Frick, had sailed from Rotterdam to Philadelphia, where he arrived in 1767. He had relatives in nearby Germantown, so he headed there and stayed for a few years. Then, sometime in the 1770s (inspired, so the story goes, by tales told by Revolutionary soldiers stationed in the area), he made his way across the Appalachians to Westmoreland County in western Pennsylvania. There he farmed until the family pushed even further west, to Ohio. Until Inez's generation, few Willicks ventured beyond a small network of towns in the Ohio River Valley. (See map, p. xviii.)

I know almost nothing about Inez's childhood in North Baltimore. I reread *Winesburg, Ohio*, by Sherwood Anderson, which is set in a town based on Tiffin,

---

[8] The population today is about 3500. Amtrak doesn't stop there; the closest station is Toledo, forty miles north.

thirty miles east of North Baltimore. I'd forgotten that, in Winesburg, nearly every character is neurotic and haunted, but it was reassuring that there was so much illicit sex going on; maybe Inez with her two out-of-wedlock pregnancies wasn't such an anomaly. And I did learn a few things about small-town Ohio life in the early twentieth century: only the main street was paved—elsewhere, the mud could be knee-deep; most people kept a cow or a pig in a shed; a newspaper reporter made six dollars a week; and if you could afford a hired girl you definitely didn't encourage her to eat with the family.

Inez must have gone to the local schools—North Baltimore High was only three blocks from the Willicks' house. I called the school, but no records exist from before 1926, when the original building burned down, taking with it Inez's grades, possibly a photograph of her as a teenager, maybe even a notation that she left school because she was pregnant. She would have been a sophomore when Doris was conceived, and a junior if she'd gone back after the birth. It's very likely that she didn't.

My mother's own life was shattered when, in 1926, as soon as she turned sixteen, she was forced by her parents to quit school and get a job, to help keep the wolf from the family door. The practice wasn't uncommon. Even twenty years earlier, the census records tell a story again and again of education vs. expedience, as they show row after handwritten row of people who made it through seventh grade or maybe some high school before they became bricklayers or tram drivers or full-time mothers.

My mother—Geraldine Goodson—had no further education, but she was smart. She was a promising Latin student when, over the protests of the nuns, she was made to leave St. John's. She had a thirst for learning that never left her, but that she never really cultivated. She never acquired the tools you need to take an interest or a knack and run with it, and she was deeply insecure about venturing even a toe into intellectual waters: If I described one of my college literature courses, her response might be, "Now is that class in the morning or the afternoon?" She was happy to provide me with books, but the only books she and my father owned were the ubiquitous *Readers Digest* condensed series.[9] I don't think it ever occurred to Mom to get a GED—if she did, she'd have had to admit she was not a high school graduate, another source of shame. Later in her life, Mom gravitated toward Elder-hostel classes in European History or Wildflower Identification and, once, a writing class where she produced a witty disquisition on the many definitions of the word *up*. I recall a modest attempt to teach herself French.

In her own way, she kept her brain busy. She followed politics closely and was a "senior intern" for Senator Lowell Weicker in Connecticut, twice going to Washington for conferences on elders' issues. She was reelected over and over as secretary of her senior center in New Haven; probably no one else wanted this job, but Mom loved it. I have notebooks full of her beautifully handwritten, lucid, and grammatical minutes of their meetings:

> We welcomed Officer Tomasso, a female police officer who walks her beat in Westville. She advised us to beware of con artists who try to sell residents a roofing job, house painting, driveway repairs,

---

[9] They were paradise for adolescents. Herman Wouk! Edna Ferber! Daphne du Maurier! A.J. Cronin! Irving Stone! Rumer Godden! James Gould Cozzens! Just typing their names makes me want to be twelve years old and curled up on the sofa, reading until I can hardly see straight.

> etc., when they are usually not needed.
> We were advised to call 911 if there is
> the slightest suspicion of something that
> doesn't sound quite right.

That sounds just like her, especially "usually," "slightest," and "quite."

Mom didn't get her small thirst for knowledge from her adoptive home. Maybe it came from her mother. It was unlikely that Inez had returned to her education after Doris's birth, but I'd rather imagine that she had. I can picture her going off to high school every morning with a happy heart, Latin noun declensions running through her head, her homework neatly done, and the book she was reading awaiting her in the bedroom she no doubt shared with a sister or two. I see her as a figure out of the Betsy-Tacy books, or an earnest booklover like Anne of Green Gables, with the idea of perhaps becoming a schoolteacher or a writer.

But, of course, neither Betsy nor Tacy nor Anne got knocked up at the age of fifteen.

WEIRD

I also can't help wondering if I am anything like Inez, if Inez went through her childhood feeling, as I did, weird—meaning out of place, unconnected, differently oriented than the rest of her family and most of her friends.

The sources of my own weirdness were various. If nothing else, I was an only child. I always had my own room, never had to compete for the last cupcake, never cried because a brother made a mean face at me or a sister borrowed my favorite skirt. This was wildly unusual in the world in which I lived, where the "onlies" were considered bratty, spoiled, and vaguely pathetic. Each of my two best friends had two siblings; every cousin was one of many; there were four Nelson kids next door, three DeStefanos on the other side. My best friend in third grade was Ann Riemer, an only child like me, but that was her only weirdness. I had others.

My father suffered from rheumatic heart disease. He was an invalid, expected to die at any time, a threat that shadowed my childhood. By the time I was seven, he became unable to work, and my mother found a job on the assembly line at General Electric. Nobody else I knew had a working mother. Nobody else's father coughed, coughed, coughed into the night, fell asleep soaked with sweat, woke at dawn with a raging headache to light a Camel,[10] drink three cups of coffee, and cough some more, sitting at the kitchen table

---

[10] Who knew in the '50s that the stress on a rheumatic heart was made worse by smoking? If anyone did, they didn't tell Dad.

or lying in bed with a cool washcloth folded across his forehead. My father's painful hacking—the famous "heart cough"—permeated my childhood like the sound of the radio or the purring of Smokey, our cat.

My father's illness had flowered from a childhood episode of rheumatic fever. The disease was a mystery to me that no one elucidated; I was told, vaguely, that "Daddy has an enlarged heart."[11] It didn't sound so bad. "Guess I'm just a big-hearted guy," he said to me, and I was expected to laugh.

Then he did die, when I was thirteen. Nothing was odder than that, more disorienting in a fathered world, more embarrassing.

I found a poem among my mother's stockpile of junk, written by me in third grade, which was when I found out about my father's prognosis:

My father and me, 1948

Little children often cry
For not 1 single reason.
Some cry every day and week
And some cry every season.

Was it my own bawling, I wonder, that inspired me?

Dad was rushed to hospital two or three times a year. I bunked with relatives while my mother hovered at his bedside, sponging his forehead and praying he

---

[11] Rheumatic fever, which begins with a streptococcal infection, is actually the inflammation of the heart, which damages the valves so that they have trouble pumping blood through the body. The heart has to work harder, which weakens it further.

wouldn't die. Sometimes I'd be taken in by my Burns grandparents, who ignored me, but whose vast attic was full of books: I found a volume of Poe, and read over and over again "The Pit and the Pendulum," "The Masque of the Red Death," and, most horrible of all, "The Tell-Tale Heart."[12]

Other times I was sent to Aunt Shirley and Uncle Jack's. Aunt Shirley was nice to me—people tended to be nice to me because I was the girl with the father who was going to die. She used to make peanut butter and mayonnaise sandwiches for my lunch box, which sound unappealing but were actually pretty good. Uncle Jack liked to make me laugh, and I laughed easily because he was funny and because I needed to. Once, I used my allowance to buy cheap gifts for my three cousins: a celluloid doll, a miniature wooden puzzle, I forget what else. They barely looked at them. I went to bed early and cried, quietly, into the alien pillow. (*Little children often cry....*)

During Dad's last hospital stay, in frigid mid-January, I was parked not with a relative but with my friend Patty Lynch, up the street. When I got up on Sunday morning, Mrs. Lynch said, "Your uncle Frank is coming to pick you up." Great! I had a huge crush on my father's youngest brother, who was dashingly handsome, not long out of college, still "finding himself." We drove in his car up to my grandparents' house. "Why aren't I

---

[12] The word "heart" distressed me throughout those years. When I was in fourth grade, my father made a "Valentine box" for me to take to school, in which my classmates could deposit Valentines for their friends, which were then distributed—your position on the social scale was countable, blatant, and public. This cruel ritual was perpetuated every year in my elementary school. Dad's Valentine box was a work of art, covered with overlapping hearts he and I had cut out of red construction paper and trimmed with gold paper lace cut from doilies—a big hit that enhanced my own popularity. But at some level all those hearts freaked me out.

just going home?" I asked him. He gave some shrugging reply. Then there was silence. I struggled to make clever conversation. Usually too shy to talk to anyone but my parents and my best friends, I blurted out a question like a character in a book—maybe that troublesome Mary Lennox in *The Secret Garden*—rather than the dreary lump that I usually was in the presence of people like uncles: "Do you have any money in the bank?" Surprised, he said he did, and I asked him, daringly, how much.

"About a hundred dollars." he told me.

My jaw dropped. What riches! For the rest of the ride he explained to me exactly why and how a hundred dollars was not riches, was barely a bank account at all, was a sign that he needed to find a new job and do something more practical with his life (he was some kind of salesman). I found this conversation deeply engrossing: I remember I thought how grown-up and sophisticated it was, how Frankie was treating me as an equal, how well I was holding up my end.

When I bounded out of the car at my grandparents' house, I was greeted by a weeping mother, weeping grandmother, various weeping aunts. "What? What? What?"

My mother asked my uncle, "Didn't you tell her?" He just shook his head. Wait—was he crying too?

"What? What? What?"

"Daddy's dead."

My father's wake was held at Fergerson's Funeral Home, an imposing stone house on Main Street that I had always admired. Now it was the scene of anguish. My eighth-grade teacher, Sister Robert, and a contingent of my classmates attended: my three or four closest friends plus another half-dozen whose names had been chosen by lot. (This seems almost the weirdest part: was everyone in my class clamoring to go, or—more likely—did no one volunteer, hence the lottery and the draft?) I walked up to the casket, took one look at my stone-dead father in his lip rouge and over-rosied cheeks, and began to scream. Even now, I shrink back in horror from the memory.

For more than a week, I refused to go back to school. Finally, my red-eyed mother gave me some kind of ulti-matum, and I went. None of my friends mentioned the scene at the wake. Various nuns would come up to me and say, pityingly, "Ah—you're the girl who lost her father, aren't you?"

At night I could hear my mother crying in her bedroom. I put my head under the pillow. Nobody talked about anything. The only grief counseling I had was one of my "nun aunts" (I had three of them) telling me that God wanted my father, and so he took him. "Why did he want him?" I asked. "We have no way of knowing," my aunt said, stroking my hand. "But God is good. Always remember that." I just nodded, didn't say anything, so that she would go away, and she did, but all I could think was that my mother and I wanted him too, and he wanted us. Mom told me years later that, when Dad was in the hospital that last time, he kept getting out of bed, in his hospital gown, pulling out the tubes, trying to head for the door and go home. He had to be forcibly restrained.

There was other weirdness. All through my child-hood, I was so shy I was unable to function in certain situations. Put on the spot, I always began to cry. When my piano teacher criticized my playing (a tricky Chopin prelude was a particular problem), I broke down in tears and was unable to speak. I would cross the street rather than talk to someone I didn't know well. I was incapable of conversation with a boy. The only adults with whom I wasn't tongue-tied were my parents.

I learned to swim, but once I became a teenager deep water terrified me. I dreaded going to the beach—Green Lake or Snooks' Pond—though it was what one did on summer weekends. I never admitted to anyone my reluctance to enter a body of water. It was a kind of seasickness combined with profound dread. I remember the relief of pulling myself up on a dock in the middle of a lake and sitting out of the water in the sun, and the burden of knowing I'd have to eventually jump in again and swim back to shore. I did it, of course. Doing things I didn't want to do—from going to Mass every Sunday to cleaning my room every Saturday—was a major part of my childhood.

The problem was that all I really wanted to do was read. I often faked sickness—I was incredibly good at this, one of my first experiences of seizing power—so I could stay home from school and read all day, with my cat on my lap.[13]

In 1904—any time, really, until the last few decades— having a baby at sixteen was probably a lot weirder than being fatherless, or too shy to talk, or waterphobic, or a bookaholic, or the only one in your entire school who couldn't wait to get out, leave town, go somewhere interesting and become someone unusual.

But maybe that—the sense that real life was elsewhere—is something that my grandmother and I shared.

---

[13] "Nobody understands me but you," I often crooned to Smokey, weeping softly, melodramatically, into his fur.

I like to think that Inez, pregnant at fifteen, found solace in books. I imagine her lumbering over to the North Baltimore Public Library in a home-made dress without a waist, a worn wool cape thrown over her shoulders, during that Ohio fall and winter—the elm trees turning yellow, the fields of wild mustard dying off, the train rumbling into the station three times a day, the B&O, bearing lucky people off to Columbus or Philadelphia. She would try to avoid the librarian, Miss Something, who used to smile at her approvingly and recommend books but now averted her eyes. She would browse through the stacks. *The House of Mirth* would have just come out, a book about a woman with worse problems than hers. Also *Maggie: A Girl of the Streets*—another "ruined" girl. The library probably had *Adam Bede*, in which the heroine is seduced by a soldier, leaves her baby out in a field, and, when it dies, is tried for murder. And *Tess of the D'Urbervilles*, same basic plot.

And the father of Doris: Who could it have been? Was Inez seduced and abandoned? Raped? In love? Oversexed, precocious, loose?

Once the spring gave way to sweltering July, her baby was born, definitely in North Baltimore, probably at home, no doubt with her mother attending: tiny Doris, about as inconvenient for an Ohio high school girl as anything could possibly be, and yet an actual little person, unmistakable, crying, helpless, desperate for milk, and wanting her mother.

DORIS

Inez's baby was raised by Jacob and Maggie. The 1910 census listed Doris, age six, as their late-in-life daughter. Her real mother, though Doris may not have known it, was miles away in Syracuse giving birth to a little sister, Geraldine. By the time of the 1920 census, Doris was still with her grandparents but identified, properly, as a "granddaughter."

By the time Doris was married, on September 1, 1928, she had been claimed by Inez as her daughter, who is named on her marriage license as her mother. (The space for "father" is blank.) Doris's wedding took place a couple of months after Inez was spotted in Syracuse, getting a look at Geraldine, her other daughter, my mother.

I try to figure out the significance of this. About to lose her first daughter to marriage, did Inez yearn for her second? Did she mean to do more than simply look and wave from the mezzanine?[14] Did she travel to Syracuse from Toledo hoping to forge a relationship with Geraldine, and did the Goodsons refuse her? ("You can have a look at her, but that's it!") Toledo to Syracuse was not an easy journey in 1928. Why did she make it? And was it her first one? Maybe she turned up every few years for a peek.

---

[14] Like the tortured Lady Dedlock in *Bleak House*, when she confronted Esther in Chesney Wold, to see her just one time ("Oh, my child, my child, I am your wicked and unhappy mother! Oh, try to forgive me!"), then part forever?

Doris—a stenographer—married a teacher and had a son, Albert.[15] The son married and produced a son himself; he and his first wife were divorced when the boy was three. (I'm sorry to say—Albert was my first cousin—that his wife's grounds for divorce were "gross neglect of duty" though what kind of duty is not revealed).[16] By the time I found these people, Albert had been dead for thirty years, but Margaret, the Maine genealogist, located a phone number for his second wife, Ginger, in Ohio.

I called her, figuring that this was it: the major breakthrough! Surely she would have some important memories. And family photos! I would see what my aunt Doris looked like, and there had to be a few pictures of Grandma Inez!

Ginger was really sweet, and she wanted to be helpful, but she was no breakthrough: she was as dead an end as those mouse-nibbled records in the Wood County Court House. Doris had died before Ginger entered the picture. Inez was alive when Al and Ginger were married, but Ginger had never met her. When Inez died, two years later, Ginger had gone to her "viewing." And? "I can't remember anything about it." Photographs? She would check: "I can't believe I got rid of that picture of Doris, maybe it's in the attic." It wasn't. "I don't really know anything about any of them," she said. "We weren't a close family." I had the feeling I had touched a nerve that had remained raw.

---

[15] I don't think I should use his real name, which is not Albert. Ditto Ginger.

[16] Katherine, my lawyer daughter, cautions, "Don't jump to conclusions. We don't get his side, only hers."

Doris Willick (l.)
and a friend, c. 1920

Thanks to the North Baltimore Historical Society, I did finally locate a photo of Doris. It's undated, but appears to have been taken when she was in her teens, in late fall or early spring, and you can see from the shadows that it's around noon. Doris is standing with Louise Adams, who lived across the street and was just Doris's age. It's logical to assume that they were friends, and this seems to be Louise's house, at 400 West Broadway.[17]

Unfortunately, Doris is the girl with her back to us, looking down at her shoes, or possibly into a Brownie-type camera. And Louise has the air of someone posing for a photograph—with a fishing rod? an archery bow?—while a second photographer, from across the street and from slightly above—out of a window?—shoots their picture. Why? And why was this one saved, while the one taken half a minute later, of Doris facing the camera, smiling, looking exactly like my mother, was lost?

No matter how I enlarge it and peer at the details, the photograph doesn't give me much. Doris might as well be a squirrel. All I can deduce is that she seems petite, like her half-sister (or whole sister? who knows?), Geraldine.

---

17 It's still there, though the Willicks' house was torn down years ago.

EMERY

I heard again from Margaret, the genealogist in Maine who discovered Doris's true identity. Intrigued by the saga and its mysteries, she had been doing more Inez research—and was rewarded with yet another strange development.

She found Inez's name tantalizingly attached to an unexpected document: the 1954 obituary of a man named Emery D. Balliet. Emery was born in 1872 in Nevada,[18] Ohio, and lived "most of his life" in nearby Kenton—both places well within that miniature constellation of small towns that encompass Inez's family history. Emery, however, died while on a visit to San Diego, and among his survivors were three half-sisters, who are none other than the surviving Willick girls, including Inez. Could Inez's mother, Maggie Willick, have had a previous marriage that produced a son?

Further research told us that Emery was indeed Maggie's child—but, astonishingly, he was an out-of-wedlock baby, born when she was a teenager. Yet another bar sinister![19] As part of some sort of bizarre and racy

---

18 Pronounced with a long a.
19 The "bar sinister"—or "bend sinister"—is a stripe on the family crest that indicates an illegitimate branch. In the course of my research into literary bastards, I found a charming 1916 short story by Richard Harding Davis, very popular in its day, about a dog named Kid whose father was a prize-winning pure white bull terrier and his mother—oh dear—a "black and tan" "street-dog." Kid narrates his rags-to-riches tale himself. He has the ability to read, to understand English (though his grammar is sometimes iffy), and to rip the heart out of any dog that calls his mother a cur.

family tradition, Inez's own mother had gotten pregnant at seventeen.

The identity of Emery's father was known, however, and here the story gets stranger. The man's name was Marquis L. Balliet,[20] an Ohio farmer, ten years older than Maggie—and married. He lived nearby, in the same north-central Ohio neighborhood. And curiously, when he had his liaison with Maggie, he and his wife already had a four-month-old son named . . . Emery. This seemed so monumentally odd that I double-triple-checked; at first I thought they'd adopted Maggie's Emery. But there are plenty of records for two Emery Balliets. Emery I died in 1935 in his Ohio town. It was a fluke that Emery II—"our" Emery, my great-uncle—died while visiting relatives in California twenty years later rather than in his own parcel of Ohio, sixty miles from where Emery I, his half-brother, was buried.

In 1880, Emery II, age eight, was living with Maggie's widowed mother, Mary Strawbridge, in Dunkirk, Ohio—thirty miles south of North Baltimore. It's likely she raised her grandson (she lived until 1934), though he kept the name Balliet. Emery seems to have had contact with the Willicks and the Strawbridges all his life: besides a daughter named Naomi, the relatives listed in his obituary are all Willicks. He may have lost touch with his father's side because Marquis died young: at thirty-five, just after Christmas in 1880.

I became intrigued by Marquis L. Balliet's name: the L is for *Lafayette*. The least interesting theory about Emery's father's name, posited by someone on his family tree, is that he was named after a ship that a distant ancestor had served on. I admit that I searched for some-

---

[20] Later spelled Balyeat.

thing that would tie the family to the "real" marquis, the French noble who aided the American cause in the Revolution. Could I be related to both Washington and Lafayette? In a story strewn with out-of-wedlock babies, what's another wild oat? And the marquis had spent time in the part of Pennsylvania where the Balliets had originally settled.[21] But I dug up nothing. The most likely guess is that the family, originally French, admired the Marquis de Lafayette, and by 1844 it was high time a son was named after him.

Like nearly everyone else in this story, Marquis L. Balliet didn't venture far from the Ohio Valley; he died in Van Wert, Ohio, only fifty miles from the Strawbridges.

---

[21] Before 1850 more settlers came to Ohio from Pennsylvania than from anyplace else.

COUSIN CLAY

I've come up with no shortage of theories, but can't prove any of them, and I reluctantly have to declare myself defeated: "Why Syracuse?" remains on the list of unanswerable questions.

But for a while I entertained the credible guess that the Willicks may have had Syracuse relatives who took their daughter in when she turned up pregnant the second time, so I scrounged through the Syracuse census records for the family names—Willick, Strawbridge, Frick—in search of a Syracuse connection.

I didn't find one, but, climbing around in Grandma Lucinda's family tree, I took a closer look at her older brother, John Wilson Frick, and my cast of characters became more interesting.

To make a long story short—well, sort of short—Jacob Willick, Inez's father, was the first cousin of Henry Clay Frick. Yes: Frick the robber baron, the steel magnate, the ruthless industrialist businessman, the strikebreaker and union buster, often cited as "one of the most hated men in America." He was also Frick the philanthropist, the Frick who was responsible for purchasing some of the world's greatest paintings and installing them at his home, which would become the wondrous Frick Collection in New York City.

Jacob Kiel Willick[22] and Henry Clay Frick were both born in 1849 (Jacob in October, Henry—always called

---

[22] The city of Kiel is the capital of the German state of Schleswig-Holstein; aside from that, I can't find a source for my great-grandfather's middle name.

Clay—in December), in neighboring towns near Pittsburgh. Jacob was the son of John Samuel Willick and Lucinda Frick. The family were never prosperous. They owned an insignificant piece of property in Van Buren, Ohio, a farm worth about $35,000 on today's market. When John Samuel died in 1876 (he was only fifty-three, but may have suffered from a Civil War wound), Lucinda moved in with her just-married son Jacob and his wife, Maggie, in North Baltimore. No doubt the Willicks were glad to have her when the twins were born the following year. Also, Lucinda's pension as a veteran's widow probably made their lives a little easier.

Clay chose his parents more wisely, at least on his mother's side. He was the son of John Wilson Frick and Elizabeth Overholt. John Wilson was considered wild and impetuous, a nonconforming dreamer with a vague desire (never realized) to be an artist. He had a Mennonite father and—worse yet—a red-haired Irish mother.[23] But he managed to marry above himself. Elizabeth's parents weren't happy about the wildness, the Irishness, the red hair he had inherited, or the marriage, but as Henry Clay Frick's earliest biographer put it, "There was no withstanding her calm inflexibility." Frick's latest biographer[24] lays it out more bluntly: Elizabeth was three months pregnant. The two were speedily married and relegated to the tiny (450 sq. ft.) three-room spring house on the Overholt property, where their children were born.

---

[23] Red-haired Irish mothers figure prominently in my family history; for a while in my thirties, thanks to Clairol, I was one myself.

[24] Martha Frick Sanger, whose frank and exhaustive tome, *Henry Clay Frick: An Intimate Portrait* (Abbeville Press, 1999), seems definitive.

Eventually, John became a farmer and, while not prosperous, raised six children without ever going into debt.[25]

John Frick's reluctant father-in-law, Abraham Overholt, was a wealthy whiskey maker. When John impregnated the boss's daughter, he was working at the distillery, making $400 a year. The booze in question was Old Overholt, which supplied the troops during the Civil War and was still being used as a "medicinal" whiskey in World War II. It continues to be made, with a picture of Abraham on the label; in a 2002 tasting profile, *Whiskey Magazine* proclaimed it: "Well rounded. Tightly combined flavours. Plenty of substance. Gingery. Rooty. Cedary. Soft, full and chewy, then builds in intensity." One of its claims to fame is that the stuff hasn't changed much since it was first distilled in 1810.[26]

Jacob Willick and his cousin Clay Frick seem to have been very different kinds of people: Clay was the kind who becomes ambitious, rich, and famous; Jacob was the kind who accepts handouts from his rich relative. He may have been ambitious—I know little about him—but if he was, it came to nothing. His three terms as town clerk, and a few years as fire chief, were about as far as he went: fairly important positions but not exactly the road to fortune.

Jacob's life was complicated by a bizarre accident in 1895. He was forty-six years old, and he and Maggie had a houseful of children. Jacob wasn't well. He was suffer-

---

[25] John was considered such a nonentity that, when somebody tried to enter him into Wikipedia, the post was taken down with the comment that, "just becasue [sic] this guy is the father of Henry Clay Frick does not assert any type of notability." His son, however, was said by an early biographer to have inherited his "dash and daring" from his father.

[26] In 2013, the caretaker at a Pittsburgh inn with a cache of vintage Old Overholt valued at $100,000, was arrested for drinking all fifty-two bottles. It took him a year.

ing from a "bad cut" he'd incurred a few weeks earlier, but he went nonetheless to a nearby town to supervise a barn-raising. A portion of the barn fell on him, and he "was in too weak a condition to jump out of the way of the falling timber."[27] He injured his spine, and one leg was crushed. He recovered, but walked with crutches for the remaining thirty-six years of his life.

Henry Clay Frick, a millionaire before he was thirty,[28] was generous to the less fortunate branch of the family, and stayed in touch with them all his life. I have several letters from Jacob to his cousin, and from Lucinda to her nephew, asking for help. In October 1907, Lucinda wrote her "dear friend and nefthew" for money to buy "feweul," which was "very high" and "the winter is so long. . . ." Frick made a note to his secretary to send his aunt $300 in cash by express mail ("You need not say anything, just put my name as sending it"); Aunt Lucinda wrote her letter on Monday and got the money on Wednesday. It was a substantial sum—more than half of a decent annual income at the time—and apparently not her first request. In this and other notes to him, she refers to previous kindness. In a note to "dear Sir" that ends "Respectfully, Jacob K. Willick," Cousin Jacob asks for help "again" through the winter ("we are very kneady"). In the 1910 census, Jacob is described as living on his "own income." Provided by his cousin? Maybe he earned it somehow (as a former town clerk he must have had some standing in the community), but a few years later he's applying to Cousin Clay again.

The two men's daughters, Inez Willick and Helen Frick, were both born in 1888 (Inez in April, Helen in

---

[27] I'm quoting from his obituary.
[28] That was always his goal, and he achieved it with time to spare.

September). Did the girls ever meet? Doubtful. Jacob and Clay might have been close as boys, but in adulthood it seems they were not ("Dear Sir"). By the time Helen was born, the Fricks were living at Clayton, the Italianate mansion near Pittsburgh that was extensively enlarged and remodeled to Frick specifications. The Willicks were renting their small house in North Baltimore, where Jacob was already the father of seven and working at the local stave factory, not yet having graduated to town clerk.[29]

Lucinda Frick Willick lived with her son Jacob and his family until she died; she was present throughout Inez's childhood. Lucinda was one of the middle children of that red-headed Irishwoman, Catherine Miller Frick, who started having babies at age sixteen and produced nine children, one every two years or so, then died, at thirty-six.[30] Lucinda married John Samuel Willick when she was twenty, and perhaps in reaction to her mother's life she had only two children, Jacob and Lewis.

Despite his infirmities, Jacob outlived his cousin Clay by twelve years, dying in 1931 in North Baltimore at age eighty-two (the town's oldest resident). Henry Clay Frick died of a heart attack at his Fifth Avenue mansion[31] in 1919, two weeks before his seventieth birthday.

Cousin Clay was agreeable to the idea of sending money to the part of the world he came from, but he never visited it again.

The art amassed by Henry Clay Frick is housed at his mansion, built in 1913 at possibly the toniest address

---

[29] Two of Frick's four children died in childhood, five of Jacob's eleven.
[30] Her husband, Daniel Frick, married again, resulting in nine more babies.
[31] Now, of course, the Frick museum.

in Manhattan (Fifth Avenue and East 70th Street).[32] The website of the Frick Collection refers to him simply as "one of America's most successful industrialists," though he has been called less benign names. He was also the object of a spectacular assassination attempt in 1892, when he was Andrew Carnegie's general manager at Carnegie's steel plant in Homestead, Pennsylvania. Frick orchestrated a brutal attempt (approved by a two-faced Carnegie,[33] who publicly sympathized with the union movement) to break the power of the iron and steel workers union once and for all by first locking his striking employees out of the plant, then building a three-mile-long fence around it topped with barbed wire, and finally calling in a private army to engage with the strikers, who would not give up. After a fourteen-hour battle and twelve deaths, the workers triumphed—but the governor of Pennsylvania came to the industrialists' rescue with the state militia and a trainload of strikebreakers. The strike leaders were charged with murder, among other crimes, but no jury ever convicted any of them.

In retaliation for Frick's major role in this shameful episode, Alexander Berkman (atheist, anarchist, pacifist, lover of Emma Goldman) burst into his office and wounded him badly (three point-blank gunshots to the neck and four stab wounds to the leg with a steel file) before Frick's workers overcame Berkman and beat him senseless. Frick was back at work in a week; Berkman went to jail for fourteen years.

---

[32] During the 1960s Joan Crawford lived across the street with her own industrial magnate husband, Pepsi-Cola CEO Al Steele. Exciting coincidence: my Pepsi grandpa, Frank Burns—about whom more to come—was a guest of the Steeles there several times.

[33] Carnegie had fled to remote a Scottish castle on Loch Rannoch, leaving Frick to do his dirty work. Frick seems not to have minded.

Frick didn't change his ways. If anything, his notoriously heartless treatment of his employees got worse: 2,500 men lost their jobs, and the workers who stayed on found their wages cut in half; the strike was a failure, and the union movement was undermined. Most workers—and the public—sided with Frick, a tendency of the oppressed to defend their oppressors that is, inexplicably, still with us.

Over the years, I've visited the Frick collection numerous times, strolled the long gallery under the vast skylight, without knowing that the mansion was built and stuffed with glorious art by my first cousin three times removed.[34] I went to the Frick again on a recent trip to New York City, and as I was standing in front of the great man's portrait—unexpectedly moved by it this time around—I eavesdropped on a gallery talk. The docent was saying how amazing that someone from such a humble background could have become one of the titans of industry. Someone in the group added, "And one of the one percent…" Chuckles all around. Except for the guide, who responded, a touch indignantly, that the one percent of those days brought the great art of Europe to America, where we are standing here enjoying it, and that Frick redeemed himself to some degree with his gift to the world of his magnificent art collection.

Frick had a taste for serious portraits of great men: the Goya St. Jerome, the Holbein Thomas More, the brooding Rembrandt self-portrait, the appealing and human Bellini St. Francis in the desert with his donkey, a blue sky, and an Italian hill town in the distance. But

---

[34] In my 1995 novel *Vigil for a Stranger*, the heroine stops in at the Frick, which seems to her like "the splendid and imposing but oddly welcoming residence of one's filthy-rich great uncle." Little did I know!

the enormous collection is wonderfully eclectic, from the frolicking lovers in the Fragonard Room to one of Constable's sunnier views of Salisbury Cathedral to the dashing and mysterious Rembrandt Polish Rider,[35] everyone's favorite—not to mention the sculpture, furniture, clocks, wall hangings, and other wondrous objects.

The last painting Clay acquired—just a few months before he died—was Vermeer's[36] *Mistress and Maid.* The mistress in her furred mantle and pearls, the red-cheeked maid delivering an obviously important letter, the quill pen and the writing implements on the table: I can't look at it now without thinking of Frick's terse notes to my relatives, delivered not by a maid but by the postal service, and wrapped around a fat check.

---

[35] Frick bought the painting in 1910 for £60,000; nearly 100 years later doubt was cast on its authenticity. The issue is still unresolved, but the Rembrandt team is winning.

[36] There are two other Vermeers at the Frick, including *Girl Interrupted at Her Music,* a whole short story in one small canvas.

GRANDFATHERS

Everyone's family history is murky in places where the rays of light refuse to shine. Straightforward sagas of weddings and begats and immaculately kept records handed down through the years are rare, I have no doubt. Still, my own story seems to have more shadows and dark corners than most, even when I detour from my mother's side to my father's.

My father was also adopted—or half-adopted. In 1912, when he was fourteen months old, his own father, Herbert William Merritt, was killed in a freakish and horrible accident, torn to pieces (arm ripped off, skull smashed in) by a locomotive that came up behind him as he crossed the rail yard where he worked. It happened during one of the massive, sudden blizzards that Syracuse specializes in. The newspaper account says he couldn't have seen or heard the train, "a monster of the Pacific type," before it was on him. ("The steam and smoke from the engines make a fog which no human eye can penetrate.") Herb Merritt was "popular among the men in the yard."

That's all I know about him, except that he came from an English Protestant family that wasn't thrilled when he married Kitty Dunn, a red-haired Irish Catholic. One of my last aunts dug deep into her failing memory and gave me that morsel of information before she died, but she could locate nothing else, and the more I pressed her the more she kept getting Herb Merritt mixed up with other relatives.

I have one tiny photo of this handsome "real" grandfather, set into a circular black frame with a pin on the back—probably a mourning piece. That and the clipping about his death are all I have left of the poor guy. He was twenty-seven when he died. *Life so short, eternity so long.*

My father's father,
Herbert Merritt, 1911

Kitty was left a destitute widow with my toddler father and my uncle Bill, age three. Bill was taken in by

Frank Burns, 1930s

Kitty's mother; little Herbie Jr. remained with his mum. She found work as a hostess at Schrafft's restaurant in downtown Syracuse, where her flaming red hair caught the eye of an up-and-coming (and reassuringly Catholic) young businessman, Frank Burns. She was saved, and then some: when Frank retired in 1958, he was a bigwig at the Pepsi-Cola Company, with a Cadillac, a hefty stock portfolio, and the distinction of having come up with the "twice as much for a nickel" gimmick in 1933 that sent Pepsi sales soaring ahead of Coca-Cola's.[37]

He formally adopted my father in 1914.

---

[37] Grandpa B. liked his Canadian Club, but Pepsi was the official family drink, viewed as a cross between Veuve Clicquot and holy water. My cousins and I probably drank enough of it in our youth to float Grandpa's motorboat (the *Pepsi*), and we had the cavities to prove it.

I remember the day I found this out: I was ten. Among the family photos and general junk,[38] I had come across a brittle newspaper clipping announcing . . . the adoption of my father . . . by my grandfather! My stomach dropped, my heart raced, and I went to my mother in tears: *What does this mean?* She told me the story—leaving out the gory details—and said not to cry, not to worry, it was a long time ago, it was nothing. She was trying to reassure me, but it didn't seem like nothing: it seemed important, dramatic, a confusion, a whirl, a mess—and, at the same time, tremendously exciting. I have a vivid memory of the green-and-black printed curtains in the living room, how as she talked I kept looking at their intricate pattern and thinking: *Nothing will ever be the same.*

But it was, of course—everywhere except in my head: there, something shifted, lurched, failed to catch the cog in the wheel. My family was not my family—my grandfather was not related to me, my dozens of cousins, my father's eleven siblings, including my three nun aunts, were only halfway related. Now it was just Mom and Dad and Smokey the cat and me, here in our little house. Just the four of us. My unspoken thought was: *against the world.*

I remember my grandfather Frank Burns mostly as a taciturn old man, always in a white shirt and loosened tie, slumped in "his" chair by the fireplace in the living room of my grandparents' white-pillared house in a posh section of Syracuse. My parents and I went "up home,"

---

[38] Including a piece in the newspaper about my other grandmother—my mother's adoptive mother, that is—catching one of her breasts in the wringer of a washing machine when she was doing the laundry, which seemed to me grotesquely, embarrassingly, improbable. And yet there it was in the *Syracuse Post-Standard*, with her name and her address—the only time she was mentioned in the paper except for her husband's obituary, and then her own.

as they both called it, for enormous Thanksgiving and Christmas dinners—and occasionally Easter—and we often dropped by on Sundays after church.

My grandmother, Kitty, would be slaving in the kitchen while Frank sat staring morosely into space, his drink on the glass-stained surface of the table on his left, a fancy pedestal ashtray on his right, for his cigar. When we arrived, my duty was to venture into the living room—I always felt a bit like a peasant approaching the throne—and utter a shy "Hi, Grandpa." He would look up vaguely and pat his knee. This meant I should sit on his lap, which I did, and give his whiskery cheek a quick kiss. He smelled—pleasantly, I thought—of booze and cigar smoke. He asked me how school was going, and I said fine. He asked me how my grades were, and I said good. He asked me if I'd been behaving myself, and I said yes. Then he'd say something like, "Well, keep up the good work," and when I stood up he'd reach into his pants pocket, take out his old brown wallet, and give me whatever bills were inside it.

I dreaded this ritual, but it had an undeniable excitement, because I never knew how much money it would be. He never really looked, just handed over the cash. It was as unpredictable as playing the slots. Once or twice he gave me five twenties. Sometimes it was only one, or a couple of tens. I never kept track. He didn't say anything—at most, he might mutter, "Here—take this," as if the transaction disturbed him: the necessity of someone in his family needing this kind of subsidy. The money was the signal that our awkward encounter was over. I'd smile and say "thank you," give him another quick kiss, and flee, leaving him to his Canadian Club and his thoughts, whatever they may have been. Then

I'd find one of my parents and hand over the dough, which would pay for my school shoes, or my new Easter outfit, or—well, I had no idea what my parents did with it. But I know it was a welcome gift for a family like mine. Grandpa was a nice man, though not what you'd call friendly.

The holiday occasions, however, are what dominate my memory of the huge Burns house on Twin Hills Drive. I loved my grandmother's cooking, but I did not look forward to the ritual family gatherings. I was sibling-less, agonizingly shy, and older than all my cousins by several years. The slew of uncles and aunts asked me the usual questions about school but otherwise, to my relief, ignored me. Every Thanksgiving, my bachelor uncle Frank showed up with a different girlfriend in tow—all of them young, glamorous,[39] and for some reason easier to talk to than my relatives. Maybe, in that crowd of Burnses, they felt as out of it as I did. (Uncle Frank eventually married one of them, which meant more cousins.) I used to try desperately to sneak off somewhere to read, but my mother would always track me down and tow me back. A low point of Christmas afternoon was my aunt Nancy's annual phone call from Germany, where my uncle Pete was stationed in the army. One by one, we'd all go to the phone. Everyone else seemed to chat merrily with Nancy and Pete, but when it was my turn it was only "fine" and "good" and "Merry Christmas" before I gladly relinquished the phone to someone more fun.

Finally, my grandmother would emerge from the kitchen, overworked and irritable, to declare that dinner was served. Pink champagne for the adults, Pepsi for the minors. On Thanksgiving, most of my gratitude was

---

[39] I remember a madly exotic blonde airline stewardess.

reserved for the fact that I was old enough to be spared the kids' table in the kitchen. Instead I squeezed in at the big table between my parents. Grandpa always carved the turkey, and always gave my father "the part that went over the fence last," also known as "the pope's nose"— i.e., the tail minus the feathers. Grandpa had gotten it into his head that my father loved it. He didn't, but he ate the nasty clump of fat and gristle anyway.

After my father died, Mom and I visited infrequently, but we always stopped in on Christmas, bringing Grandpa a bottle of whiskey, as my father had done every year. After Grandpa's massive retirement dinner in New York at the Commodore Hotel in 1955, Pepsi gave him a trip around the world with my grandmother.[40] He was retained by PepsiCo as a "national management consultant," but, whatever that meant, as the years went by it didn't fill much of his time. He and my grandmother had given up their summer cottage and the cabin cruiser (the *Pepsi*). Grandpa didn't golf, didn't travel, didn't read much besides the *Wall Street Journal*, didn't putter in the garden, didn't go anywhere that would require a new tie or cuff links. Whiskey was a safe present, and the tall gold-wrapped gift bottles would pile up under the tree.

My grandmother Kitty died in her late sixties, but Grandpa Burns—retired, bored, and ailing—lived to be ninety-one, too old. One of my nun aunts, now an unstable ex-nun, lived "up home" and took care of him. Gradually, his old friends died off, and that made him not only sorrowful but angry. I was in my early thirties the last time I saw him. He was propped up in a hospital bed that had been imported to the dining room where the vast table used to be; it was clear that he felt lousy. There was

---

40   I have a postcard she sent from Paris complaining about the food.

no Canadian Club, no cigar, no old leather wallet, but the cheek I kissed felt the same, and we had just as little to say to each other. At his jam-packed funeral, the bishop (in black vestments) conducted a Solemn Requiem Mass, and I surprised myself by breaking down in tears in the middle of the *Agnus Dei.*

The grandfather situation on my mother's side is much simpler. Grandpa Horace Goodson was born a Georgia Protestant, and he worked on the streetcars in Syracuse. He died when I was four. He's so shadowy in my memory that he barely exists.

I don't know if he collaborated with my grandmother, Cora, in her various oppressions of their adopted daughter: keeping her out of school to run errands or do child care,[41] locking her in the cellar if she complained,[42] making her walk across town to give money to ne'er-do-well Uncle Johnny, who abused my mother in some way she resolutely refused to specify. Maybe my grandfather paid no attention, or tried to step in. My mother didn't talk about him with either rancor or affection: she didn't talk about him at all.

Horace Goodson, 1940s

---

[41] Cora gave birth to seven children of her own, starting five years after she adopted my mother.

[42] All her life my mother was terrified of enclosed spaces, the dark, and rats.

The only interesting story I ever heard was from one of my mother's sisters: When my aunt was a very little girl, my grandmother used to make Horace take her with him on Fridays after work when he went off to blow his paycheck. My aunt recalls a derelict house in the black section of town, people coming and going, and a front porch where she was made to sit and wait. Sometimes she'd doze off. After a while he'd emerge, they'd walk home together, and he'd say, "If you tell your mother where I was, I'll kill you." Then, when she got home, my grandmother would say, "If you don't tell me where he was, I'll kill you."

Nobody killed her, of course, and when she told this story it was for laughs. But for me it seemed an insight into what it was like to grow up in the Goodsons' succession of small, crowded, ratty apartments. In 1933, not long before my mother married my father, she took a photograph of her young siblings grouped around the back stoop of their place on North McBride Street and, with a mixture of exasperation and affection, captioned it "Tobacco Road."

Back in the early days of my quest, Horace Goodson provided some food for thought as I thought about the "Why Syracuse?" question: How, why, and exactly when did Inez—a girl who'd probably never been east of Sandusky—make her way from a sedate Ohio town to the big city of Syracuse? Syracuse is a long way from North Baltimore—nearly 500 miles on modern highways, no doubt much longer in the early 1900s, though it was possible to get there on the good old B&O, which conveniently ran through Inez's home town: three trains a day going east.

Did she become pregnant again in North Baltimore and go to Syracuse to have the baby? Did she take a trip to Syracuse for some reason and have a liaison that ended badly? Was she someplace else entirely when my mother was conceived? During those years, she appears in no city directory or census—the usual places where obscure relatives lurk. Unless she was using an assumed name. From what I've learned about Inez, this seems possible—I see her in a red wig, living in Milwaukee or Houston and calling herself Zeni Frick—but is definitely not verifiable.[43]

All I know for sure is that, not quite five years after her first child was born, Inez had her second out-of-wedlock baby in Syracuse on April 3, 1910, at St. Mary's Maternity Hospital and Infant Asylum, on Spring Street. The hospital was run by the Sisters of Charity—the order of nuns whose headdresses (back in the days when nuns wore such things) were like a pair of billowing sails. Inez named the baby—my mother—Geraldine Anna,[44] and she was adopted at nine months by my "grandparents," Horace and Cora Goodson.

I did consider the idea that Inez had been sent away in disgrace to give birth and have the baby adopted— that maybe one Willick bastard had been enough for her parents to handle. But sending her as far as Syracuse would have been pretty drastic. There were foundling hospitals aplenty in Ohio and Pennsylvania. And the

---

[43] Not that I haven't tried.

[44] My mother was told at some point that she was named after the popular soprano Geraldine Farrar—a famous eccentric who, when she premiered as the Goose-Girl in Humperdinck's opera *Königskinder* at the Met in 1910, trained her own flock of geese, causing, according to the *New York Times*, "much amusement" when she appeared with a live goose under her arm. I own a postcard, c. 1910, of the Strand Theater in Syracuse; the marquee reads "Geraldine Farrar—*Carmen*."

Willicks weren't Catholics; Jacob had a Mennonite background, but he and Maggie were Lutherans. Inez seems to have practiced no religion at all. So why the nuns?

An explanation for the Catholic angle came to me when my mother and I were first embarking on the quest. Once it floated into my mind, it hung there with such urgency that gradually not only Mom and I but also her sisters and my cousins began to take it as a kind of wishful truth. In my first novel I used it as the basis for the plot.[45]

The theory was this: Inez goes to Syracuse for reasons we'll never know, and let's say she's staying next door to Horace and Cora. Horace is from Savannah, with a slow southern accent, and he's a randy devil (I knew him only as paunchy old Gramps in a cardigan and suspenders, smoking a pipe, but family legend pegs him as a skirt chaser), and he seduces young Inez, who becomes pregnant. What to do? Horace walks down Spring Street, past St. Mary's Maternity Hospital,[46] every day on his way to work (he's a driver on the trolley cars), and, as his girlfriend gets bigger and bigger, he directs Inez to the good sisters, and they take her in.

The baby is born. At that point, the Goodsons have been married for three years and still don't have a child. Horace has a soft spot for babies and for Inez: he talks Cora into adopting little Geraldine. And at some point he confesses the truth—or Inez spills the beans—or Cora figures it out. At any rate, Cora knows whose baby it is—

---

[45] Complete with a happy ending: the Mom character and the Inez character are brought together in a reunion engineered by the "me" character. I couldn't help it; it was my first novel. Really, it's not as bad as it sounds. *Family Matters*, 1979.

[46] The word *hospital* in this context had nothing to do with illness; it was used in an older sense, indicating that it extended hospitality to people in need.

and this always seemed a convincing explanation for why she treated my mother like Cinderella.

My Grandpa Goodson theory also shed light on something that baffled me from the beginning: how had Inez known to look up the Goodsons in 1928 so she could get a glimpse of her abandoned daughter? The Goodsons knew Inez's name: it was on the adoption papers, to certify that she agreed to the adoption. But how did Inez know theirs, let alone where to find them eighteen years later? I assumed that was proof of a deeply personal connection.

But my theory was shaken in the cozy wood-paneled reading room at the Amherst Public Library when I learned from a hefty tome called *The Encyclopedia of Adoption* that, in the early twentieth century, "confidentiality of the identities of the birth parents and adoptive parents was not commonly practiced." My mother's adoption was formal, certified by the State of New York, but even within that official framework plenty of adoptions, in fact, were arranged informally by the parties themselves—and were, de facto, what are known today as open adoptions.[47]

Gradually, I began to find more holes in the theory. Most glaringly, even eighteen years later, would Cora have agreed to let her husband's old flame have a look at their love child? This does not sound like my grandmother.

It's more likely that Inez and the Goodsons were hooked up when Cora and Horace applied to St. Mary's for an adoptable foundling. As a condition of relinquishing her, Inez may have demanded to know who was adopting the baby, or the Goodsons may have insisted on meeting the woman who had given birth to their child.

---

[47] The Willicks' adoption of Doris, their daughter's child, was never formalized.

My evidence for a more direct connection—Horace's reputation, Cora's bad mothering, an iffy resemblance between one of my cousins and me—is not much more than a large gray cloud that's shaped something like Grandpa Goodson.

My mother, however, was particularly fond of this foggy scenario and was grateful to me for concocting it. Horace may not have been a perfect parent, but he was a familiar one, and she loved him. And giving him a spot on the family tree made her only half illegitimate.

But now that she is dead, I'm forced to chop off that branch and go back to square one. The problem is that the square is blank.

My "real" maternal grandfather—the one I don't have a photograph of—has stubbornly remained a zero. I know absolutely nothing about him. The space for "father" is empty on my mother's adoption certificate. Her birth certificate has not turned up, despite diligent searching of Vital Statistics records in both Syracuse and Albany.[48] Even if it could be found, the chances are that only Inez's name was recorded—though I admit I'd hoped that the Sisters of Charity might have forced out of her the name of her collaborator in sin.

But somehow, somewhere, somebody got Inez pregnant in July 1909 and disappeared without a trace.

---

[48] It apparently exists: there's a record of a birth certificate for one "Geraldine Willis," born on my mother's birth date at the Foundling Hospital in Syracuse. But finding the record of the record has not led to the record itself.

PART II

FACT AND FICTION

The dead are at our mercy.
~Virginia Woolf, *To the Lighthouse*

ICE CREAM

O n a warm day in late spring, I drove with my dachshund, Freddie, to a nearby dairy farm. This part
of Massachusetts is rich in cows. At Cook's, if you take
your ice cream cone outside, you can gaze over green
fields in a trance of bliss or walk over toward the barn to
watch the cows slopping feed out of their troughs. Sometimes a glossy black hen or two will come mooching over.
Fred tends to be set in his ways, and I was trying to get
him used to surprises like sudden mooing noises and fat
chickens rising suddenly into the air, so we spent some
time with the cows.

I usually get a black-raspberry-chip cone, but today,
for the first time, I ordered the flavor called "Inez": a
dark vanilla studded with tiny bits of coconut, almonds,
and chocolate.[1] I'm not a big coconut fancier, but it was
pretty good, and I thought it might inspire me.

The genealogical quest I had embarked on was
getting me down.

Genealogy is a passion—even an obsession—for
many, and there's a great satisfaction in learning about
long-ago people who are related to us. We have the
vague, unprovable idea that we also learn something
about ourselves if we know where our mother's mother
was born, and what wars our father's grandfathers fought
in, and the names of our sad distant cousins who died
in childhood, and the resting place of a great-aunt who
lived to be 104 and was part Penobscot.

---

[1] It's named after a particularly beloved cow.

But that collection of facts, dug up obsessively and with difficulty from a scattered array of sources, is never much more than names and dates and locations: the equivalent of a pencil sketch on a napkin when what you really want is a big oil painting. Now and then a photograph may come to light—in my case, precious few until my mother started pointing her Kodak at people in the '20s. And photos aren't always helpful: my first husband's mother's attic yielded up dozens of portraits, beautifully preserved, many of them framed ovals of people with elaborate hairdos and fancy ties and leg-o'-mutton sleeves and expressionless faces. Who were they? Who knows?[2]

I'd been pondering the surviving Willick children, starting with Maud and Mabel, the twins, in 1876 and ending with Doris in 1904. I managed to find out where they lived, whom they married, where they're buried, and what their children were named.

But—so what? What does all this mean? And what does it have to do with me? Are these long-gone strangers my "family" in any meaningful way? Have they influenced me? And who were they "really"?

These are questions to which ancestry research doesn't provide answers.

When I was a kid, I snooped. Not only did I annually have an intimate acquaintance with my presents long before Christmas morning, but I was also an expert on what was in my parents' bureau drawers, coat pockets, handbags, and wallets. I wanted to know things. Not higher mathematics or why the caterpillars swarmed to our willow tree or the history of the Baltic States. What

---

[2] My mother used to instruct me sternly, "Always write names and dates on the back!"

I wanted to know was: Who were my parents? Why were they the way they were instead of some other way? What did they do when I wasn't around? Who were they before I was born? What did it mean when Aunt Mena said "Hernando's Hideaway" was "a sexy song" and my mother, with a glance at me, shushed her?

I have not changed much, though I've learned to keep my curiosity under control. I don't read anyone's mail or poke around in bureau drawers anymore. But if someone wants to confide in me, I listen with interest, and what I hear often stays with me for a long time.

On the other hand, if I could find a cache of letters from my long-dead ancestors, or an intact bureau drawer from the house on South Second St., I'd swoop in with the appetite of a vulture. I know Maggie died in 1935, but was she fat or thin, pretty or plain, and how did she get along with her live-in mother-in-law, Lucinda? I want more details about Hester and Raleigh, taken by diphtheria within a month of each other, about Charlie's drowning at age ten in Blocker's Pond, and about poor Ralph, who died at twenty-four of typhoid fever contracted in France during the First World War.

And why was Jacob's brother Lewis such a loser? Or *was* he? He may have been a lovable layabout who was tolerated because he was good with the kids and could keep the stove going. Or maybe he was a writer who couldn't hold a job because he was obsessed with his great novel, the one that would have revolutionized American literature if he'd just gotten it into the hands of Maxwell Perkins instead of dying in 1911 of consumption. Was the manuscript burned up in a fire? Destroyed by his sister-in-law Maggie because it was a roman à clef that blew the lid off the Willick family secrets? Or maybe stolen by his niece Inez, who admired his work but who left it behind on the train to Syracuse and the conductor took it home to use for toilet paper....

But wait—Uncle Lewis's novel doesn't exist.

Writing history, biography, family chronicles, you work only with facts. Imagination functions as a way to figure out where to get the facts, to find links between them, maybe see patterns providing clues that can be followed. But you have to beat your imagination down, restrain your thirst for stories, for satisfaction, for closure. The sad truth is that you can't—or shouldn't, anyway—make anything up.

A fiction writer, on the other hand, has infinite power. Her only constrictions are the demands of her story's interior logic, the capabilities of her characters, and the limitations of language.

When I was thirtyish I worked as a reporter for our local "alternative" paper, the *New Haven Advocate*. It was the first time I'd been paid to write, and I loved it, but after a while I knew I had a problem. When a story wasn't quite as fascinating as it had promised to be, or an interview subject wouldn't oblige with a snappy quote, the impulse came creeping up on me to embellish things a bit. I could see—not to beat around the bush—that I was right on the verge of manufacturing material, like Jayson Blair at the *New York Times*, who was forced to resign in disgrace in 2003.[3] I quit the *Advocate* and started writing a novel.[4]

---

[3]   The HBO TV series *The Wire* used this concept brilliantly in its last season: a Baltimore newspaper reporter is discovered fabricating stories, but he not only doesn't get busted, he's awarded a Pulitzer.

[4]   *Family Matters.*

Forty years later, sitting on a picnic bench while the cows alternately munched their dinner and gazed at Fred with their own brand of curiosity, I realized that, all along, as I researched the Willicks, I'd been thinking like a novelist, whose quest is to reach deeply into the imagination, to gradually discover a reality as robust and vigorous as her little black dog, or the dairy farm near her house.

Slowly the idea came to me that I could make things up—or rather, I could have it both ways: along with the factual history, I could write a parallel story, one that fills in the holes and knits up the ragged ends, that provides motivation and freckles and a pair of red bloomers and a novel-writing uncle. I could tell my grandmother's tale twice: once sticking strictly to the facts, and then a flip side where Inez soars above the dry census records and yellowed newspaper clippings, where the loose jumble of information comes together like a pattern in a kaleidoscope, or the lost pieces of a jigsaw puzzle that were under the sofa, and my scattered, improbable, gap-toothed family history makes sense. I could take the huge sprawling mess of real life and tidy it into the comparative neatness of fiction.

I finish my ice cream and corral Fred, and when I get home I sit down with a new page: *When she comes in from school, they're sitting at the kitchen table waiting for her.*

I can see Jacob's crutches leaning against the wall by his chair. I can see Grandma Lucinda—she's close to eighty, and maybe her hand shakes as she picks up her coffee cup. Maggie's there, of course. Weeping? Angry? And Inez is a schoolgirl of fifteen, almost five months pregnant and starting to show.

The story spins itself. I begin to enjoy "characterizing" these people. My crippled great-grandfather is all bark and no bite. My great-grandmother is still deeply scarred by the drowning of her son Charlie in 1896. My feisty, bookish, impulsive grandmother blithely tells not one but two whoppers in order to get what she wants....

Actually writing the story of their lives seems more of an invasion of their privacy, somehow, than sitting around with my daughter, speculating about what their motivations might have been, what made them tick. In a way, I'm horrified at what I'm doing. In another way, I revel in it.

AGNES

1903–1906
North Baltimore, Ohio

A ll she's ever wanted to do is read. "She gets it from Clem," Bessie always says. Her mother likes things to come from somewhere: Agnes gets her love of books from her father's brother, her dark hair from her father's side of the family, her stubbornness from her aunt Sarah, who died before she was born. Or maybe from George Washington, to whom her family is related on Bessie's father's side.

The baby, of course, she gets from Jesse Lyman Zorn, and if her uncle hadn't passed on to her that love of reading, her waist would still have measured $24\frac{1}{2}$ inches and she would not have had to tell a summerful of lies.

She meets Jesse at the library, where he has a job after school. He's a senior at North Baltimore High, two years ahead of her, and they have never spoken to each other, but she knows who he is because everyone knows who everyone is in North Baltimore. He's the star of the debating club, and he pitches for the baseball team, and his girlfriend is Mary Corbett, who is famous for fainting in biology lab in the middle of dissecting her frog.

Agnes discovered Dickens over the summer. The library has his complete works, in a set bound in beautiful brown leather, each volume with a red ribbon for a bookmark. One day in September, when she is standing in front of the Dickens shelf, Jesse appears beside her and says, "My favorite is *Bleak House*. What's yours?"

She says she hasn't read *Bleak House* yet, she's only read *Great Expectations* (twice) and *David Copperfield* and *Little Dorrit*. He takes down *Bleak House* and hands it to her. "Meet me here next week and tell me how you like it."

She laughs. "How can I read this in one week? I do have to go to school, you know."

His smile almost makes her knees buckle. "I have faith in you."

She blushes. Why is he even talking to her? "Two weeks," she says, partly because she knows she'll need two weeks and partly because she feels like being ornery. What right does he have to smile at her like that?

He raises an eyebrow. His eyes are a clear gray-green, glittering and narrow, like fish. He says, "I'll give you two weeks, not a minute more."

Two weeks later, she's there after school, expecting nothing, but he is leaning against the Dickens shelf with his hands in his pockets. He stands up straight when he sees her. "Well?"

"I finished it this afternoon in study hall."

"And?"

She had a whole speech prepared—designed to impress him—about Dickens's love of justice in all his other books but how, in this one, things were more complicated. She also thought they could chat a bit about the fog that swirled through the story from start to finish. But when the rays of his smile beam down on her, she forgets what she meant to say. "I have never read such a book," she stammers out. "I could sit right down and read it again."

"You are very pretty," he says. "And you like Dickens. This seems a miracle."

That makes her so confused that she starts to babble about the English court system, about which she knows nothing, and they stand there talking until Miss Truitt swishes over and shushes them.

She's there again the next week, and so is he. The third week, he pulls her into the alcove at the end of the stacks and kisses her. The only boys she has ever kissed are her friend Emma's older brother, Tim—a wet, sickening, sour-breath kiss in their back hall—and Ross Huddle at a party where they were playing Post Office until the hostess's mother walked in and sent them all home. That had been somewhat better, but kissing Jesse is a revelation to her, like a confirmation of something she has always known but didn't know she knew.

They kiss for several long minutes, and then he leads her down a short flight of stairs to a storeroom and very softly closes the door behind them. Shelves filled with stacks of papers and old books line the walls, and there is a worktable in the middle of the room with a pot of paste on it and a Mason jar full of pencils, a teapot and a pile of cups and saucers. She sits on the end of the table and Jesse stands in front of her, and they stay there kissing until Miss Truitt rings the buzzer that warns the library is about to close. Jesse says, "Wait here. Don't make a sound."

In ten minutes he's back. "I have a key," he says. "Not a single soul on this earth knows we're in this library."

She doesn't know much about Jesse Zorn, with his thin, clever face and a smile that could melt ice. But she is well aware that they live in different worlds. Mr. Zorn owns the glass works in Findlay; Agnes's father hasn't been able to work since an accident at a barn-raising six years ago. The Zorns live in a big brick house on North Tarr Street, the Millers in a small frame one on South Second. Jesse has only one sister, not a houseful of noisy brats, much less a crazy uncle living in the attic. And Jesse Zorn is an important person in the high school where Agnes Miller is a nobody.

And yet, from that first day, it seems to her that they are so much alike it's as if they are one person, split down the middle in some ancient time and place and rejoined in North Baltimore, Ohio, in 1903. She thought this when they met the first time at the library, and, not long after, she read it in Plato's *Symposium* in Mr. Delby's class: that men were children of the sun, women of the earth, and humans were punished when they threatened the gods: they were cut into two pieces and spent their lives trying to find their missing half.

The next time they meet in the storeroom, he pulls up her skirts. She is terrified, but now there is a glitter to her days, a light illuminating the stolid sameness of her life.

They meet three more times. Nobody knows about them. They are each other's secret.

Agnes doesn't know that what they are doing will make her end up pregnant: that is the simple, ridiculous truth. Growing up with brothers, she's familiar with the oddities of male bodies, and when she was ten her friend Edith explained to her how boys' anatomy vs. girls' made a certain kind of sense, though for what reason was not entirely clear to either of them.

She knows instinctively that they shouldn't be doing it, but when Jesse pushes against her, and insists, and thrusts himself into her, she gives in. And it happens so slowly, it happens along with so much else, such a warmth of skin on skin, so many kisses and murmurs. *How can anybody be so soft and pretty? I think about you all the time. You are just the prettiest thing....*

She doesn't know that listening to his murmurs, murmuring back, kissing (so pleasant) and what follows (so painful) will end in a swelling stomach and the need to throw up every morning before school.

And she doesn't know that the significant fact isn't that she's been singled out, made special, but that— as her family will point out to her over and over in the months to come—for a bright girl, she has been very, very stupid.

Uncle Clement, her father's only brother, has lived with the family since Agnes was eight. After Gilbert's accident, Clem and his crates of books arrived in North Baltimore from Toledo. He was wounded fighting the Cheyenne in Colorado, and his right eye is made of glass. He helps out with the boys, plays checkers with Gilbert, keeps the stoves going, does anything heavy that needs to be done. On the fifteenth of every month he gives Bessie four dollars from his army pension.

Clem made himself a bedroom in the attic, where along the north wall he piled his books. Most of them are about history, or about travels to faraway places like China and Australia. Besides the books, there is a cot bed, a wobbly table next to it with an ink well and an oil lamp and his pipe tobacco, and a wooden box full of notebooks and papers.

The room is cold. Clem says the books insulate the room and keep him warm, but he has woken up more than once with ice in his red beard. Agnes likes to visit him up there in the quiet attic. Sometimes they just sit together, him hunched up on his bed, her on the floor, both of them with their books, sometimes raising their heads to speak, but mostly reading.

Or Clem scribbles in his notebook. He is writing a novel about a tramp named Tiberius Humphrey who is making his way from Ohio to the Klamath River in California, where a long-lost relative is supposed to have a goldmine. Clem spent a year out west when he was a young man—doing what, nobody knew, not even his brother. He says he has dreams of going out there again, but for the moment he has to be content with writing about somebody else's journey.

"When is he going to get there?" Agnes asked him.

"It doesn't matter," he told her. "Maybe never. This book isn't about getting to a destination, it's about a journey."

She climbs up to the attic one day in early February. Uncle Clem is writing in a lined notebook, sitting on his bed with a muffler around his neck and Bingo the cat draped over his feet. He holds up his left hand and says, "One moment, Agnes." He writes another word or two, blots what he's written, and closes the notebook with a little smile. "Tiberius is traveling across the state of Nebraska in a flatboat on the Platte River. You may not know this, but, although Nebraska is completely land-locked, it has more miles of rivers than any other American state. I hope you'll get to see it someday—go in the summer. The Great Plains are a vast expanse of gold. A beautiful part of the world, enormous and empty. Very different from Ohio."

Agnes sits down on the end of the bed, dislodging Bingo, who leaps to the floor and sits, licking a paw. "I need to talk to you, Uncle Clem."

He sets his pen on the table and leans back. "Talk away, my dear."

He doesn't interrupt while she tells him the story—it's not very long—beginning with Dickens last October and ending just that morning before school, when she jumped down from Mrs. Ober's hayloft, landing hard, twisting her knee, and waiting, waiting, for something to happen, but nothing did except that she limped all day.

"Don't ever try that again."

"I won't. But I don't know what to do."

Uncle Clem doesn't speak for a while. Maybe he is waiting for her to cry, but she isn't going to cry, no matter what. She just looks at him, noticing as she always does how his right eye is a brighter blue than his left eye. It doesn't move, of course, while the other one does, so he often appears to be cross-eyed.

"Well, Agnes," he says. "There's not much you can do except to pop that baby out when it's ready."

She had hoped for something else. She'd decided that Uncle Clem would be the one she would tell because she knew he wouldn't judge her and because he hadn't spent his whole life in Wood County, Ohio, like everyone else in her family. Maybe he would know of some old woman in Toledo who has a magic potion, or a doctor who will do him a favor.

"Oh," she says. "Well." Bingo jumps up to her lap and settles down again. "Then I suppose that's what I'll do."

She tries to imagine herself with a huge front end and a lap with no room for a cat to curl up. How could that happen? She's always been short and skinny. But her sister Helen, even tinier, was so big with her twins she could hardly get out of a chair.

"Are you going to tell me who sired this child?"

Agnes stares stonily at a pile of books: a geographical encyclopedia in six volumes. "No, I am not."

"Agnes—"

"You can all take turns torturing me until I scream, but I'll never tell."

"Jesus Christ almighty."

"Please don't get mad at me. I came to you because I can't tell them."

"They're going to have to know, and pretty soon."

"Mama will have convulsions and Papa will murder me."

"Agnes? Will you please stop being melodramatic?"

"I'm sorry." Now she wants to cry. Her knee still hurts, and her favorite blue skirt doesn't button around the waist anymore, and it has snowed every day for the past week. "It's just that everything is so awful."

"Let me think."

She scratches the back of Bingo's head to start up her purr. Uncle Clem fills his pipe and lights it, paces over to the window under the peaked roof and opens it a crack, then sits down, leaning back against the head-board. Her uncle's puffing on his pipe and the cat's purr are the only sounds.

"I'll tell your mother, and we'll let her tell Gilbert."

Then she does start to cry, and blubbers out her thanks.

"I suppose Bessie will be thinking of Emery."

Emery is Agnes's half-brother. Everyone knows that her mother gave birth to him when she was seventeen, and he was raised as a Trowbridge by Bessie's mother in Kenton, not an hour away from the Millers. He comes over for Sunday dinner every couple of months. They all take him for granted. Agnes has forgotten the name of Emery's father—a local farmer, married to somebody else. He died long ago, when Emery was little. Emery works at the post office and is engaged to Caroline Graves, the first-grade teacher at Powell Elementary. They all love Emery, but Bessie has never said anything about how he was gotten—not to Agnes, anyway.

She blows her nose and wipes her eyes on her sleeve. "Maybe she won't be so mad at me."

"Agnes—it's not about people being mad at you. That's the least of it."

"Then what is it about?"

"Nobody can make this right if you won't tell us who the father is."

"When you talk about making it right, you mean getting married."

"That's the usual way."

"I'm only fifteen."

"And how old is he?"

She presses her lips together and shakes her head.

Uncle Clem exhales tobacco smoke with a loud sigh. "You are a stubborn girl."

She's used to being called stubborn. "I don't care. I'll never tell. Never, never, never."

"All right. We'll see about that. For now, the important thing—" He puffs on his pipe for a minute. She waits for the important thing: she knows that, if her uncle says it's important, it is. "The important thing is that we don't let this ruin your life, Agnes."

"How do you know?" her mother asks.

"I don't get my monthlies."

"How long?"

"Not since October. Last time was right after school started up."

"Four months." Bessie's eyes drop. Agnes sucks in her stomach. "You're showing. Why didn't I see it? And why did it take you so long to tell me?"

"I wasn't sure what it was."

"Agnes." Her mother's voice is weary. She closes her eyes, raises her hands to her head, and rubs her temples. Slow, circular motions that speak more than anything else of trouble, trouble, trouble. She does that for a long minute, and then she abruptly drops her hands and opens her eyes. "Don't you learn anything from all those books you read?"

Agnes thinks of Hetty Sorrel in *Adam Bede*—pregnant, but how? After a walk in the woods? And then deserted, ending up in Australia as a convict, her baby dead.

"Who did you do it with, Agnes? Who's the boy?"

Agnes clamps her lips shut and shakes her head.

"Was it Jeremy Batterly?"

"No."

"Ross Huddle?"

"No!"

"Somebody older, Ag?" Bessie pauses. "Was it Mr. Hibbing?"

"No! No! No!" Agnes stands up to leave but sits down again and hides her face. "It was nobody! It was nothing. It doesn't matter who it was!"

"Stop your crying," her mother says. "You're going to have to tell sooner or later. Papa will make you."

"I won't tell! I'll kill myself. Is that what I should do? I'll slash myself with a knife. I'll wait for the train and lie down in front of it. I'll get Father's army pistol and blow my brains out."

Bessie comes over and holds her. "Hush, hush, crazy girl. Stop your crying. When are you due? Next summer sometime. We'll work it out. It will all come right, Aggie."

Agnes knows it will not all come right. She doesn't want to have a baby, to get fat and have to endure the pains—that much she knows: it is painful to get the baby out, much, much more painful than it was to get it in. She was only six when Robert was born, but she remembers being waked up in the dark by her mother screaming and how it was still going on when she left for school. She'd heard Helen talk about the delivery of the twins. She knows about the blood, the filthy sheets put to soak, the pain that's so bad nobody can even describe it. The women always stop talking about such things when the boys come in, but they keep it up in front of Agnes and her sister Sally. Sally once said, "I'm never going to have a baby. Never!" Agnes hadn't been quite so sure—women kept doing it, after all. How bad could it be? And besides, it's just something that happens—how could you help it?

Now she knows more. Her ignorance embarrasses her. And it will not come right. Her father's wrath will burn down the house. Her grandmother's tears will drown them all. She is fifteen, and she will be sixteen when the baby comes. What will happen to it? Will she have to stay home from school to nurse it and tend it?

And Jesse, Jesse: when will she see him again?

"I don't want this baby," she says, weeping again. "I don't want this to happen."

Bessie says, "Hush now, quiet down, don't worry, we'll figure it out," and Agnes presses her forehead against her mother's comfortable middle and quiets down.

When she comes in from school the next afternoon, they're waiting for her at the kitchen table. Sally
is at eighth-grade choral practice, Robert and Sam never
come home until it's almost dark. It's just Mama and
Papa and her Grandma Lu, who looks like she's been
crying all day: nothing is more lugubrious than the gaunt
Frick face with its long nose and hollow cheeks and severe
expression. When her father and her grandmother smile,
they look wonderfully, unexpectedly merry. But neither
of them is smiling now.

"Sit down, Agnes," Mama says. She is not smiling
either. She pushes over a piece of cornbread and a glass
of milk. "Eat."

Agnes isn't hungry, but she knows her mother will
nag her until she eats, so she stamps the snow off her
boots and hangs her coat on the hook and sits at the table
and takes a bite of cornbread.

"Especially the milk."

She has a sip of milk, which doesn't taste right.
Maybe it has gone off? Mama would never pour away
milk just because it has gone off. And the cornbread is
stale, tasteless. She thinks about dunking it in the milk,
but decides against it.

Her father gets right to it. "Who is this hoodlum?"

She says nothing, just gazes down into the glass of
milk she doesn't want. She hears her father exhaling
hard through his nose, which means he is angry but not
yet livid.

"Agnes—is it somebody you're fond of?" Mama asks.
Agnes knows that, if she tries to answer, she will cry, so
she just gives a nod.

"Then Aggie, why—"

"No!"

"You could just—"

"No! And I will not talk about it."

Another long silence. Papa's snorts continue for four or five breaths, and then he says, "Well, one way or another, what we figured was that after your birthday you can leave. You'll be sixteen, so that's perfect."

"What does that mean: leave?"

"Leave school, Agnes. Leave North Baltimore High School."

"And what does that mean: perfect?"

"It means you'll be old enough to quit school without anybody giving us a hard time."

Outside somewhere a dog barks. The clock ticks. Otherwise, a heavy afternoon silence descends on the kitchen. Into it, she speaks again: "What does that mean: quit school?"

"That's enough from you." Papa pushes back his chair and reaches for his crutches as if he were going to get up. But he doesn't. He leans back again and rakes his fingers through his hair and makes a face like he is being strangled. "You know damn well what it means. You'll not be going back, you'll be home looking after that baby."

"But I don't know what it means, Papa," she says, keeping her voice soft and agreeable. "You don't mean next fall? You mean just for a while? I'll go back in September?"

"No. That's not what quit school means, missy."

"Uncle Clem says the important thing is that I don't ruin my life."

"Clem." Papa would spit if there were a spittoon handy. "Who do you think's going to look after that child if you don't? I doubt that he's going to do it."

"I don't know." Agnes folds her arms across her swollen chest. "Mama?"

Papa starts to stand up again, but Mama puts out her hand on his arm. "Don't, Gilbert."

He pulls his arm away. "Don't what, Bessie? She needs to take the responsibility for her own mistakes." He stops and folds his arms the same way Agnes has hers folded. She sets her hands back in her lap. He says, "All right, Miss Agnes. Let's do it this way. You tell us who the father of your mistake is, and we'll see about letting you stay in school."

She stopped throwing up a month ago, but now her throat constricts. It isn't just the sour milk. She can't speak for half a minute, then she looks him in the eye. "What do those two things have to do with each other, Papa?"

He stares right back at her. "You give me something, I'll give you something."

"Why do you want that from me?"

"Agnes!"

Mama says, in the calm way she sometimes has, "I'll take care of the baby, Gilbert. Let her stay in school." Not so much calm as resigned, maybe. Ever since Charlie drowned, she has a way of suddenly sitting back quietly in the middle of an argument, quitting, as if to say: *Just let it happen. What does it matter?*

Her grandmother speaks for the first time. "You stayed home and took care of Emery, Bessie," and Agnes turns to give her a look that says: *You're supposed to be on my side.*

"I did take care of Emery," Mama says. "But I wish I'd been able to stay in school instead."

Grandma Lu nods. "That's what I meant. And you graduated from high school, Gilbert. You and Clement. I made sure you boys did. I wish I'd finished, too. In them days hardly anybody did, but I wish I'd had some schooling and learned something in my life." Agnes has never heard her say such a thing before. She reaches over to squeeze her grandmother's old, wrinkly hand. "That would be best, Gilbert," Grandma Lu says, squeezing back. "Aggie's too smart not to finish school."

"Smart." Papa lets out one of his snorts. "If she's so smart, why is she in this trouble?"

He sits there shaking his head, but Agnes feels a flame of hope. "Papa? They'll let me take my final examinations here at home. I know they will. They'll send work home for me. They did that for Jack Halbach when he had diphtheria." She is always careful to pronounce it *dif*, not *dip*. "Mr. Meyers went to Jack's house the minute the quarantine went off and made him write some of his final exams and for some of them he just asked him questions, and Jack passed everything."

"Why should I give a damn what Jack Halbach did? He wasn't expecting a child!"

"Well, neither am I. I mean, nobody really knows I am. I can leave school next week. I can have a fever. A disease."

His eyes drop to her waistline and slide away, back to her face. "You think they don't know?"

"I'm not showing so much. And suspecting isn't the same as knowing. It could be Mama's baby." She raises her voice. "This could be my sister I'm carrying."

The idea stuns her with its simple brilliance, and she has to stop and take a breath.

Her father says, "Now she's become a lunatic on top of everything else," but Agnes can see that the idea interests her mother.

"Well, why not, Papa? If Mama agrees to it. And if people suspect something else, they'll stop after a while, or they'll lose interest in it. Or they won't. I don't care."

She has realized this only recently, in the space between the last time at the library and the day she told Uncle Clem. It came to her in Latin class one morning as she looked around at her classmates, who were doodling, daydreaming, passing notes. Thinking Virgil is funny because of Virgil Bendix, who sits on the steps of the post office singing and wishing everyone who passes a happy anniversary. She doesn't care if she is talked about. She doesn't care whether Emma Bartz and Edith Mercer ever speak to her again. She only cares about one thing, finishing high school. No, two things. The other one is keeping her secret.

Papa repeated, "You don't care. Did I hear that right?"

Agnes turns her attention to the yellow-checkered oilcloth that covers the table. It is rubbed bare in spots, so you can see the weave of the cloth. On it rest her mother's plump hand with the thin gold band, her coffee cup (pink roses) and saucer (plain blue), and the half-inch of cold coffee Mama left, as she always does. Also, folded on the oilcloth, her grandmother's hands, with a twining pattern of raised greenish veins on the backs. And her father's right hand, made into a fist, clenching and unclenching. *Notice everything*, Mr. Huebner said, and so did Uncle Clement. *If you want to be a writer someday.* So she concentrates hard on the chipped cut-glass sugar bowl that serves as a spoon repository, a dozen or so of them leaning back against the edge, including two that are real silver with the F monogram and two that are cheap dull tin and the rest that are—

"Agnes."

She raises her head.

"Your father asked you something."

"I'm sorry, Papa. What was it?"

"You said you don't care what people think? What people? Your friends at school? The people in this town who've known you since you were born?"

"No. I don't care." She knows it is the wrong thing to say, but she has to say it because it is true. "In five years, what will it matter?" She holds out her own two hands, palms up, and sees how thin and white they are compared to the other hands at the table, which are red and old. She puts them back in her lap. "But if I don't graduate, that will matter."

"Matter to who?" Papa asks.

To whom. "It will matter to me."

"You weren't raised to have these ideas."

Agnes chances a smile. "Papa? I wasn't raised to have them, but I was raised to say them if I needed to. To be honest. Wasn't I? So I'm saying that I don't want to quit school. I love school. I'll do anything. I'll tell lies about this baby, and I'll pretend I had rheumatic fever or whatever you want. Typhoid. Consumption. The Black Plague."

He bangs his fist on the table—she was waiting for it—and the cup rattles in its blue saucer. "Don't try to be funny, miss! This isn't a joke."

Her grandmother says, "I know it's just your way, Aggie, but you're tempting fate to talk like that about sickness and fevers." She reaches in her apron pocket for her handkerchief and balls it up in her fist, handy in case she needs it.

Just your way. What does that mean? That she doesn't belong in this family, never had, she belongs somewhere else—Nebraska, California, the foggy streets of London,

England. Anywhere but there. *Finish high school and get out, somehow, someday.*

Then her mother reaches over and tucks back a piece of her daughter's hair that has come loose, and she smiles the way she has done, all Agnes's life, when she touches her hair—the frizzy curls that all her girls have gotten from her, though Agnes has brown hair like her father and her brother. "Aggie," Mama says, with that tenderness in her voice, and Agnes feels she never wants to be anywhere but in this shabby kitchen, with her mother taking care of her.

She sniffs back, again, the threat of tears. "I'm sorry, Grandma. I'm sorry, Papa. I'll take care of the baby until September, but then I want to go back to school so I can graduate with my class."

"And then what? Get a job someplace reading books and writing poetry in Latin?"

"Well, I hope so," she says, and that makes Grandma Lu laugh, and then her mother.

"Oh, Gilbert," Mama says. "She'll get married like everyone. And she'll be a better mother if she's had some schooling."

"And if people don't know she's got that baby," Grandma puts in.

Mama's face lightens suddenly, and she begins to laugh. "I'll have another baby. I'll do this for Agnes, Gilbert. What's another baby?" She sobers up again. "And we've lost so many." *Charlie*: the thought goes around the table, and the image of the way he looked when they pulled him out of Blocker's Pond.

"You spoil her, both of you," Papa says finally, wearily. "But that's not news to anybody, is it?" He stands up. "I'll find out who that child's father is. He should help out. He should pay some money for raising it."

"No." Agnes lifts her chin in a way that she knows her father will find pert. "He should not. If we need money, I'll write to Cousin Clay."

"You will not!"

Mama smiles. "You should know by now when your daughter is joking with you, Gilbert." They are all aware that only Papa and Grandma Lu are allowed to beg from Cousin Clay.

"Joking." Papa makes a disgusted noise, hauls himself up, arranges a crutch under each arm, and swings over to the door. He takes his coat off the peg. It has begun to snow again, and Agnes can sense her mother wanting to say: *Wear your scarf, Gilbert, put on your hat.* But she doesn't. He shrugs on his coat—nobody helps him, he never lets anybody help him—and goes out, slamming the door.

Mama said, "He'll be all right with it in the end."

"He's going down to Tully's."

"That's none of your business. Agnes."

She looks at her mother: mild blue eyes, red cheeks, double chin, untidy blonde hair gone white at the temples. She senses that her mother wants to add something. "What, Mama?"

"You should just tell us. You know some fathers would beat it out of you."

"But I don't have a father like that. Thank the merciful heavens for small favors."

Her mother sighs. "Drink up that milk, you need it."

She drinks the milk and eats the stale bread, because at the Millers' wasting food is the worst thing you can do.

The last time she met Jesse in the storeroom was just before school let out for Christmas vacation. She told him she couldn't meet him anymore—no reason, she just couldn't.

"Don't say that, Agnes. What will I do without you? You're like nobody I've ever met before."

"Well. I'm sorry. I just can't see you anymore."

"Can I ask you why?"

"I have to go home and read a book."

That made him laugh. "There—you see? That's what I mean."

She couldn't believe she'd never hear him laugh again. She leaned her head on his shoulder. She loved the smell of him, even his sweater.

He drew away to look at her. "Aggie—you're all right, aren't you?"

In the dim library on a late afternoon in winter, his eyes were more gray than green. His light brown hair fell across his forehead past his eyebrows. All she wanted was to lie down back on the table again and lift up her skirt.

She put on her coat. "I'm absolutely fine," she said, and pulled her wool hat down over her ears.

Sally comes home from school and says to Agnes, "Some people are talking about it."

"About what?"

"About how my sister looks like she's going to have a baby."

"Who?"

"Archie Sweet. He said you're no better than a streetwalker."

"Really. And what did you say back to him?"

"I asked him what a streetwalker was."

"And what did he tell you?"

Sally's face gets so red you almost can't see her freckles. "You know."

"Well, Archie Sweet can go directly to hell and take his pimples and his buck teeth with him."

"You will owe me this for the rest of your life," Sally says. "You'll have to do every single thing I ask you forever, or I'll tell everybody the truth."

Agnes knows that is nonsense—Sally would never want anyone to know her sister is having a baby—but she thinks it best to do what she knows Sally wants: she hugs her and kisses her and begs her to keep the secret and tells her she depends on her, she'll never get through it without her.

Sally says she won't tell, and she insists that they prick their little fingers with pins and mingle their blood. Agnes doesn't point out the silliness of it—they're sisters, their blood is already mingled! She just gets a straight pin from Mama's dresser top. They stick their thumbs and squash them together, and when Agnes sucks the blood from her thumb she realizes she's sucking Sally's too and that makes her gag.

Then, on a cold day in March, when Agnes is walking home from school, Jesse catches up with her. It's her last week of classes. On the coming Saturday, she is going to be too sick to go to Edith's sixteenth birthday party, and by Monday she will be in bed with a high fever.

"I want to talk to you." She doesn't say anything, just walks faster, but he keeps pace beside her. "Agnes," he says. "We're in trouble, aren't we?" She keeps going. "You're going to have a baby. Am I right?"

She stops then and looks up at him. He is suffering, she can see that. There may even be tears in his
eyes. "Yes."

"I'm a brute."

"No. You're not a brute. You're—" She can't think
how to go on, so she stops.

"Listen," he says. "Agnes, listen to me. I miss you so
much I'm going crazy. I want you to know this. I'm in
love with you."

"Don't say that."

"I will say it because I mean it. I've never known
anybody like you."

"You said that already."

"I'll say it again. I've never met anybody like you. I
didn't expect this to happen. I thought—I don't know
what I thought, Agnes, but I have gotten to love you."

They walk in silence along the snow-rutted road
while she tries to take it in. What does it mean, he loves
her? And does she love him? Is that what this is? The
sleeves of their wool coats touch as they walk. She tingles
with the awareness of him beside her, looks down to see
his galoshes, unbuckled, striding along beside her brown
boots. The low winter sun hangs in the air in front of
them, at the end of Main Street, and she thinks, knowing
how foolish it is: not a brute, a child of the sun, a sun god.

"But there's this," he goes on, when they're almost at
her street. "I don't want to get married. I'm only seventeen. I'm going off to college in the fall. I'm going to be
a newspaperman. Or maybe a lawyer."

"Like Mr. Vholes in *Bleak House*?"

He laughs again. "What kind of girl are you, who
can make a Dickens joke in the middle of a serious
conversation?"

"I wasn't aware this was a serious conversation."

"It's the most serious conversation I've ever had with anybody. I wish you would slow down so we can talk properly."

"People should not see us together."

"All right, all right. But, Agnes, listen to me." They stop again and face each other. His nose is red with cold, his eyes squint against the sun. She could look at him forever. "I can't be a father to this baby. I can't—we can't—"

"You don't have to keep saying it. I heard you the first time."

"But I need to say this. I want to be with you. I will be with you someday. I will. We will. We'll get married. But not now. Do you understand?"

All those *I wants, I wills,* make her angry—or almost angry. "How do you know what I want?" she asks him. "How do you know I would marry you if you asked me?"

His face is stunned. "Well . . ."

"This is what will happen," she says. "My family is going to pretend that I'm ill. Nobody will see me. I'm going to miss school. We're going to pretend this is my mother's baby. My little sister."

He gapes at her, and she lets him do it for a minute before she goes on. "I will never tell a living soul that you're the father of this child. Is that what you want me to say?"

He lets out the breath he has been holding. She can see the relief in his eyes. "Yes. But I also want you to say you love me and that somehow, some way, we'll be together."

"I suppose I can say I love you. The rest of it . . ." She shrugs. "It's like something in a book. We are not characters in a book. Who knows what will happen?"

"Say you love me."

"All right. I love you."

"But you wouldn't marry me if I asked you?"

"I never said that."

"This is mad," he says.

"Maybe."

They turn the corner and, when they come to her house, he suddenly lunges forward and stands teetering on a rock in the front yard. "This can be our post office," he says.

"You have to go now, Jesse. You can't stand here on a rock talking to me."

"I'll leave notes for you under this rock. I'll do it as often as I can. We can write to each other. No names, just you and me. Tiny notes. Look." He jumps off the rock, lifts up one side, and tucks a dead leaf under it. "Like this."

She has to giggle. "It's not a difficult concept to understand."

He ignores that. "I'll write to you and you'll write back. Little bits of paper."

"Jesse."

"It's all we have, Agnes. Listen to me! I don't want to lose you."

"What about Mary Corbett?"

"What about her? She's read about four books in her whole life, and I hate kissing her."

"Do you like kissing me?"

"You know the answer to that."

"Say it anyway."

He jumps off the rock and stands beside her. His voice drops to a whisper. "I would rather kiss you than do anything else." Then it becomes a whisper she can hardly hear. "Except just one other thing."

She begins to tremble. She really thinks she might fall down in a faint. And that is when she first feels the baby kick. At first she thinks it's part of the faintness, but it happens again and she gasps. How does she know what it is? Nobody has told her. But she does.

"Jesse, you have to go."

"I'll leave you a note. Tonight! And write back to me. I'll walk by and look under the rock. Whenever I can." Far down the street, Agnes can see Sally with her friend Ida. "Will you do it?"

"I'll try."

"Aggie? We're in a pickle, that's for sure. But it will all work out, you wait and see."

She learned later that Jesse always said that: *It will work out. Everything's fine, you wait and see.* For the kind of person he is, that is always true. She isn't sure yet if she is that kind of person—so far, it doesn't seem so.

"You've got to go," she says again, and this time when she looks at him she sees tears in the corners of his long, fish-shaped eyes. "Jesse."

"I'm sorry for this. I wish things were different."

"I don't wish it had never happened."

"My God, Agnes, how can I not kiss you now?"

"You have to go." She heads toward the house, the baby fluttering in her stomach, and at the door she turns. Sally is only half a block away, but she asks, "How do you know it will all work out?"

"Because we love each other. We know that now, and that's all that matters."

She goes up the steps and in the front door, knowing he's watching her, not turning around, feeling—what was a good word? Exultant! In spite of everything—yes, exultant! And what had ever made her exultant before? A 98 on a Latin test? She has been so stupid it's hard to imagine such staggering stupidity is possible, but at least she is living, she is no longer sleepwalking, she is in love, someone loves her, and—yes—*that's all that matters.*

The first note reads: I LOVE YOU LIKE THE THUNDER LOVES THE LIGHTNING. THE LIGHT-NING IS THE REASON FOR ITS EXISTENCE.

Neat printing on white paper, a bit damp but read-able. She doesn't find it until the next week. She doesn't know how long it has been there. In that house full of people—eight of them in five rooms and an attic—it isn't easy to sneak out to the front yard to look under a rock. She is supposed to be in bed with chest pains and short-ness of breath and a temperature of a hundred and two: rheumatic fever.

She ponders the note for a day or two, wondering if it's a quotation from Shakespeare or a Dickens novel she hasn't read. She hopes he made it up. She decides it's beautiful, and has the pleasing thought: *He is trying to make me think well of him!*

She borrows books from Uncle Clem, mostly about journeys—*The Innocents Abroad* by Mark Twain, and *Travels with a Donkey* by Robert Louis Stevenson—but her greatest loves are novels. Sally picks up books that Miss Truitt at the library chooses for her: *The Mill on the Floss, Hard Times, Jane Eyre, Tom Sawyer, Little Dorrit,* which she has already read but happily reads again, and *Our Mutual Friend,* which she knows Jesse loves. "Tell your poor sister she can keep these as long as she needs to," Miss Truitt always says. But Agnes gobbles them down and wants more.

On Agnes's birthday in April, Helen drives over from Tiffin in her new buggy with a box of her old maternity clothes—her idea of a birthday gift. She doesn't hide her disgust at Agnes's condition. Helen has always been easily disgusted, but a whole new world seems to have opened up since she married Roger the preacher.

"Once this is over, I hope you're planning to behave yourself," she says.

"Mind your own business."

"And it's a scandal that you won't tell anybody who did this."

"It would be a scandal if I did."

But Helen has made a spice cake, and they sit in the kitchen amiably enough, with cake and coffee. Bessie joins them. She doesn't complain, but Agnes knows she must be as restless as she is herself. The two of them are in the house together all day, withdrawn from the world. How much does it bother her mother, Agnes wonders, not to be able to go to the store or the park, or to take her long walks out to Blocker's Pond, where Charlie drowned—not to the cemetery where he was buried, but to the pond, where he was last alive. Now she spends hours just sitting at the kitchen table drinking coffee or knitting, lost in thought, looking out the back window— at what? The outhouse? Agnes wonders, not for the first time, what people who never read books think about.

She pours coffee into her mother's favorite cup, the one with the pink roses. "Mama and I considered the idea that she could go down to Deter's with a pillow under her waistband," she tells Helen. "But we tried it and we couldn't get it to look right."

"I can't believe you can tell these lies, Mama. I can't believe you're letting her get away with this."

"I know what I'm doing," Bessie says, with the closed-in look she gets on her face. She picks up her knitting, a white lopsided thing that is meant to be a blanket for the baby. "I want this child."

Her daughters look at her, then quickly at each other and away. Helen shrugs. "You people do things your own way."

"You people!" Agnes says. "As if you're not related to us!"

"Sometimes I wonder."

"You're not the only one."

"Girls."

They stop squabbling. Agnes passes the cake. Helen tells her she's carrying low, which means she'll have a boy. She suggests that she name it Theodore, after the president.

"I'm naming it Percival Montmorency," Agnes says.

Helen shakes her head. "Why are you like that?"

"I do hate all this dishonesty," Mama says once or twice. Agnes doesn't. *Minima de malis,* Mama! The lesser evil! Besides, telling lies makes life more interesting. They force her to use her brain—like math problems, but more fun. Like writing a book, but easier. Making dishonesty plausible is part of what she thinks about as she sits at the window hemming flannel diapers and watching winter turn to spring.

It's her idea to send the boys down to Van Buren, to help out on Uncle Dan's farm. *Aggie's sick,* Mama writes while Agnes dictates. *She needs quiet if she's ever going to mend. And the boys get so wild.* It's Agnes who gets Sally to spread the story around school about the night they were sure she was going to die—how her face got as white as a sheet and they thought she'd stopped breathing. And it's Agnes's idea to have Sally bring Edith Mercer over so she can wave at her through the parlor window, with a flutter of her hand and a wan smile.

Grandma Lu comes home lugging a pail of buttermilk from Mrs. Deter: *It's for Agnes, the best thing for the fever.* They all hate buttermilk, but Mama makes a pie out of half of it and a cake out of the other. *Our family has had its share,* Grandma Lu says to the women she runs into in town, and that's a truth nobody can argue with.

Agnes doesn't know what Papa is saying down at Tully's Tavern—men probably don't talk much about such things—but the rest of them have learned, and pretty quickly, to become a lying family. Agnes knows it bothers everyone, and she courts their forgiveness by taking over all the cooking, frying Papa's eggs in the morning, grilling bread for Uncle Clem to take upstairs with his coffee, making oatmeal for the rest of them, and in the evening devising supper out of potatoes and carrots and onions and chicken necks and whatever else Grandma brings home from the market.

Uncle Clem is the only one who doesn't have to lie. He hardly sees anyone, doesn't sit at the bar at Tully's with his brother, just stays in his room scribbling in notebooks and smoking his pipe. Sometimes, in the late afternoon, he ambles around the back yard in a rectangular pattern, along the fence and past the outhouse and the old chicken coop, and back along the Walnut Street side, over and over: it's what he calls a "thinking walk"—he says he got the idea from Charles Darwin. And then at supper he gives them the latest news of Tiberius Humphrey. When summer comes to Ohio, Tiberius is approaching the Colorado border. "Sounds like he's getting close to California," Agnes says.

"I might have to send him on a detour up through Wyoming and Idaho."

"I wish I could go with him," she says, which makes Uncle Clem chuckle, but not Papa.

It's hard to tell what Papa is thinking because he doesn't talk much. Agnes tries to keep out of his way, but one morning she is sitting on the couch in the parlor reading *Middlemarch*, with Bingo on her belly, when Papa sticks his head around the door. He has stopped asking her who fathered the baby; like Mama, he is defeated rather easily, though not until he has blustered and stomped around. She knows that the world, which to her is a storehouse of wonders, is in her father's eyes a terrible place, full of disappointments and disasters: his daughter's predicament is probably no more than what he expected.

"The patient is feeling a bit better today," Agnes says. "She is able to come downstairs."

He ignores that. "What's the book?"

"It's about a good woman and her disgusting husband and the handsome man she really loves but doesn't know it until the end. This is the second time I've read it."

"Sounds like a lot of nonsense."

"It's less like nonsense than anything I can think of."

He just stands there, leaning on his crutches. Then he sighs. "Well, I hope you're happy."

"I can't say I'm entirely happy, Papa. Considering."

"I mean the reading," he says. "You've finally got plenty of time to read."

"Yes." She smiles at him. "I like it when you cheer up and look on the bright side, Papa."

"Don't be smart, young lady." He says goes back down the hall. It's a sound she will be hearing in her head even if she lives to be an old lady: the rhythm of her father's crutches as he makes his way around the house.

Uncle Clem helps her with lessons, especially geometry, which is not her strong point. Her grades in any kind of mathematics have always been embarrassing. She likes making diagrams on graph paper, though she doesn't always understand them. Her uncle is surprisingly good at it. He also has a fund of knowledge about American history, especially Henry Clay, the Kentucky senator Lincoln admired. Cousin Clay the millionaire was named after him, and Clem doesn't have much use for either one of them. Agnes feels she has to stick up for Cousin Clay because he is so generous to them—another of his large checks arrived in April, between her birthday and Sammy's, so they've been eating whole chickens instead of just necks and backs—but her uncle says Clay has built himself a ridiculous chateau in Pennsylvania where he lives like a prince while he pays pittances to his employees at the steel mill, then sends a check to his crippled Cousin Gilbert or his old Auntie Lu and pats himself on the back. Just like Henry Clay himself, who railed against slavery but had a houseful of slaves at his plantation in Virginia. "He treated his slaves well, is what all the books will tell you," Uncle Clem says. "Whatever that means."

Agnes writes a paper about Henry Clay for her history class, calling him a hypocrite. Her uncle approves it, but Miss Rembert sends it home with a note saying she should have done more research and only gives her a 79.

Mostly, though, her teachers are easy on her, poor Agnes, sick in bed and feverish through all this glorious weather, except for Mr. Phelps, her Latin teacher, who plagues her with long translations from Livy and Cicero. Once she has a nightmare about the ablative absolute. She has always loved doing Latin, but during that long pregnant spring, she gets to love it even more: the precise structures, the way you can pack so much into a phrase, the glimpse into a lost world—it all makes a comforting distraction from the muddle of her life. Sometimes she does extra exercises just for fun.

Mr. Phelps has the Latin II class write notes to say they miss her, with various attempts at "get well soon" in Latin that run the gamut from "este bene" to "mox convalesce." Sticking to English, Ross Huddle writes that he hopes she won't have any permanent heart damage— a danger Sally has happily spread around—spelling it "damidge."

When she gets the highest grade on the Latin final, Mr. Phelps sends her a book of Cicero's speeches, with the inscription: *In omnibus requiem quaesivi, et nusquam inveni nisi in angulo cum libro.* A volume of Cicero isn't what she would have chosen to curl up with in a cozy corner, but she likes the sentiment, and she likes owning a book that's all in Latin. She would have preferred Catullus's love poems, which she makes Sally bring her from the library (she says Miss Truitt gave her a funny look), but Agnes copies down her favorites, in both Latin and English. She writes out the one about the thousand kisses (*basia mille...*)

and means to leave it as a note for Jesse, but she isn't sure how good his Latin is and doesn't want to be showing off.

One day, she wakes up early and decides to make bread. Mama is sleeping late, Grandma Lu is upstairs praying, Uncle Clem is in the attic, and Papa has already gone out, probably hanging around the firehouse with his old cronies. Before ten o'clock, she has three fat loaves rising in the sun. She tears a piece of paper out of her Latin notebook and writes: I'M A GOOD BREAD-MAKER, I'LL BET YOU DIDN'T KNOW THAT, AND I LOVE YOU LIKE THE FLOUR LOVES THE YEAST. She pulls her mother's big shawl around her fat self and runs outside—oh, the beautiful fresh air! oh, the ray of sun that bursts through a cloud as if just for her!—and puts the note under the rock.

Toward evening there's a rainstorm. She can see the rock from the living room window, like a turtle in a sea of mud. She doesn't know if Jesse has gotten her note or if it has disintegrated in the general mess. Then comes a warm spell, and she goes out very late one night to find a note that says: I LOVE YOU LIKE THE MUD LOVES THIS ROCK.

Before she can answer it, he sends another: I THINK OF YOU ALL THE TIME THAT I'M NOT THINKING ABOUT BASEBALL. I LOVE YOU LIKE THE CATCHER'S MITT LOVES THE PITCHES I THROW PAST THE BATTER. LAST WEEK EXCELSIOR 6, BUCKEYES 3!

She can't think of anything clever, so she just writes: CONGRATULATIONS. I WISH I HAD BEEN THERE and, in tiny letters, *I miss you.*

She imagines him pitching at the baseball games. She saw him doing it the year before, though she hadn't paid much attention. All she had was a vague memory of his long, lean body winding up the ball. She knows he'll be graduating at the end of June, and she will not be there to sing in the chorus at the ceremony. She'll be home with her huge belly in one of her sister Helen's ugly maternity dresses, frying eggs and cutting up onions, tired out from sleepless nights, the baby kicking her insides to bits. And she knows Jesse's taking Mary Corbett to the senior prom. She hopes it's true that he doesn't like kissing her. She hopes kissing her is like kissing a brick.

Sally goes to the graduation and says the chorus sounded fine without Agnes. Better, maybe.

Always, she is aware of the baby, not only the presence of the huge, kicking, flailing thing inside her but the unfathomable idea that it's a person who will grow up and do things and have a big sister named Agnes. She wonders if she'll be able to get through her whole life keeping the old lie alive.

Mama's fiftieth birthday is on the Fourth of July. Unexpectedly, Cousin Clay sends a check, and Mama has a new shirtwaist, sprigged with flowers. They put the flag out, and Helen and Roger and the twins come over with a big cake. Roger looks at Agnes's enormous belly but doesn't say a word, as if what she has under Helen's old plaid dress is a bushel of potatoes, not a baby. He says grace before lunch, and ends, "We thank thee Lord for all blessings present and to come," which Agnes thinks is sweet of him.

Nobody else is invited. The neighbors will find that odd. And Mama's best friend, Rose Covell? Agnes has a sneaking suspicion that Mrs. Covell knows the truth. Even granted that Mama is old, the pregnancy is difficult, she isn't feeling well—she and Mrs. Covell have been friends since they were both new brides, and she would never cut Mrs. Covell out of her life. Agnes wants to ask her mother, but she wonders about the awkwardness of life after the baby is born: Mrs. Covell knowing the truth, Agnes knowing she knows, Mrs. Covell knowing Agnes knows she knows, but neither of them able to say anything about it. And so what is the point?

She eats too much cake and has a bad attack of heartburn afterward while she's watching the fireworks through Uncle Clem's attic window. Then she can't sleep. She goes out to the rock at two in the morning—the air still smells of gunpowder—and finds a note: FOR THY SWEET LOVE REMEMBERED SUCH WEALTH BRINGS, THAT THEN I SCORN TO CHANGE MY STATE WITH KINGS. In very small letters he has added: *Forgive me.*

She thinks: Well, if anybody had found that, they would have known right away that Jesse Lyman Zorn wrote it, because who else in North Baltimore, Ohio, would quote Shakespeare on a note he hid under a rock?

She takes a chance and scribbles back: BASIA MILLE. In return he writes: DEINDE CENTUM. She finds it late on the night of July sixth. *Kisses, kisses, more kisses.* How could she have doubted his Latin? She goes up to bed but doesn't sleep. At first she just weeps with longing for him—the only person in the whole world who could recognize a line from Catullus and quote the next one!—and then, around three A.M., her water breaks, and she knows she's in for it.

Her labor goes on for a whole hot day and night and part of the day after. Grandma Lu sits in a chair in the corner of the room the whole time, sleeping, then wakes up to pray—her lips moving, her head nodding—then dozes off again. Helen drives over with a bag of swaddling clothes. She had her twins less than a year before, and Agnes is glad she's there. It's even more terrifying than she'd expected. Mama keeps her calm, tells her everything is going just the way it's supposed to. She reminds Agnes that she's given birth twelve times, counting Emery, and they all think about Leo and Hester and Raleigh, and poor drowned Charlie, and Hazel out in California and hardly ever writing home. But all the babies were born alive—"healthy and kicking," Mama says. And here she is herself, fifty years old, rubbing her daughter's back with her strong hands.

The whole time Agnes is in labor, trying to endure it quietly, trying to distract herself with Latin verb declensions, she tries not to think about Jesse's last note: sweet love remembered, *basia mille, deinde centum,* a thousand kisses, and a hundred more—and here she was while he was—what? Pitching a baseball. Walking out with Mary Crowley. Lying in a hammock reading a book. But that was the way of it. In between the pains, when she lies panting on the filthy, sweaty bedclothes, the tears leaking out of her eyes and into her ears, her mother wiping them away, her grandmother mumbling to Jesus in her corner, Agnes thinks of what she will write to him: *There's no need to forgive you, but if there were I would forgive you like the flower forgives the bee, like the tree forgives the wind . . . .*

She feels she has a moral duty to believe it: that Jesse is not to blame for this. And then during her last contractions, when there are no pauses between them, before the last push, the tearing surge of pain before the release, the thought comes to her that she hates him maybe even more than she loves him—*I hate you, I hate you, how could you do this to me*—and she isn't sure if she is saying it out loud or just in her head.

Helen catches the baby, and when she says, "Oh, Aggie, it's a girl, it's a perfect little girl baby, praise the Lord," Agnes is so astonished the first thing she does is laugh.

Helen washes the baby and quiets her screaming, and Mama wipes Agnes's face with a soft flannel, murmuring, "My brave girl, my darling girl." They put the baby in her arms. She doesn't look like anything but a bald bundle of redness and noise, but by the third day Agnes can see that there is something of Jesse in the slightly pointed ears and the way her eyes are placed in her head. But not enough, thank the heavens, for anyone else to notice.

She checks every day once she's able to get up and go outside, but it isn't until August that she finds another note under the rock: I NEED TO SEE YOU. WHEN? HOW? WHERE?

Agnes doesn't answer it immediately. Dorrie is waking her up every few hours all night long; her frantic need for milk is almost frightening. If Agnes can't open her dress fast enough, the baby screams so hard she can't calm down to fasten on, and that makes her scream even more. Agnes's breasts are big and leaky, her stomach is slack. She tries to imagine being with Jesse. Seeing her woebegone face in the mirror, she knows she is nobody's darling.

At the same time, mothering that baby is so all-absorbing she can think of almost nothing else. Just watching Dorrie sleep holds a fascination Agnes never expected. She remembers when Robert was born—Mama's last baby, a slobbering, dirty, noisy creature Agnes had kept her distance from. Now she can understand what a miracle the rest of them had seen in him, born only two months after they had all been awakened by Mama's sobbing cries when she found Leo motionless in his crib, looking like wax. The perfection of babies, the simplicity and innocence of everything they did, the way they want nothing else but to live and to grow. Dorrie's rosebud of a mouth opening and closing while she sleeps, as if she is dreaming about milk—her only pleasure. Then comes the fixity of her gaze on her mother's face, and something like a smile when Agnes picks her up. She jumps when there is a loud noise, or cries. She turns her head toward the sound of her mother's voice.

They've named her Doris Lucinda, but she's always Dorrie. Sometimes Agnes calls her Little Dorrit, which nobody in the family but Uncle Clem understands. "I hope she grows up to have more gumption than that girl," he says.

Mama is completely taken with Doris, and with a kind of quiet joy joins into the pretense that the baby is hers, carrying her into town and over to Mrs. Covell's. Sometimes Agnes thinks that she's gotten away with nothing, and that half the town must be aware of the truth. How could Mama not tell Grandma Trowbridge and Emery when she goes to visit them in Kenton? Helen and Roger know: why wouldn't Roger's brother Bill, who works at the livery stable, hear about it? Sally has probably made her friend Ida Rupert swear her own blood oath that she'll never tell anyone. And Ida doesn't tell anyone but her sister Susan, who only tells her boyfriend Pete Zewicki, who only tells the whole junior class at North Baltimore High School.

In spite of the baby's crying, the house is quieter than usual. The boys won't be back until September. Robert sends home a misspelled note to say he wants to stay, work with the horses, he wants to be a farmer, why does he need to go to school, but Papa says no—Agnes is glad of that—and Uncle Dan will be driving them home in time for school. By then she will be back in school herself, cured of her illness and with a new baby sister at home.

A week after Jesse's note, she wakes up in the night in a panic. Time has flown by. He will leaving for Syracuse, in the middle of New York State, to enroll at the university there—Syracuse because his father went there and because, Agnes suspected, he wanted to get as far away from North Baltimore as he could. It was one of the things they had talked about in the library after the other business was done: leaving, just to leave, they had to leave. "I feel like a wild animal here," Jesse said. "Shut up in a cage. Do you ever feel that way?" Yes, she did. "I thought so. I could see it, Agnes. From that first day. It was in your eyes."

She doesn't know exactly when he's leaving. What if he has already gone? She gets out of bed and finds a piece of paper.

They meet at midnight behind the outhouse, where they can be seen from Mrs. Ober's bedroom window if there's a moon, and there is. Uncle Clement is occasionally inspired to take one of his "thinking walks" in the middle of the night, smoking his pipe and ambling around in the dark. And Papa always sleeps badly: he could be sitting at any window, thinking his black thoughts.

Agnes doesn't care. She leaves the baby with her stomach full, sleeping peacefully, though she knows this cannot be counted on, and creeps out the back door, avoiding the bad step, wishing she had taken a shawl because the nights are already cool, fall is not so far away. At first, everything is black except the ivory disk of moon in the sky. She stands for a moment until she can make him out at the end of the yard, watching for her, and she runs.

They stand with their arms around each other. The familiar smell of him, his arms holding her, her head on his shoulder where it belongs: *This is enough*, she thinks, but then they begin kissing. It doesn't really matter that she's haggard and exhausted and her hair is a rat's nest and the moon shines down on them like a lamp.

"We only have two more weeks," he whispers. "I'm leaving on the sixth."

She can't help it, she starts to cry.

"No, listen." He speaks quietly, quickly, in her ear. "I have an idea. You can start going out, Agnes—can't you? You've made a complete recovery from your awful illness. I want you go to the dance at the grange hall Friday night. I'll be there too. We'll dance together—once, twice—by the end of the night, maybe three or four times."

"Jesse—"

"Listen, my honey. We fall in love. Right there in front of everyone! We look at each other with stars in our eyes, as if we've never seen each other before! I walk you home! Why didn't we ever notice each other before? And now here we are, and I'm leaving in two weeks." He holds her away from him, and in the moonlight his eyes are shining. Jesse has a way of looking happier than anybody in the world. "In those two weeks I court you like you've never been courted before. We go out walking together. Your parents invite me to supper. My parents invite you to supper! I call for you on Sunday morning, and we walk to church together and listen to Reverend Archer's asinine sermon."

Asinine sermon, whispered in the dark, makes her giggle. She knows there's something wrong with this conversation, that Jesse is turning something serious into a game they'll play together, but in spite of herself she's getting caught up in it. "We walk home from the ice cream social holding hands," she whispers back. "When you leave me at the door, you kiss me—just once."

"Maybe twice."

"I suppose that's a possibility."

"Your father will yell at you, but you tell him you're in love."

"Amor vincit omnia, Pater."

"Veritas!" He laughs and holds her tighter. "And the night before I leave we have a picnic in the park and we sit on a bench. I put my arm around you and ask you to wait for me."

"And I think about it for a minute but then say I will."

"You darn well better say you will!" He looks into her eyes. "And you will, Aggie. Won't you? I'll be home at Christmas. It's not even four months. And in the meantime we'll be able to write to each other. Aggie—we'll be *going steady.*"

Agnes doesn't know the expression, but it has the right sound. She clings to him. He kisses her again. They say that they love each other. Then, from the house, she hears Dorrie cry. Jesse raises his head; the light in his eyes has dimmed. "That's her?"

"Little Dorrit," she says, but he doesn't react.

"I guess you'd better go, then," is all he says, and when she turns he suddenly pulls her back. "Aggie," he mumbles into her hair.

The cry is now a wail. "I'll go to the dance," she says. "I promise," and runs back to the house.

They make it last for almost two years. They are a couple, a pair. Everybody knows it. They are Agnes and Jesse, Jesse and Agnes, and her parents are happy that, after the Doris problem, she's found such a nice boy, who has such a bright future.

The summer of 1906, their second summer, Jesse doesn't come home because he has a job at a newspaper, the Syracuse *Post-Standard*, as a copy boy.

I can't believe my luck, he writes to Agnes. *Mr. Carlson says if I do well the first month he'll let me try some writing. Think of it! It's really the first step on the road to being a journalist—a newspaper reporter—I'm never sure what to call it, but I know it starts here.*

She reads the letter on her way to work, taking the long way, reading it twice before she puts it in her pocket. The cheeriness, the excitement, the—yes, that was the word—*exultation* of it makes her want to sink down in a heap on Main Street and cry. She takes it out and reads it again.

My job is all about the 5 C's, he writes. She doesn't care what the 5 C's are, but he tells her anyway: *Clear, Correct, Concise, Comprehensible, Consistent*. The 5 C's make him happy. Not—when she thinks about it—that it takes much to make Jesse Lyman Zorn happy. He ends it: *Be glad for me! Love, Jesse.*

What she doesn't write back to him is: *We have not seen each other since April, and now we will not see each other until*

Christmas. Is this part of your unbelievable luck? Or is there a sixth C, Jesse? Cruel!

What she does write is: *Of course, I'll miss you, but your job sounds perfect. I like my job at Ellis's too, though you might not believe it. At Ellis's the 5 C's are Coffee, Crullers, Chicken, Coleslaw, Codfish. Mr. Ellis says I get bigger tips than any waitress he's ever had.*

That is true. She went to work at Ellis's two days after her high school graduation. At the end of her first week, Mr. Ellis said, "You're a born waitress." Not that it's a difficult job—who wouldn't be a born waitress? What did you need to know? How to balance a tray? Remember who ordered what? Be polite to the customers? That's how she was brought up. Wasn't everyone? The hardest part is keeping her curls tucked back neatly under her cap.

She tells Jesse about the tips because she thinks it might make him jealous. But she doesn't tell him that Mr. Ellis calls her a born waitress.

Besides, it's as clear as sunlight: Jesse's father probably has a dozen old pals out there in Syracuse, men who were in his fraternity at the university, and he's gotten one of them to give Jesse a job. She doesn't need to wonder why Mr. Zorn couldn't have found his son a job in North Baltimore, at the *Beacon*. Or even the *Courier*, in Findlay. The answer is obvious: Jesse's parents want to keep him from her.

After that dance at the grange and the ice cream social, after the rapturous Christmas holidays and the Everyman volume of Keats's odes Jesse gave her and the gold locket he sent for her birthday with his picture in it, and after that first summer, when he came home calling her Agnès—he was learning French, and he would say her name with his eyes half-closed, and make it sound so soft, so seductive. *Je t'aime, ma chérie. Ma petite ange. Ma vie…*

After all that, had his parents finally got what they wanted?

Ah, that summer. She had never been happier in her life. They talked and talked, long hours of thinking about their life together. Someday.

"We'll live in a city, in our own house."

"A whole room with nothing but books."

"A big bed."

"A fireplace."

"I'll buy you a dog, and a hat with roses on it. We'll go out dancing on Saturday nights."

He brought home with him a tin of something he called Jimmy hats. She was still afraid, but they climbed up to the loft of the abandoned barn at the end of the town road and did it anyway. Sometimes he rented a buggy and they would take the road toward Findlay, where there was a long, dusty path with empty fields on either side, and they would leave the horse in a lay-by and hold each other in the middle of the tall grass. Then drive home in the dark and talk about their house full of books and their big bed. Brass, they decided. And what kind of dog? Something small and frisky.

After a while she stopped being afraid, or maybe she just stopped thinking. That first summer, Jesse worked for his father at the glass works, running the printing machine that made labels for the bottles. "Like young Master Dickens," he said, with a grin, and told her that Dickens was forced by his father to work in a factory pasting labels on tins of bootblack. On Friday nights Jesse always had ink under his fingernails that would disappear by Monday morning. Once she found half a dozen smears of ink on her white petticoat and had to bleach it out so Mama wouldn't find it. When she encountered Jesse's parents in church or on the street, they looked at her as if they could see her lying in a field with their son, her skirt hiked up around her waist. They never did invite her to supper.

You're so small, he was always saying. She knows her waist has become flabbier, but he could still circle his thumb and first finger around her wrist in a loose bracelet. He touched her collarbones, bent her leg to kiss her bony ankle. *You're like a bird*, he said. *You are my beautiful curly-haired canary.*

She fitted a Jimmy hat around him and then—oh, then, it was all so familiar, so alive, so perfect. *You are me. I am you. Nothing will ever change that.*

All through the next school year, he wrote to her two or three times a week, sometimes just a note to say he missed her, or to tell her what he was reading in his literature classes—*The Education of Henry Adams*, Emerson's essays—books Agnes looked at in the library but found she didn't want to read. Or he said he couldn't wait until Christmas, or Easter, or summer, when they would be together. He sent a telegram on the anniversary of their first time in the back room at the library: "I love you, and can hardly wait to love you even more." For her graduation, he sent a spray of white roses with a card: "For my darling, with all my love." She had a white dress with long puffy sleeves and a satin sash, and Mama bought her a new corset that pulled her waist to where it had been before Dorrie was born. She sent Jesse a copy of her graduation photograph, carrying the roses, signed with her love, and he wrote back, "I am starving for you."

And after all that, and the kisses and the vows and the house full of books and the big brass bed—after all that, she thinks as she plods to work clutching Jesse's letter, Mr. Zorn has concluded that a young woman with wild hair and a strange uncle and a wayward brother and a father who is unable to work, a young woman whose only claim to fame is the North Baltimore High School Class of 1906 Latin Language Prize, is not a fit mate for his only son.

This is what she believes. Has to believe. Because otherwise she has to believe that what the letter is really saying is that Jesse is staying away because he is tired of her.

He has never laid eyes on his daughter. The two or three times he had supper with the Millers, Dorrie was already in bed. Maybe, that first summer, he glimpsed her on her travels with her uncle Clem. Clem started taking a new kind of "thinking walk," pushing the baby around town in the old wicker perambulator, even after she was big enough to walk, just because they both liked it—Dorrie in her sunbonnet, sitting backwards, hanging onto the sides with her tiny hands, the top folded down so she can look at Clem while he talks to her. Agnes knows they are a sight: her tall, red-bearded, bowlegged uncle pushing a baby around the village, talking to Dorrie about his book as if she can understand everything he says. Jesse must have spotted them, but if he did, he never said so. Once, when Dorrie was sitting on the porch with Agnes and Sally, Jesse passed by the house with a wave and said he was in a hurry, he'd see her later. He never mentioned Dorrie, never acknowledged the fact that she existed.

And what did Agnes expect? If he had picked Dorrie up and bounced her on his knee and played peek-a-boo with her, that would have been, somehow, even stranger. And maybe someone would have noticed something about her ears, the shape of her eyes. Still, on the rare occasions when Dorrie's name comes up, she wishes he wouldn't look as if he didn't hear it.

Not long after her birth, Dorrie is weaned to a bottle and turned over to Mama, and by the time Agnes goes back to school in September, the baby is Mama's girl completely, Mama's late-life surprise. Sometimes it seems that even Papa and Grandma Lu have forgotten who gave birth to that baby.

But Doris still gets put to bed with Agnes in the tiny bedroom under the stairs. This is partly because there's no other place for her. Uncle Clem and his books and papers have the attic, the boys are crowded in their small room, Sally sleeps in with Grandma Lu. Mama and Papa have the back room on the first floor—Papa sleeps so badly even the cat is banished from their bedroom.

But the baby sleeps with Agnes partly because Agnes won't give her up. During the hours she's asleep, she belongs to her, her Little Dorrit.

That second summer, Agnes aches for Jesse. It's easier from Monday to Friday, when she goes home from Ellis's so tired she can hardly keep her eyes open and sometimes wakes up in the middle of the night with the lamp gone out and her book flat on her chest. But on her days off, when she finishes the chores, she takes long walks by herself, and that's when she has time to think and remember and miss him.

He writes a letter from Syracuse every Friday, which arrives every Monday. At first she sees this clockwork regularity as proof of devotion, but the absolute unvarying promptness begins to seem more like proof of duty than of constancy. She wonders, irritably: Does he never feel the need to write to her on, say, a Tuesday? Or get an irresistible urge on a Sunday? She remembers their notes under the rock. She never knew when one would arrive, and that made every day rich with the possibility of joy. Now she almost dreads Mondays, knowing one of his drab notes will be in the mailbox.

She answers every one of them the day she gets it. And longs to write to him again before the week is out, but she never does—or not more than once or twice.

Late in June, she begins to go out with Rudy Killian. Rudy works in the office upstairs at Guthrie's general store: he is the junior bookkeeper. He's short but heavily built, with an Irish brogue like a vaudeville comic and reddish hair slicked back with pomade. He comes into Ellis's every day for lunch: a ham salad sandwich and a cup of sweet tea—never coffee. Same thing, Monday through Friday, and he always leaves her a fat tip.

The day they got to be friendly was the day he ordered liver and onions. She glanced up from her order pad and stared at him. "Did I hear you correctly?"

He said, "I thought that would get a rise out of you," and they both began to laugh—more out of silliness than anything else. She knew he always ordered the same lunch, but had never noticed before his bright brown eyes and funny turned-down smile. Never really looked at him, she supposed—he always came in at the busiest time—and later he said he was always trying to catch her eye, and liver and onions was the only way he could think of to get her attention.

He invites her to the opera house to see a variety show with a comedian and a magician. She doesn't want to go out with him. From the beginning, Rudy strikes her as slightly ridiculous, though she can never pinpoint why. It isn't just that his ears stick out. Maybe it's something about those bright eyes, always eager, like a dog's eyes. She tells him she doesn't know him well enough. And that is true: she hasn't any idea who he is. His parents are in Ireland; he says he sailed to America when he left school, to live with his aunt and uncle, Mr. and Mrs. Ryan, over on Cherry Street. She doesn't know them, either, but she knows who they are. Mr. Ryan was a fireman with Papa years ago, before Papa's accident. Rudy asks if he can call on her sometime and meet her parents, and that very evening, after supper, there he is at the door. Mama welcomes him—Papa is in his room lying down, as he often is in the evening—and then she and Rudy sit on the squeaky porch swing together, Bingo stretched between them. Sally hears them laughing and peeks through the door but she doesn't join them, though Agnes wishes she would. After a while Uncle Clement comes out. She introduces him as her uncle Pumble-chook, and Clem raises his hand as if to slap her and she giggles, but Rudy just looks confused, so she says, "This is my uncle Clement," and Clem sits down with them, smoking his pipe. The two men start in on a long talk about motorcars.

It's a soft summer evening. She is wearing the blue-and-white striped dress that Helen made for her. She's thinner, thanks to the waitressing, being on her feet all day, but her breasts have kept some of their fullness.

Rudy can't take his eyes off her, at least not until Dorrie comes waddling over to the screen door looking for Uncle Clem.

Clem opens the door, scoops her up, and sits back down in the rocking chair with her on his lap. She is almost two years old and sweeter than any child Agnes has ever seen, with her big blue eyes and the stick-straight hair she got from the Fricks, cut in bangs. Rudy gives her his big smile and says, in his lilting voice, "What have we here, then? A little lamb? Or a puppy dog? Or maybe a baby goat?" Dorrie gives her funny crow of laughter, and in that instant Agnes forgets that Rudy needs a haircut and hasn't read Dickens.

"This is our Doris," Clem says, and Rudy looks from Dorrie to Agnes and says, "Well, you don't have to tell me you two are sisters."

They go to the opera house for the variety show, and the next week for *Uncle Tom's Cabin*. Agnes has seen it before, so she hardly cries, but she can tell that, when Eliza runs away with her baby son, Rudy is trying to keep himself from sobbing.

Jesse's parents are sitting two rows ahead of them. Mr. Zorn, who looks like an older, stouter Jesse, nods with raised-eyebrow cordiality, possibly even the trace of a smile, when he spots her at intermission, but Mrs. Zorn's eyes slide past her and away, and none of them speak. Jesse's Monday letter described in detail how he was asked to rewrite a story handed in by Albert Bass, the City Hall reporter whom she knew he disliked and considered incompetent, and he did the job so well that Mr. Carlson, the editor, considered giving him the byline but decided against it: "Next time, though!" Jesse wrote. "And then I'm on my way." At the very end, he added, "I hope you're well, my Aggie, and are not missing me too much. Love, Jesse."

My Aggie. And *me* missing *him*! Where was *I love you like the thunder loves the lightning?* All winter, he had signed his letters: *With mad, crazy love to my darling girl.* Or *Your obsessed Jesse.* Once he quoted from a Byron poem he read in his literature class: *We love too much and yet cannot love less.*

And now it is only *Love, Jesse.* It means nothing. When he writes to his mother, his sister, his aunt Clarissa Zorn over in Findlay, no doubt he ends his letters *Love, Jesse.* And his letters to Agnes have become—how can she even think this?—they have become boring. He never writes about anything but his job, the politics of his office, the dreary news from the city of Syracuse. A former mayor involved in a financial scandal. A train derailed. A big new building going up. Even his handwriting seems careless. She imagines him tossing off the letter and mailing it on his way to meet another girl and take her out for supper. She can almost see her, tall and dark-eyed, something like Mary Crowley but a better kisser.

She can't sleep all that hot Monday night. She lies soaked with perspiration beside the baby, listening to her soft breathing: the very existence of this tiny person beside her is proof of how they had loved each other, how they could not love less. Her tears mingle with the sweat on her face. At some point she begins to shake, as if it were January and she's freezing, like Eliza crossing the ice. She tries deep breathing, she tries curling herself around the comfort of Dorrie's hot little body, she tries reciting poetry to herself: *Forlorn! The very word is like a bell/To toll me back from thee to my sole self!* She can think of nothing more cheerful.

After a while she gets out of bed and goes down to the back yard. She sits on the steps. It isn't much cooler outside, but a tiny breeze comes and goes, and she opens the front of her night dress and lets it cool her breasts and her neck. She says to herself: *You have been a fool.*

She sits there until the sun comes up and the crows begin to call from tree to tree. She looks up at the torn pink clouds, and she decides she will wait a week, or even more, before she answers his letter. *La belle dame sans merci*: she will be like that.

She lets Rudy kiss her the next time they go out, and not because she likes his odd, prim kisses. She doesn't. If nothing else, it seems wrong to kiss someone so short: head-on instead of tipping her head back. She doesn't really like Rudy's big red mouth and thick fingers. He never seems more ridiculous to her than when they are locked in an embrace. She doesn't want to kiss anybody but Jesse, and whenever Rudy's eager face approaches hers she remembers Jesse bending down to her with that little smile.

But she does it anyway, thinking: I'll get used to it. And eventually, she does.

Jesse's Monday letters get shorter as the summer goes on. Hers to him are even terser, sometimes just a few lines scrawled above a quick "Love, A." She hopes her handwriting indicates that she has a lot on her mind, not much time to think about what she's writing. *All well here,* she writes, the double-L's a wild scribble. *You know what N. Balt. summers are like.* Occasionally she tosses off something like: *I did have an interesting time at the firemen's carnival,* or *Good picnicking weather!* But if he cares what that interesting time involved, or who takes her on picnics, he doesn't let on. His letters are like a challenge to see how much boredom she can endure: he's thinking of moving to a different rooming house, he says, on East Willow Street, from which his walk to work will be about seven minutes shorter. On his day off, he walks to a nearby park, where you can sit on a bench and see the whole city. Mr. Carlson has had electric ceiling fans installed in the newspaper offices. He finally gets a byline, for a story about a runaway carriage that injured six people, and he sends her the clipping:

RUNAWAY ACCIDENT
NARROW ESCAPE OF ELDERLY WOMAN
by J. L. Zorn

Mrs. Dorothy Ptak, age 68, narrowly escaped death in an accident which occurred Tuesday evening at half past nine o'clock at the corner of Herald Place and North Clinton Street. She was in a two-seated carriage with her son, Thomas Ptak, and a friend, Constantine Kehler, when the horse, owned by Kehler, who was also the driver, became frightened by a westbound streetcar and made a dash for liberty.

Entirely out of control, the animal crashed into the large iron trolley post in front of the Palace Restaurant, throwing the occupants of the carriage to the pavement. Mrs. Ptak was hurled between the post and the wreckage of the carriage. When she was extricated it was found she had escaped injury with the exception of a few scratches. Her companions likewise were uninjured.

The horse was bleeding badly, while the carriage was smashed to splinters. The horse, which will recover, is valued at $250 and the carriage at $100.

Extricated, she thinks scornfully. What a showoff. She writes back with congratulations and adds—as laconically as she can manage—"Glad about the horse." But she keeps the clipping in an old candy box in the drawer next to her bed, where she keeps all his under-the-rock notes and all his good letters and all his dreary letters. And—God help me, she thinks—she takes them out and reads them over and over, even the story about Mrs. Ptak.

Rudy knows nothing about poetry, and he never reads a book. They don't have much to talk about. He likes playing Parcheesi, Agnes likes checkers, and so they play both. Often they're silent together, which she finds uncomfortable at first, though she gets used to that too.

But Rudy can sing. He has no shyness at all about breaking into song. When they sit together on her porch, his warm, true tenor will suddenly ring out: "Just a song at twilight, when the lights are low . . ." Or the waltz from a new opera, *The Merry Widow*: "Hear sweet music softly saying 'I love you' . . ."

Sometimes as he sings he gazes at her, and she feels it would be rude to look away but misleading to gaze back at him, so she directs her eyes somewhere to the left of his left ear, which sticks out more than the right one. He can harmonize effortlessly, which Agnes can't do, but she can hold onto the melody while he weaves around it, and they sound good together. One night Mrs. Ober and the Rupert kids and the Phelans from around the corner all gather on the Millers' steps to listen.

Rudy is a soloist in the choir at the Catholic church. Agnes goes with him one Sunday to High Mass. Grandma Lu is opposed to her doing this. Grandma scarcely ever misses a Sunday at St. Luke's, the Lutheran church around the corner from them, and she considers Catholics no better than witches. But Papa hasn't been to church since the accident. And Mama doesn't care because that's Mama. So Rudy picks her up, and they walk arm in arm to St. Augustine's.

Uncle Clem goes with them. Clem makes the rounds of all the churches, a different one every Sunday. He shows Agnes the chart he's made: he checks them off, one by one, then starts over. He always says, "None of them is worth anything, so why not try them all?"

She asks him, "Why try any?"

"Intellectual curiosity."

"I don't see what's so intellectual about church."

"Absolutely nothing, as any idiot can see," he says, and that's the end of that.

Rudy sits in the choir, and Agnes sits with her uncle. When Rudy sings the *Sanctus*, Clem nudges her at one of the high notes and whispers, "Hang on to this guy, Aggie. A voice like that is nothing to sneeze at." Agnes digs her handkerchief out of her bag, takes three quick breaths, and lets out a dainty sneeze. Clem pretends it doesn't make him laugh.

She doesn't intend to hang on to Rudy, but he sticks to her. She works the lunchtime shift at Ellis's, and when she gets off at three o'clock, Rudy is usually waiting for her. He has talked Mr. Guthrie into letting him leave his ledgers and his adding machine for half an hour so he can walk her home. He works until seven to make up the time.

"Now there's an example of true devotion," Uncle Clem comments. "You're not going to find that too often." He's always on Rudy's side, and when Agnes ask him why, he just mumbles something like "He's a solid citizen" or "Don't underestimate old Rudy." She has the feeling that Clem knows Jesse is Dorrie's father. Mama asks her several times how Jesse is, and Sally badgers her about why her boyfriend isn't home for the summer. But Clem never mentions his name, and that omission is like an enormous boulder between them. She climbs the stairs to the attic less often, and has begun to lose interest in Tiberius Humphrey, who is stuck in the town of Casper, Wyoming, working on a cattle ranch.

In spite of everything, Agnes is unable to stop believing that somehow Jesse's philosophy—that everything will work out if you just give it time—will combine with her own—everything will work out if you just give it a kick—and the result will be more like Plato's philosophy: they are two halves of a soul who have found each other and reunited.

She can't figure out how that can have stopped being true—or, if it is still true, why they are writing each other these awful letters.

She sets her mind to the task of enjoying Rudy's company. It should not have been so difficult: she's aware that he's a very sweet man, and, though he isn't a reader, he's smart. He takes a piano lesson every Saturday afternoon from Mrs. Sanders on Poplar Street, just as Helen and Hazel did when they were little, before Papa had to stop working and all such frivolousness was knocked out of their lives. In less than a year, Rudy has already become a good pianist. "I'm good at numbers and good at music," he says with his easy grin. "And that's about it."

The Ryans have an upright piano, with keys as yellow as old teeth, and Rudy gives her a few beginner lessons on it, teaching her some of what he has learned. Mrs. Ryan likes Agnes. Soon Agnes is calling her Aunt Molly, like Rudy does. Aunt Molly sits and plays Parcheesi with them, and teaches them how to play gin rummy. Sometimes while Agnes and Rudy are fooling around at the piano, she makes a batch of macaroons or oatmeal bars that she brings out with two cups of coffee and a pitcher of milk. Agnes sometimes imagines marrying Rudy Killian. He's doing well at Guthrie's—his salary is twenty-one dollars and fifty cents a week. She could quit her job and settle down with him in a nice house like the Ryans' and have babies. While Rudy was at work all day, she could read and cook and make a flower garden, and Mama and Doris would come over, and Doris would be a big sister to her children, and she'd read them all stories.

When she isn't with Rudy, this fancy is especially appealing. Then there he is riding up to her front door on his yellow bicycle, or fumbling with her buttons on the back stoop, and he is just Rudy: a broad face under a straw hat, rattling on in his brogue about his job or the folks back home.

He's a little homesick, and he likes to talk about taking a trip back to Ireland to visit his parents, who are getting old, and to see his brother Paddy's triplets, born in the spring, and he says he wants to talk his sister Maureen out of becoming a nun. He sailed to New York from the port of Londonderry on the *Caledonia* four years before, going third class, but he has dreams of traveling back in second class, in a stateroom that he might have to share with only one person if he buys the ticket far enough in advance.

"I'm hoping I can go next summer," he says one evening when they're sitting together on the piano bench. "I'm saving up money for a ticket."

He has just sung for her a song she's never heard before, playing the accompaniment while he sings: "I Dreamt I Dwelt in Marble Halls," which he says is from an Irish opera called *The Bohemian Girl*. Agnes didn't even know there's such a thing as an Irish opera, but she doesn't say so.

"I hope you can do that," she comments, absently. The song stays with her: *that you loved me still the same, that you loved me, you loved me* . . . It's about everlasting devotion, and it has made her think of Jesse.

Rudy picks up one of her hands from her lap and holds it in both of his. "I think I can save enough for two tickets, Aggie. We could take a trip to Ireland on our honeymoon."

It's a hot night, but a chill goes through her, bringing a vision of her future life: Rudy Killian snoring in bed beside her while she lies awake and stares out the window at a dark blue sky and a huge creamy moon with flickers of clouds passing across it. It lasts only a few seconds, but it's as real as the music on the stand in front of her.

Gently, she withdraws her hand. "I don't know, Rudy," she says, and begins to stammer something about how they haven't known each other very long, but he shushes her and says, "I don't expect an answer right away, Aggie. It's a big step. But I wanted you to know I think about it. It's what I want, and I hope you'll come around to it too."

Oh, he is so decent. And he loves her—or she supposes he does, though he doesn't say so. *I love you like the thunder loves the lightning:* that's the kind of love she wants, and she doesn't just want it to be given to her: she wants to feel it, to give it back. She knows what it's like to love somebody that fiercely, and she will never settle for anything less.

Or so she tells herself sitting on the piano bench with Rudy. At the same time, she wonders if she's had her one romance and might never have one again, and if she will end up marrying Rudy, or somebody like Rudy, and lie awake watching the moon. As if Dickens had married off Little Dorrit to John Chivery, whom she doesn't love, instead of Arthur Clennam, whom she does.

By the time autumn arrives, Mr. Ellis has put her on the supper shift, working five nights. The money is good, but by the time she gets home she's beat. She hates not reading before she goes to sleep. All summer she's been struggling through *War and Peace*, but the war parts don't hold her interest. She gives up and rereads *David Copperfield* instead, but even that is slow going.

She sees too much of Rudy. She begins telling him not to come over on Saturday mornings, that she's too busy with chores to see him. After she has wrung out the laundry and hung it up and put the bread to rise, she has time before her shift at Ellis's, and she plays with Dorrie, teaching her the ABCs or just listening to her soft chatter about her dollie, whose name is Buckle. Or she goes out to the back steps where she can usually be alone, reading, the smell of mown grass all around her and Papa's overalls flapping on the clothesline and Bingo the cat rolling in the dust at her feet. But sometimes Rudy rides over on his bicycle to help Robert with his sums—Agnes never should have let that happen—and then he wanders out and talks to her. He has no idea that someone with her nose in a book might not want to be disturbed. Sundays are worse—she often goes to church with Rudy or Uncle Clem, and then Emery and Grandma Trowbridge come to dinner, and sometimes Helen and Roger. Even with the boys and Doris and Helen's twins eating in the kitchen, they are a crowd, elbow to elbow around the dining room table, but Mama usually invites Rudy to squeeze in, and he never refuses.

Every time he joins them, laughing at Uncle Clem's jokes and listening to Papa's tales of the Great Fire of 1891, it's as if another bar of her prison clangs into place. The two grandmothers refer to him as "Aggie's young man," and from the kitchen one afternoon she hears Robert in a singsong: "Aggie loves Rudy, Aggie loves Rudy," until she goes out and smacks him.

Jesse's classes have started again, which means he takes the trolley up to the university every day. He still works for the *Post-Standard* on Saturdays. By the middle of November he hasn't said whether he'll be home for Christmas, and Agnes can stand it no longer. She puts a P.S. in one of her letters: *Do you plan to condescend to visit your hometown for Christmas?*

Before she mails it, she looks at those words for a long time. She hates them. She hates being flippant and snotty. She hates not being able to write: *Please come home for Christmas, Jesse, I miss you like the smoke misses the fire.* The foolish tears roll down her cheeks—how did this happen, how can things have changed so much? But finally she

takes two deep breaths, wipes her eyes, seals the envelope, and takes it to the post office, where Virgil Bendix,
the idiot, wishes her a happy anniversary.

His next letter is only five words and a question mark:
Do you want me to? And her return is only one plus an
exclamation point: *Yes!* It gives her such relief to write it,
as if one of the songs she's struggling with on the piano
has ended in a rich and satisfying chord.

And then for three weeks she doesn't hear from
him at all.

Guthrie's has a fancy Christmas party every year,
with an orchestra and a champagne supper, and Rudy
invites her to it. The party is on a Saturday evening—
Agnes's night off—and she can't think of a reason not
to go, so she says she will, and that's when Rudy says
something that makes her want to crawl into bed and
stay under the covers until 1907: "I have a present for
you that I think you're going to like." His grin falters for
a moment, then returns. "At least I hope you will, Aggie."

She doesn't have anything nice to wear—her only
good dress is her white summer one—and she doesn't
care, she'll wear any old thing, but Mama and Sally
devote intense thought to the problem, and finally
Agnes decides she does want to look pretty after all those
months sweating and being rushed off her feet at Ellis's.
She wants to be pretty, but not for Rudy. She wants to go
to the party, but not with him. She wants Rudy never to
have come into Ellis's for lunch that day. She wants Jesse
to walk in the front door, sling her across his shoulder,
and carry her away.

Mama finds an old green-striped silk dress of
Grandma Lu's at the back of her closet—ancient, but

in good condition—and Helen alters it, letting out the waist and adding some lacy trim on the sleeves. Mama suggests she wear her hair tied back with a black ribbon, with just a few curls in front. Helen says she can borrow her fringed shawl. Sally says, "I don't know how you can marry somebody like Rudy. I'm going to marry a cowboy," and Agnes says, "I am not going to marry somebody like Rudy! And I'm definitely not going to marry Rudy!" Sally just smirks and says, "You wait."

All she can think about is the horror of the Christmas present Rudy is going to give her. And whether or not Jesse will come home.

When she leaves the restaurant on the Thursday night before Guthrie's party, Mr. Ellis's automobile is parked, as always, under the lamp in the street in front, like a big shiny insect. Leaning against it as if it's a fence post is Jesse—hands in pockets, wearing earmuffs, his face expressionless—watching her come out the front door and down the path. She is strangely calm, and she walks slowly. Even in the dimness, she knows him right away, though as she gets closer he looks different—older, taller, maybe. Or has she simply forgotten his face?

Without a word, he holds out his arm and she takes it, and they walk down Main Street. It's a frigid evening, but there has been almost no snow, so the brick paving is clear, the mud along the sides frozen into ridges. They get as far as West Maple, and neither of them says anything. Then, under the gas lamp on the corner, he stops and faces her. "Your letters," he says.

"What."

"They were horrible. Short, full of nothing, as if you couldn't think of anything to say to me."

The cold air creeps under the collar of her coat, and at the same time she is hot all over. Her breath starts to come in the kind of shaky snorts Papa makes when he's agitated. She clasps her hands to her chest, pushing hard through her coat as if she can slow down her heart. "Your letters," she says, and her voice comes out in a kind of gargle. "They were horrible. Short, full of nothing, as if you couldn't think of anything to say to me."

They look at each other. He becomes familiar again. His odd, light eyes, silvery in the dimness. His unruly sandy hair. And the feeling that used to be so powerful, so impossible to resist, that ebbed away over the summer and fall, begins to return, caught somewhere in the air between them.

She says, "Something has gone wrong, Jesse."

"Do you know what it is?"

"No!"

"I do."

She holds her breath. She doesn't want to hear it. She can't help remembering how, the Christmas before, they had made their own snug cave of warmth, pressed together in the buggy Jesse sometimes borrowed, or standing at her front door in the dark.

"What, then?"

"Agnes." He puts his arms around her. She can feel the grip of his fingers through the wool, and his warm breath on her forehead. "It's too hard to do this long distance. If we are going to be together, I need you with me. By my side. I need you to be there. Not here. I need you to come to Syracuse."

She puts on the silk dress and lets Mama fix her hair and tie on the ribbon, and she goes to the party with

Rudy. They've cleared the middle of Guthrie's first floor, pushing all the merchandise to the sides and covering it with red cloths. There's a raised platform at one end and the Guthries' spinster daughter on the piano, but—a bit surprisingly—Rudy's musical talents don't extend to the dance floor, so she is spared his arm around her waist and her breasts against his broad chest. They sit out the dancing at a table with his friend Ed, who works behind the counter at Guthrie's, and Ed's girlfriend, Winnie. Agnes went to high school with them both but remembers almost nothing about Winnie except that she was a dunce in Latin and only took a year of it. Ed had played baseball with Jesse. Winnie and Ed can't dance because Winnie fractured her ankle and has a plaster cast sticking out from under her skirt. Ed asks Agnes if she wants to dance. She has had two glasses of champagne, and would have liked to, but Rudy says, "You can get that idea right out of your head, pal!" and puts his arm around the back of her chair.

All through the meal—chicken with a sauce on it that even Ellis's wouldn't have served—he keeps grinning at her, as if they share some wonderful secret. The suspense is killing, and she is almost glad when Winnie says she really has to go to the little girls' room and hobbles off on Ed's arm, Rudy says, "I guess I told you I've got a present for you, Aggie," and reaches into his pocket.

Of course it is a little velvet box, dark blue. He waits for her to open it, but she can't make herself do it, she just sits gaping at it, and he finally springs it open himself and holds it out: inside is a gold ring with a tiny blue sapphire set into it.

When she looks at the ring box all she can see is Rudy's big paw holding it. "Ag?"

She reaches over and closes the box with a snap. "I can't accept this, Rudy. I just can't." She wants to say she is sorry, but she isn't, she's just relieved that it's over at last. Then she sees his face, bewildered and hurt—stunned, in a way. Like Charlie used to look when anybody yelled at him, as if he couldn't believe everybody didn't love him. Then she is sorry, but she still doesn't want to say so.

"I thought we were going to get married, Ag. Not now. But in a year maybe." She just shakes her head. "You mean not ever?" he asks—exactly like John Chivery to Little Dorrit.

"Yes. Not ever."

He takes a deep breath, lets it out with a whoosh, and sits shaking his head. He says, "I'll be honest with you, Aggie. I didn't expect this." He puts the ring box back in his pocket and says, "I don't know what to do now."

She can't look at him. She looks down at her hands twisting in her lap. She feels pretty sure she's done something wrong, but she doesn't know what it is.

AGNES

The B&O Railroad
April 1907

Agnes doesn't sleep well that last night, dozing in and out of crazy dreams. When she can begin to see the pearly light behind the tree out her window, she knows it's time to go. Dorrie lies beside her like a tiny furnace, and Agnes stays curled around her for a final minute. She's so used to the heat of that little bundle. The small, even breaths have lulled her to sleep for nearly three years. She wonders if she'll ever be able to sleep again without her daughter beside her.

Mama's little daughter.

She draws away carefully, not to wake her, and gets out of bed. The cold is a jolt. It's not until that minute, when she stands there shivering, up at dawn, with the dark house around her and the silent world outside her window—that she really understands what she is doing, what an immense thing it is, and at the same time she stops being scared. The excitement of it is almost enough to warm her up. She has waited so long for this.

There's just enough of a break in the dark to help her see and not stumble. She buttons up her shoes and takes her bag down from the hook, ties the blue scarf over her hair, pulls the covers up around the baby—they still call her *the baby*, she is so tiny—and kisses her warm face, softly, softly. *Goodbye, Dorrie. I'll be back someday*—not at all sure that is true.

She opens the door, and then she thinks the baby has made a noise, her puppy noise, they call it. She waits, but hears nothing more. She leaves the door ajar, not wanting to chance another squeak of the hinges, and tiptoes down the stairs. She can hear Papa's snores all the way to the kitchen. She gets her coat and goes out the back door into the near dark of the spring morning. First the outhouse, so jittery she can hardly pee. She hears the pulse beating in her ears. Mrs. Ober's pig, Swiney, mutters softly in her pen next door. Agnes slips back around the side of the house, past the forsythia bush and the white cross on the grave of Thomas, their cat before Bingo.

She stands on the front walk, getting her bearings, half expecting a shout from the house behind her: Mama roused by a noise no one else can hear, Uncle Clement prowling around, the baby crying.

But there is nothing. Nobody is out, not a milk wagon, not a drunk staggering home, not a dog. Only a rabbit on the lawn—was that a rabbit? Two rabbits. In the silence, she hears the cry of a lone bird. Around the corner on Main Street a cart goes by at a slow clop. She waits until it passes before she heads into the chilly wind, her bag hugged to her chest, glad of the scarf around her head. She has folded the money into the envelope that holds Jesse's last letter and has pinned it inside her camisole, except for three dollar bills for her trip in the pocket of her coat and another three in her leather purse.

The cigar store, Deter's Grocery, Ellis's, the pool hall, the livery barn, Hoffman's drugstore. A light on above the saloon. She keeps to the shadows. She is walking east, toward where the sky is warming to a rosy orange, but Main Street is dark, so that when she comes around the corner to the station, the lamp in the window is so bright she has to blink.

Her teeth are chattering with the cold, but she doesn't go in, though she can see the stove glowing. Mr. Bartz is on night duty in the station, narrow eyes and turned-up moustache, Emma Bartz's uncle, who worked with her father at Town Hall years ago. She imagines him later, at home. *What is that Agnes Miller doing, off to Philadelphia in the dark?* It would be all over town by noon. She will do better to buy her ticket on the train.

Sally knows she is going, but Sally doesn't know everything. All she knows is Philly, Mama's cousins on Walnut Street, and a possibility of a job as a waitress in a hotel there. "What hotel?" she asks. *The Hotel Astor.* Sounded grand enough. *They pay six dollars a week, plus tips.* "Six dollars! You've only ever been a waitress at Ellis's, they'll never hire you at a fancy hotel."

"They train you," Agnes tells her. "They pay four dollars a week while you're being trained, then up it goes."

She sees Sally believing it: her sassy sister, distrustful of everyone, and yet Agnes has always known how to make her believe anything. It's all about details.

"The uniforms are black and white," she says. "You wear a white cap and an apron with a ruffle."

Sometimes she wishes it were true. A fine hotel, a pay envelope—it sounds a lot easier to believe in than Jesse Lyman Zorn and a boarding house in a city in New York State that she can hardly imagine. She barely knows where it is, only how to get to it, and she has a feeling this is a roundabout route she's taking, not the cheapest or the quickest, but it's the only way she has been able to figure out.

The early morning train is scheduled to come in at 5:28, and according to the station clock, it is right on the minute. The noise and smoke and steam frighten her—as they never do when she just stands in the station on a normal day, watching the big locomotives chug in and out. But she leaps onto the step and lets the conductor pull her up. She stands there feeling dazed, suddenly a little sick, thinking she can jump right back down again and go home and they'll never know she's left. The conductor looks into her face and asks, "Where you going, miss?" She says, "Philly," and he says, "Seats to your right. Keep a tight hold on that bag, young lady." He turns and calls, "All aboard!" out into the gray morning, but nobody else is there. The train starts, and the light from the station window is whisked away.

Half a dozen people occupy the car, a couple of dozing men and a woman in a big hat, and two other women together, with a tiny baby and a boy about Charlie's age when he drowned. He has Charlie's brown slash of bangs and thin shoulders. She goes to the back of the car, as far away from them as possible, and takes a seat by the window. The conductor comes through the car and she hands over money for her tickets. "Change trains in Philly," he says.

She puts her head back, listening to the noisy, measured clack of the wheels. She has planned this for so long that the reality overwhelms her. She closes her eyes.

But what she's left behind pulls at her. In spite of herself she begins making a list of the things she doesn't want to think about. The baby. Mama. Grandma Lu. And her birthday in two days, on Friday the thirteenth. Robert kept teasing her: "You're jinxed! You're Bad Luck Aggie!"

Not anymore. Her birthday is how she knows she really wants to do this and isn't just fooling herself into it—that she hasn't even waited for her birthday gifts, even though she knows Mama and Papa are giving her the wristwatch with the expansion band that she saw at Rheinheimer's. And she will not be there to open it. And that will show them how important this is to her, how it would have done no good to try to talk her out of it—not that they had the chance.

They would give the wristwatch to Sally, she thinks gloomily. But she doesn't care. Maybe they will save it for her, hoping she'll be back at Christmastime. And will she? Will she ever? And if she does, will they want to see her? Or will this be what turns them all against her for good?

The question that has plagued her for a week returns to plague her again: should she have left a note? It was too risky, she had decided. What if they came after her? Better to write to them when she arrives. *Dear Papa, I hope you have forgiven me by now. Darling Mama. Dear Grandma Lu. Dearest Uncle Clem, don't think badly of me.* . . . But now that she is on the train she imagines Mama waking up, looking in on her and Dorrie, finding her missing, frantic until Sally gets up and the news hits them like a thunderclap: Left home, gone to Philadelphia, made me swear not to tell. . . . *And why? Our Agnes? Why?*

She opens her eyes. She licks a finger and rubs at the filthy window. The train has picked up speed, and the world outside is rushing by. She takes off her coat, folds it, sits on it, remembers the money in the pocket, takes out the three wrinkled dollar bills and puts them into her skirt pocket with her handkerchief and two hairpins. She looks out of the window: woods, long pauses of fields, then a house or two, a block of stores, a station, a house or two, fields . . .

When they get to Tiffin, she can almost see her sister Helen's house, past the tracks and two streets over. She imagines Helen and Roger saying their morning prayers and getting ready for the day. Helen will be disgusted when she hears the news. Agnes imagines them praying for her.

She falls asleep but wakes up when the conductor comes down the aisle bawling, "PIIIIIITTS-burg! PIII-IIIITTS-burg, ladies and gennamen. PIIIIITTS-burg!" Agnes pushes back her hair, adds a hairpin, smooths her skirt. The April sun pours in the window, getting past the grime. She has never seen anything like the Pittsburgh station. *Notice everything:* millions of people, everyone in motion, flickering lamps, a crowd of soldiers in uniform. Porters with dark brown faces and hands, pushing carts. Piles of fancy luggage. And a buzz: Voices? Machinery? The hum of a huge city?

Pittsburgh. Somewhere in it is the Frick Building, built by Papa's cousin, who will be at his desk by now—doing what, she cannot imagine. Making money. A funny thought. It is his money pinned to her camisole, part of his last birthday check to Grandma Lu, a big one. What would they do without him? What would they do if he died, or decided he'd given them enough over the years? She sees him as a bearded man like Papa, with the same lean cheeks and turned-down eyes, but wearing a suit and a vest and a silk tie, smoking a cigar. Barking orders, slamming his fist down. The building is twenty stories high, made to be taller than Mr. Carnegie's building. He and Carnegie were once friends and partners but had a falling out and now are enemies. "They no longer do business together," Papa says in that way he has when he talks about his cousin, as if he has heard this from Clay himself. But he hasn't. She doesn't know where he's heard it.

Grandma Lu always calls him her dear nephew. He never comes to see her, never writes a real letter, just sends money. Sometimes she writes him a letter asking for the money, sometimes it just arrives, like the birthday check. When Grandma Lu slipped Agnes the money, tied up in a handkerchief, she whispered, "Keep it for when you need it. And say a prayer for your cousin Clay."

People get off the train, more people get on. The seat beside her remains empty, and when a large woman with a huge bulging bag approaches, Agnes is relieved when she moves on. Then a man sits down without even a glance at her. A dapper Cousin Clay kind of man. He arranges his trousers and crosses his legs and begins to read the Pittsburgh *Gazette*.

People are still lurching down the aisles, but the train is off again, spitting out noisy jets of steam. The conductor says over and over, like a mechanical man: "Altoona next stop. Altoona next," and they pull out of a tunnel and into the sunshine. Pittsburgh rolls by in a blur of dirty buildings. Then countryside again. Another state, but it looks just like Ohio.

She has nothing to read. The less she carried with her, the better, she'd thought, but she hadn't anticipated the long, empty hours. She'd thought about stealing a book from the library. *Adam Bede*, which she'd read twice while she was pregnant, painful though it was. She wishes she had it with her now. Or maybe something less tragic. Dickens would be best. *Bleak House. Great Expectations.* Something she could read over and over. Or make another attempt at *War and Peace*. She'd decided that stealing would bring bad luck—but why didn't she at least bring her volume of Keats? Or a notebook, a diary in which to record her adventure. Sally said, "You'll never be the same again," and Agnes dismissed it—her sister always reached for the highest drama, as if their lives were Shakespeare. But it is true, she knows it, and it is worth writing about in a diary that she could show Uncle Clem someday, and maybe he would be proud of her.

By now they know she is gone. There will be tears—Sally's for sure, because she would be blamed for aiding and abetting. Mama—what would she do? See to Dorrie, hold her, give her a cookie. Uncle Clem would go for one of his walks and think—what? That she was not the girl he thought her to be? Or that she was.

And Grandma Lu . . .

Don't think about Grandma Lu, or any of them. Think about the rooming house in Syracuse, on East Willow Street, Mrs. Anderson's, one of the better places in that part of town, Jesse wrote. He has moved to a bigger room in anticipation of her arrival: sunny, with high windows. At night you can pull the curtains or leave them open to the moon and the stars. He has acquired a typewriter, and a Kodak camera, and a mongrel dog named Reggie.

She touches the stiff outline of his letter where it is pinned to her camisole. If she closes her eyes, into the brownish purple behind her eyelids comes Jesse with his laughing eyes and his pointed ears and his hair falling in his face. *What's more real,* she writes in the diary in her head: *What we imagine or what we do? It's always surprising that thoughts can be more alive than life.*

The man next to her puts his hand on her skirt. She feels it on her thigh and opens her eyes. She looks sideways at his face: handsome, with a small gray moustache. She glares at him. He takes his hand away and returns silently to his newspaper. Then she can't think of anything but his hand.

She finds the train out of Philadelphia with only seconds to spare, and leaps up the metal stairs. "You're all right, miss," the conductor says. "You made it, don't you cry now," which is when she realizes she is crying. She has lost her blue scarf, and her hair has come down. She's shaking as she sinks into a seat, and so hungry she feels faint. There was no time to buy anything to eat in Philly. But the woman sitting next to her gives her a piece of cake from a metal lunch box. "I'm on my way to meet my husband in Binghamton," she says. Agnes says she is meeting hers in Syracuse. Now there's a coincidence, the woman says. Her name is Dorothy Thompson, and Agnes says she's Hazel Pratt, which is her California sister's married name. She closes her eyes and pretends to sleep, and at last she does sleep, shushed by the noise of the engine, waking now and then to peer out into the dark. Once she sees a shed on fire in a field: orange blooms lift toward the heavens, then disappear. And further on, an enormous farmhouse lit up, every room, in the middle of the deep black night—the loneliest sight she could imagine.

Oh, it's a long ride. She feels as if she's been on a train all her life. She knows to lean her head back and open her mouth to relax her head for sleep. Knows not to breathe when she uses the ladies' toilet at the rear of the car, the tracks rushing by under the hole in the floor. She finds out where the dining car is and eats a bread roll with meat in it. What kind of meat? It doesn't matter, it tastes so good, she could eat four of them. Coffee, bottled lemonade, a packet of cookies. Once she gazes out the window for hours—the landscape always changing but always the same—and when she asks the conductor the time, only thirty-five minutes have passed.

She begins to feel like Tiberius Humphrey, who is still making his way to California. The last Uncle Clem told her, he's in the southeast corner of Idaho, crossing Bear Lake on a steamer. "He'll be in Nevada before much longer," he said, but Agnes consulted a map and had her doubts.

Her seatmate gets off at Binghamton, in the dark, and she has the seat to herself all the way to Syracuse.

She wakes at sunrise, chased by a dream: her brother Sammy in a red knitted cap saying, "Everything exploded, they never knew what hit them." Out her window, brown fields, two horses under a tree, a man with a lantern. And then, in the light of morning, the conductor is swaying down the aisle bellowing, "SAIR-acuse next stop! SAIR-acuse station next!"

Jesse described in a letter how the train went straight down the main street, through the center of the city, just like the streetcar in Toledo, but this is a big locomotive and six cars, noise and steam, chuffing past the hotels and fancy shops and apartment buildings and bicycles and automobiles. A man standing in the aisle laughs and says, "Well, don't this beat all?" A green trolley car stops to let the train go by. Women pull their skirts back but barely give it a glance. On a corner she sees a man with a red beard like Uncle Clement's—for a ghastly moment she thinks it's him. In a shop window, there is a mannequin in a long silver gown. In a barbershop with a red-white-and-blue pole, a man in a chair getting a shave.

A bank like a church, a town square with a statue of a soldier on a horse, a theater showing, of all things, *The Bohemian Girl,* starring Geraldine Farrar. Agnes tries to remember the words to "I Dreamt I Dwelt in Marble Halls," but they're gone.

Then the train is at the station, everyone milling into the aisles. She goes down the steps, clutching her bag. *Let him be here let him be here.* The conductor takes her elbow while she jumps, and when she looks up Jesse is coming toward her, waving his hat and hanging onto a rope with a small black dog at the end of it.

PART III

FACT AND FICTION

Se non è vero, è ben trovato.
~Italian proverb[1]

---

[1]   Which can be translated, very loosely, as: "If it's not true, it ought to be."

COUSIN DUKE

Not long after Agnes stepped off the train in Syracuse, I received an email from my cousin Duke.

Six months earlier, wanting to leave no research stone unturned, I had spat into a test tube and invested $100 in a DNA analysis, which would decode my genetic heritage and compare it with those of other people who have spat into a test tube and sent in their payment. A small sampling, but I hoped it would yield something unexpected that might provide a clue to the identity of my lost grandfather—that missing one-quarter of my family history. Maybe an exotic snippet of Mediterranean or African or Native American genetic material. No such luck. In the past, whenever I've been asked about my ethnic background, I always said, "Irish with a little bit of English and some French." (The French was purely my mother's romantic invention.) Now, should anyone ask, I'd revise that to: "Mostly English, a lot of Irish, and some German"—not exactly an earthshaking development.

However, the test did provide a significant beam of light: Cousin Newland ("Duke") Hingley. The DNA project matched us up. We sent a few emails, then had a long talk on the phone. Our mothers were first cousins, we're second cousins: Duke is the grandson of Inez's youngest sister, Mary Fay Willick Wills. All three of Inez's sisters who lived to adulthood ended up in California. Duke, part of that migratory branch of the family, is a few years older than I am, a retired LAPD motorcycle policeman living in the Sierra Nevadas with his cat.

Duke has done plenty of genealogical research, though when we talked he hadn't yet gotten to the Willicks or the

Strawbridges.[2] I was able to tell him more about both families than he knew, including the Pierson ancestors and the link to George Washington,[3] as well as more recent news. He had no idea his great-aunt Inez had had two out-of-wedlock daughters and was barely aware of Doris's existence—probably because she, like Inez, stayed in Ohio. Inez had visited her sisters in California. Duke was almost sure he'd met her when he was a child; he had no real memory of that but did recall his mother and grandmother talking about Inez, though not what they said.

We had a pleasant chat, and I was intrigued to hear from an actual Willick, but Inez remained the usual frustrating dead end.

Then, toward the end of 2013, Duke called again. He told me that his mother, like mine, had been the repository for the family archives—and Duke had inherited everything. After our first phone conversation, he had rummaged through the stack of boxes stored in the back of a closet, a chore he'd been meaning to get to for years. He pulled out what he figured I'd find interesting and sent it off to me. "Expect a big packet of stuff," he said.

It was in my mailbox two days later. I consider myself a tough old bird, but when I opened it my hands were trembling and I had to sit down. Inside was a thick, rich stew of photos, letters, post cards, birth certificates—years of Willicks and Fricks and Strawbridges.

---

[2] The rest of his family had kept him busy: he photographed the 1210 gravestone of a Viking ancestor in England, drove cross-country in his motor home to Boston to see the grave of a Pilgrim ancestor who founded the town of Barnstable on Cape Cod, and flew to Hawaii to check out a dairy farm that used to be in the family.

[3] Turns out Duke is a "double Washington," related to George and also, through his father's family, the Balls, to Martha.

It was staggering. Suddenly, here was a chunk of my lost family history—people I never knew but who are bound to me nonetheless, more kin to me than the dozens of cousins I grew up with but to whom I'm related either sketchily or not at all. Here's a huge group of Willicks under the apple tree in the backyard of the North Baltimore house. Here's Inez's sister Mary Fay and her handsome cowboy husband as they marry, produce children, get old. Here's another sister, Maud, in 1912 perched rather dashingly in the sidecar of a motorcycle driven by her young son. Here's Grandma Lucinda Frick in her sixties, holding a baby, looking stern. Here's Inez's young brother Ralph just before he died of typhoid fever, and here are his stricken parents after the funeral. Here is the elusive Doris, my mother's sister, a brooding, dark-haired teenager.

And here is Inez—eighteen photographs of her.

The earliest is dated March 1, 1909. (See cover photo.) Inez is twenty years old, a bosomy girl with an hourglass figure (possibly helped along by some tight corseting), her hair piled high under an impressive hat— deeply into the then-fashionable Gibson girl look. Her face is innocent, thoughtful, self-possessed; it's hard to believe that she has a four-year-old daughter and that, a few months later, she would have another bun in the oven: my mother.

Inez, 1914

There's a blank in the photo collection from 1909 to 1914— for me, alas, my grandmother's most crucial years. But the 1914 picture is intriguing: Inez stands on a tiled floor, wearing a plain white skirt and simple frilled-collar blouse, a hole punch hanging from a tie around her waist.[4] Behind her is part of a poster with just the ends of words visible, fuzzy but readable:

NARD
CKHAM
OUSE
DANT

My daughter, Katherine, used her impressive research skills to elucidate a few things. The poster is advertising *The House Discordant*, a silent two-reeler released in July 1914,[5] starring Hazel Buckham and Robert Leonard. Inez is a cashier, or "box office girl," as they were called. How-to manuals for theater managers emphasized the importance of the cashier: a "lovely box office attendant" was as important as electrified marquees and colorful posters for enticing moviegoers inside. In the photo, Inez looks tidy and trim, and she still has her wasp waist, even after two children. Her abundant curls are held in place by a band. She isn't what you would call "lovely" or "enticing." A smile might have helped, but she's not supplying it. Her expression verges on grim. Did she hate her job? Just having a bad day? The photograph is both a trove of information and an enigma. [6] But it seems clear that this is no flibbertigibbet, certainly no floozy. She has

---

[4] It's exactly like the one on my desk. Hole punches were invented in 1885 by a Massachusetts man named Benjamin Smith—as usual, the Internet provides more riches than anybody would ever need, including the website Hole Punch World.

[5] Same year as *The Perils of Pauline.*

[6] Despite strenuous digging, neither Katherine nor I could discover the location of the theater. In 1914, motion picture houses were springing up all across the country (there were two in North Baltimore—pop. 2300), and this unmemorable movie was playing in dozens of them.

a strong face. In both photos, she looks modest, confident, dignified—nobody's fool. And is there a trace of defiance? As in: *I'm not who you think I am.*

Apparently, all the Willick girls struggled with their weight; their letters are full of pounds lost or gained.[7] Inez was hefty throughout her middle age. There's a photo of her with her mother taken in the early '30s, not long before Maggie died. Plump and cozy-looking in all her earlier photos, Maggie was pared down at the end— sweet-faced as ever, and with a crown of frizzy white hair. Inez was in her forties and stout. Her abundant brown curls are shorter—she's the only brunette daughter. Despite her plus-size, she bravely wears a dress printed with large flowers, and I think it suits her. In many of her pictures, in fact, she's adventurously fashionable: there's a shot of her at her chubbiest wearing a kind of Op-Art print dress with an asymmetrical pleated skirt and a pair of many-strapped, pointy-toed high heels, looking like a formidable matron in a *New Yorker* cartoon from the '30s. Maybe she got her taste in clothes from her mother, who at the age of eighty is wearing a rather snazzy polka-dot dress.

Inez and Maggie
Willick, 1930s

I don't know when she left her box-office-girl days behind, but by the early 1920s, after a year or two in Youngstown, Ohio, waitressing at the Hotel Salow, a well-respected local fixture, Inez took her Spanish name to a city that also has a Spanish name—Toledo, on the

---

[7] On the back of one photo, Mary Fay has written: "Inez when she was fat, fat!"

western end of Lake Erie. She was back in the vicinity of her roots, in the city that, when she was a girl, was connected by a trolley to her town. She probably knew it fairly well.

In Toledo, Inez lived for a while with her sister Mabel in an apartment; then, at some point, she rented a small white cottage (built in 1872) on Stickney Avenue. According to the City Directory she lived alone, but— who knows? Her house was in what's now part of the historic Vistula district north of the Maumee River, Toledo's oldest neighborhood. Her brother, John, lived nearby with his wife, Pearl.

The bits of her work history that I've uncovered have shown her waitressing in hotel dining rooms, so (this is what happens when you step into the maelstrom of research; there's always a new eddy to be sucked into) I've spent some time trying to figure out in which Toledo hotel Inez might have been working. I lit on the Hotel Secor; according to the Toledo *Blade*, it was the city's "first true luxury hotel," with 400 rooms and a fancy restaurant, and it was a short walk from Inez's cottage.[8]

At some point she met a man named Peter Franger, who was originally from Buffalo but lived in her Toledo neighborhood; he was working as a cook, his consistent profession throughout the 1920s and beyond. I can picture them flirting in the kitchen at the Secor as Inez (in her wire spectacles, bobbed brown hair, and black-and-white uniform, size large) loads her tray with a platter of Sirloin Steak ($1) or Cold Capon, Tongue, and Lima

---

[8] The Secor closed in 1971 and was taken over by the Ohio Bell Telephone Co., which, according to the *Blade*, "tore out much of the original interior of marble columns and decorative plaster, and covered marble flooring with office carpeting [and] harsh, damaging glue."

Bean Salad ($1.25). A piece of Huckleberry Tarte for dessert was thirty-five cents. The hotel had no wine list—Prohibition was the law of the land—but it was famous for its excellent coffee.

I struggle to keep my head above water in this particular whirlpool, but I wonder: if Peter had worked in a high-end hotel kitchen, wouldn't he have called himself a "chef" in the census and in the Toledo city directory? Or hadn't food snobbery surfaced yet? Maybe in those days a "cook" was just as likely as a "chef" to wear a toque and make a tarte. And, of course, I have no way of knowing if Inez was a smartly dressed waitress in a posh dining room getting large tips, or a Mel's Diner kind of waitress who calls you "hon" and knows that you like your eggs over easy.

I give it up. I flounder toward the shore, to the facts as I know them. Whatever their cooking/waiting credentials, Inez and Peter took a day off and got married on a Thursday, September 9, 1926, traveling down to North Baltimore from Toledo for the ceremony. She was thirty-eight, he was forty.

Doris was probably present; she would have been twenty-two, two years away from her own wedding. Inez's sisters were all in California, so perhaps they did not attend. Grandmother Lucinda had died years before, but Maggie and Jacob Willick were still alive, relieved perhaps to see their daughter married off at last.[9]

Peter was divorced, with three grown children—a handsome, dapper guy who, in his photographs, always looks relaxed and happy. It intrigues me that, two years after she was married, Inez took her trip to Syracuse to

---

[9] Cousin Henry Clay Frick had died in 1919, so there would not have been a wedding check from New York.

get a look at her lost daughter. Did she wonder, now that she was respectable, if things could change? Did Peter—father of three—urge her on, maybe even accompany her? More unknowns.

After whatever happened to Inez at fifteen, after whoever was the father of her second child in 1910, my errant grandmother certainly deserved love, or at least contentment. I think the Frangers had a good marriage. Duke sent me the memorial booklet from Peter's 1946 funeral, in which Inez wrote—with obvious care, in her neatest penmanship—the details of his life and death. "My dear husband," she calls him, notes the time of his death down to the minute, and gives his age as "58 years, 11 months, and 36 days." There was a service at the Lutheran church, though the Frangers were not churchgoers: "Rev. Slater delivered a very beautiful sermon for one he never knew and quoted a few scriptures from the Bible."

My grandmother was a young widow, only fifty-seven. There's a lovely image of her from a few years later, white-haired, no longer pudgy. And seemingly active: the photo was taken in Toledo with her "bowling club," and she's definitely the oldest member. As her

face ages and slims down, she begins to remind me of my mother, especially in this shot, maybe because of her plucked eyebrows and general air of glamour—and that small, droll smile. But, try though I may, I can't find a strong resemblance.

Doris, however, looks some-thing like Katherine in several of the photos—especially as a young

Inez in her 60s

flapper in her dropped-waist shift taken with her bespectacledfriend Louise (I think). Doris was eighteen. There's a second shot of her in the same dress, in a family lineup, where she looks sullen, impatient, longing to escape and go out with her friends—or maybe I'm just projecting.

Doris Willick (r.) and a friend, 1922

The fatherless Doris was close to her mother and grandparents all her life. If she knew the secret of her parentage, there's no evidence of it. Despite the wealth of Duke's family archive, I've found no clues as to who fathered either of Inez's children. It's a door that stays stubbornly closed.

But the photographs have told me a lot. They show a close family, children devoted to their parents (one photo of Maggie and Jacob is labeled "darling Mama and Papa"), and much travel between Ohio and California, where all three of Inez's sisters settled.[10] The photos have yielded the source of my younger granddaughter's frizzy blonde curls that have mystified both sides of our family: at least four Willicks had that wonderfully wild hair, a gift from the Strawbridges via curly-haired Maggie. Great-grandfather Jacob has straight dark hair and the

---

[10] I've had to relinquish the idea that Inez was the adventurous sister. Mary Fay married her cowboy in Iowa, lived on a ranch in Wyoming, ended up in southern California. Maud and her husband had their kids in North Baltimore, then hauled them all out to L.A. Mabel had a mysterious early husband (in a rakish photograph, he has the air of a gambler) before she too lit out for the territory and settled near her sisters. Inez decamped to New York State for a few years, but spent the rest of her life back in Ohio, not far from the town where she was born.

Jacob Willick, c. 1909

angular, long-nosed Frick face—a masculine copy of his mother Lucinda's. In old age, his hair gone white, he's a benevolent figure with an impressive moustache—and always with a crutch under his left arm. The packet even contained several photos of Emery Balliet, son of the teenage Maggie. One photo of him is labeled (I think by Mary Fay) "good ol' Emery," which may mean—well, anything, but he seems a good-looking and pleasant fellow. The Willicks in general are not smilers, but Emery is an exception: he's usually in mid-grin, and in old age retains the thick, curly Strawbridge hair.[11]

The package Duke sent me contained a letter written from Inez in Toledo to her sister Mary Fay in California on February 20, 1936, not quite two months after Maggie's death. Written in pencil, it covers eight pages, both sides, in a firm, no-nonsense hand. She begins with an apology for taking so long to write: "It seems I can't get my mind settled on anything anymore since Mama died. I just think of her all the time and can't seem to get over it."

Inez is a vivid and leisurely letter writer. She envies Mary Fay's California climate and complains about the frigid weather in Ohio: "people freezing, homes burning, gas explosions," and adds, "I nearly freeze waiting for the street car at night" (she was still waitressing). One cold morning, on her way to work, "Who should drive by me

[11] As does Cousin Duke. None of the Willick men seem to have gone bald.

but Myron Frick and Charlotte," her second cousin and his wife, in town for a Frick funeral. Myron got out of the car to chat, though he didn't offer her a ride.

But most of the letter is about Maggie's death. Inez and Doris were with her in North Baltimore during her last illness, and it was Inez who found her mother dead: "It was just two minutes of seven when I went in and kissed her twice and then I said, Doris, her face is so cold, and Doris lit the lamp, and she was gone," adding, "She just slept away, and was in no pain or suffering at the end."[12]

She writes at length about Maggie's funeral, the beautiful flowers, the kindness of neighbors, the many mourners. No reference to God or religion except to say that, at Maggie's request, "The Old Rugged Cross" and "Help Somebody Today"[13] were sung by a quartet, two men and two women. The funeral cost $300; "the government" paid $100 of it, maybe because Maggie was the widow of a veteran. The letter ends with the hope that Mary Fay's carbuncle has healed, with love from Inez and Pete.

Possibly the most fascinating artifacts in the package are Inez's report cards from sixth and seventh grades. They don't contain much information, but what they do say tells me something about who Inez really was.

She was absent from school fairly often—a total of fifteen days in one term, nine in another. I wonder: Was she ill? Faking sickness, like I used to, so she could sit in bed and read all day? Was she made to stay home and

---

[12] A particularly Inezian detail notes that Maggie must have known she was close to the end: "She told Doris she didn't want a coffin with blue silk lining."

[13] The chorus goes: "Help somebody today,/Somebody along life's way;/Let sorrow be ended, the friendless befriended,/Oh, help somebody today!"

help her mother? Was she rebellious—playing hooky to hang out with her friends? According to the report cards, her deportment was pretty good, and her "application," only fair in sixth grade, improved greatly in seventh. As for her grades, she was a hopeless arithmetic student (her lowest grade, at the end of sixth grade, was a shameful 10), but got 90s in spelling, reading, and composition. She was on her way to becoming the bookworm, Dickens buff, and Latinist I invented, the ancestor I can thank for my love of reading.

Which brings me back to Agnes, who has just arrived at the railroad station in Syracuse. It's 1907, and there's Jesse, and the black dog.

What to do with her?

Getting the torrent of information from Duke was like breaking a long fast with a dozen double-chocolate brownies and a pint of ice cream. I spent a whole day just sorting the huge, glorious jumble into roughly chronological piles and trying to identify who was who in the stack of photos. I spent hours scanning and emailing so that Katherine and I could ponder them together. The collection was both a treasure and a befuddlement: it told me so much, but also so little. A grandmother myself, I had acquired a grandmother. These images of the real Inez are significant beyond their surface details: somewhere in her enigmatic eyes lies not only me, but my mother, my daughter, my grandchildren—the source of our existence.

Some societies have two categories of ancestors. There are the recently dead—the "living dead"—who are still remembered by at least one person who knew them. And there are the immense throngs of the "truly dead," who have been gone long enough that nobody remembers them as they were when alive—people who are now, at most, a name, a set of dates, maybe a famous nose, or a story that's been handed down. Every one of us will die, have a brief sojourn among the "living dead," and then, gradually, as the people who knew us die off, we'll become buried under the generations until we're nothing but a small leaf on the family tree.

Who remembers Inez Willick? Who knows what made her laugh? Did she put sugar in her coffee, like my mother? Was she a good soprano, like Katherine? Did she, like me, hate to wear shoes? I doubt that anybody has thought about her in many years. Her siblings are dead, Doris is dead, and so is Doris's son—Inez's only grandchild besides me. Katherine and I talk about her. Cousin Duke and I talk about her. But we aren't remembering her: there's nothing to remember.

Absorbed in the wealth of Willick data, I shoved Agnes to the back of my mind. But slowly, after a few weeks, I began to think about her again. At first I considered abandoning her there in the Syracuse train station. But I found that I wanted to keep her alive. She may be nothing like my grandmother. But she may equally plausibly be very much like her. Despite all I now know, the slate remains somewhat blank: *Tabula rasa est*, as Agnes and Jesse would certainly put it. I would have to make a few minor adjustments—add a few more pounds, for one thing—but my Agnesized version of Inez has become no less real just because a framed photograph of the real Inez is staring at me from across the room. In a way, Agnes has become even more vivid to me, because now I can see her face.

In my novelist's fantasy world, as long as Agnes is alive, Inez will keep a toehold in the land of the living dead.

Years ago, in New Haven, I was part of a writing group. One of its members, the author of a widely acclaimed first novel based on her wartime childhood in Czechoslovakia, was struggling with her second, about the breakup of her marriage to a Yale academic. She changed people's names and substituted Harvard for Yale, but otherwise both novels were completely auto-biographical. In the new one, she was having trouble clarifying the actions of her heroine—i.e., herself. I suggested that she devise a bit of backstory that would solve the problem.

She was both puzzled and horrified. "It wouldn't be the truth!" she said. "How would I even *do* that?"

Another writer in that group, terrified of alienating anyone she actually knew, even by accident, set her stories in places and peopled them with characters so remote from her own life that she was never really able to get a handle on them.

I see these two writers as the extremes on a continuum on which I'm struggling to keep my balance near the middle.

All my writing life, one of the great joys of writing fiction has been reaching into my imagination and pulling out what I need to tell a story: I've hardly ever used my own life or anyone else's as material for my novels. Now and then a shred of fact will creep in, whittled down or fattened up. A house I knew well ended up in one novel, though I had to install an apartment over the garage. The brother of a friend turned up in another book, heavily disguised, and a boy I knew who died young appeared in another—middle-aged, balding, very much alive. Even in my first novel, based on my mother's adoption, the events bore little kinship to reality by the time I was finished with them.

When you write fiction dredged from imagination rather than memory, you can put in anything you want as long as it serves the truth of the story you're telling. Virginia Woolf wrote about the exhilaration of "making up" during her long walks over the downs near her house in Sussex. I know exactly what she meant as, over the years, I've walked in Brooklyn, New Haven, Amherst: one foot in front of the other, mind roaming free.

But the made-up part of the Inez saga is a hybrid. It's neither fact nor fiction that I'm writing, nor is it a nonfiction novel or a fictionalized biography. There isn't much to go on. I feel like an anthropologist trying to reconstruct a human history from a skull and a thighbone. Generalization is possible, given the location of the bones and their age and perhaps a bead necklace found nearby. It might be possible to deduce cause of death. But how that person laughed and walked, what she ate for breakfast, whom she loved and hated, remain eternal unknowns.

My first novel was published in 1979; over the years I've published eleven more. I know how to write a novel: you devise a story, then create characters to people it. Or you invent characters and dig out the story they live in. Or you overhear a conversation on a train or stop at a used bookstore or observe a dog walker in Greenwich Village, and the novel-writing area of your brain lights up: You're off and running.

But with this book I'm in alien territory. As I push my way forward, I'm creating my own grandmother, a woman I never knew—trying to look through her glasses in an attempt to turn real life into fiction that reads like real life. I feel something like Uncle Clem's Tiberius Humphrey, who is traveling from Ohio to the Klamath River in California. I can't make the story up, any more than Clem can move the Klamath River to Indiana to make his hero's journey quicker and easier. Despite the enormous gaps in it, Inez's story is a collection of facts, the way a moth-eaten sweater is still recognizably a sweater. Or (I keep resorting to metaphors, the last refuge of the confused writer) it's like those Iron Chef challenges where the task is to produce an edible dish using only kumquats, oysters, and half a cup of peanut butter. The ingredients have been dumped in my lap. Whatever I invent has to be respectful of them. And a pleasure to consume.[14]

I struggled with all this as the winter advanced and a series of snowstorms made Amherst beautiful but too icy to walk in, and I was stuck inside with the dog, the stack of photographs, and the book I was writing. The pictures of Inez made her more real, but also made me feel even more like a trespasser. Whatever else it tells me, her expression in her earlier photos is not saying, "Here's permission for some over-fanciful future granddaughter to invade my privacy by making things up about me."

But a hundred years have passed. The fanciful grand-daughter is already deeply involved in the story of a girl named Agnes Miller, and she finds herself staring back at Inez with a reflection (inherited?) of her determination. The later, twinkly, happy photos are more welcoming—or so I like to think. And the granddaughter's head is swarming with ideas. There's a persistent image of a

---

[14]   In his memoir *Boy Detective*, Roger Rosenblatt says a writer requires "the desire to see what is not there, and to make it at once orderly and beautiful."

travel-weary girl arriving stepping off a train, madly in love. And what of the rooming house on East Willow Street, the park bench, the dining room at the Yates Hotel, the nuns at the foundling hospital . . . ?

The granddaughter feels vaguely apologetic toward the woman in the photographs. But she's not going to quit now.

AGNES

1909
Syracuse, New York

Every morning but Sunday Jesse goes to work at the
newspaper as a full-time reporter on the City Hall
beat, and every morning Agnes and Reggie, the dog,
stand at the window to watch him go. She loves the confident way he walks, hands in pockets, hat at an angle.
Jaunty, she thinks: *that's my Jesse.*

He has made up his mind: he wants to be a lawyer,
not a reporter, and maybe get into politics. Meanwhile,
he's learning all he can by observing, talking to people,
covering City Hall and the courthouse, getting to know
the workings of the city's politics. She can imagine him
in a courtroom. He'll be a splendid lawyer. He would be
a splendid anything.

When he's out of sight she goes down to the kitchen
and gets a second cup of coffee and a sweet roll if there
are any, a piece of bread if not, with a corner of it for the
dog. Jesse never needs anything in the morning but a big
cup of Mrs. Anderson's sweet, milky coffee, but Agnes
always wakes up hungry.

She isn't due at work until eleven. What she likes
to do is have breakfast by the window, sitting in the big
armchair with her feet up on the sill, reading or writing
one of her difficult letters home. Reggie lies on the rug
until she makes the slightest move to get up, when he
springs to life, ears up and tail whipping back and forth.

She says, "Oh, you funny old Reggie dog, you!" and he prances over to the door, knowing it's time to go out.

She replaced the rope with a braided leather leash, bought with her first paycheck along with a yellow tie for Jesse and a pair of red bloomers for herself that made him laugh. The second paycheck took them out to supper at the hotel, mostly for the fun of sitting in the dining room dressed to kill and ordering a meal from Mr. Carmody himself, the manager of the dining room at the Yates Hotel (also the maître d') where Agnes works. "Why, good evening, my dear," he said. He recommended the lamb shanks, then took a dollar off the bill, winking at Jesse. "Don't think we do this for all our waitresses. Just the prettiest ones."

"You'd better watch that old goat," Jesse said when he'd left.

"He's only a goat for the waiters."

Jesse raised his eyebrows. "Really! Well, jolly good for him!"

It's one of the things she loves about Jesse, that he doesn't pass judgment on anyone, not even on Cousin Clay, no matter what they read in the papers about him. "There's always another side," Jesse insists. But of course he needs to have her think well of Cousin Clay: if they're going to ask him a favor, they have to believe in his benevolence.

But they are not going to ask him a favor. She will not do it. Except for one other small matter, it's the only thing they have argued about.

On a morning in May Agnes finishes her coffee, clips on Reggie's leash, and steps out onto East Willow Street. Their north-side neighborhood seems like a town in the middle of the big city. For fun, soon after she arrived, she paced out the shape of North Baltimore, less than a mile in each direction, and inside that compact shape is everything they need: shops, parks, the library, their favorite cheap restaurants.

But Syracuse is not much like the town of North Baltimore. For one thing, though she's been there for two years, she hardly knows anyone. She can walk down the streets, anonymous, hugging her new life around her like the beautiful blue paisley shawl Jesse gave her for Christmas. And most of the streets are paved. She scarcely sees a cow or a pig, and the sidewalks seem to go on forever, the farms and fields not a short walk away but somewhere far beyond the busy downtown and the university and the tall spires of the churches. On some streets there are almost as many motorcars as horses. Her walk to work takes her past the Erie Canal that, like the railroad, cuts right through the city's busy center, boats and barges loaded down and ready to move out. Where? Everywhere. Syracuse isn't just a place where people live, it's a place where things happen, people and things arrive and leave, change is everywhere. She loves being in a city. She must have said to herself a hundred times: *I'll never go back.*

On this May morning, she walks, as she often does, to Schiller Park, to the top of the hill where Jesse took her when she first arrived: you can see the city down below, and the lake in the winter. She likes it in the warm weather, when the path is dry. It's good for Reggie, she thinks, to climb the hill, and there is a bench where she likes to sit while he sniffs around.

Today there is someone on the bench—the first time that has happened. A woman about her own age, with a long, sad face that brightens when she sees Reggie. She says, "Oh, what a darling little fellow! What kind of dog is that?"

"He's a mutt. Probably part dachshund."

"He's kind of fat."

"I bring him up the hill to give him some exercise."

Agnes lets Reggie off the leash and sits down. The woman wears a tweedy wool skirt that has been patched near the hem—neatly, and with similar material, but you can see it. She introduces herself as Olive Webster. It turns out they live only a few blocks from each other— Olive and her husband are on Highland Street, near the grocery.

"Are you married?" Olive asks her right away. It's what women always want to know. Married or not: nothing is more important.

Agnes still grits her teeth, but she has learned not to hesitate. She says, "Yes. My husband is a newspaper reporter for the *Post-Standard*."

"Really?" The woman stares at Agnes as if she doubts her. And so she should, Agnes thinks—but it's the job that has amazed her. "You mean, if I pick up the paper I might see something he wrote?"

"Very likely."

"Well." Olive frowns over at Reggie, who is briskly digging a hole at the base of a tree. "That would be something."

Her own husband, Clarence, Olive says, has just gotten a job as a motorman; they took him on at the streetcars not even a month ago. The Websters have come up from Georgia, where her husband's family lives, and he was glad to get a job so quick.

As Olive talks, Agnes becomes fascinated by her eyes, which are brown, with deep purple shadows below and heavy brows above. *As if her eyes are trying to hide.* Is that a good metaphor or not? She thinks not. *As if her eyes are peering out of a dark room.* Not much better. Agnes doesn't think she'll ever be a writer. She can't really imagine being like Uncle Clem, stuck in an attic writing in a note-book for hours every day. She'll let Jesse be the writer in the family—although there's nothing poetic about what he writes for the newspaper. Mostly grim accounts of crimes and accidents.

Like a pair of wild animals in a den . . .

She gives it up and sits back on the bench, glad to have the sun on her face. Olive keeps talking, laying out her unremarkable life story. She is originally from Oswego, she says, but most of her family lives in Syra-cuse now, her mother and father right around the corner from her, they all like Syracuse better than Oswego. Agnes doesn't know where Oswego is, so Olive tells her, in detail, and says she never liked living so close to the lake, it was so cold in the winter, and if Agnes thinks the winters in Syracuse are hard she should try going up to Oswego some January. Olive sometimes gets work as a seamstress for Mrs. McCraigie, over on Division Street near Pompeii. Pompeii? "Our Lady of Pompeii Church," Olive says, looking startled again. "Where do you go, then? Assumption?"

"My family is Lutheran."

"Lutheran! Well! My husband's family down in Georgia is Baptist, but he converted when we got married. I've never met a Lutheran before. My moth-er's sister, back in Ireland, married an Episcopalian. I get them mixed up, all those churches. Why don't they just say Protestant? I've never met him—or her either. They have a farm in some little town. I suppose they're been happy enough. Six kids, one a priest in Dublin."

"Good for them." Agnes stands up, finally, and calls Reggie, and he comes running.

"Now there's an obedient doggie!" Olive stretches out a hand and snatches it back when Reggie licks it.

Agnes bends down to attach the leash. Olive's shoes need resoling badly, and she isn't wearing stockings, you can see a slab of her leg, dead-white with dark hairs on it. "We'd better go," Agnes says. "I have to be at work soon." She still has to do her hair properly before she walks down to the hotel.

Olive asks her where she works, and gives Agnes her astonished look again. "Imagine that! Working as a waitress at the Yates Hotel!"

"Yes, it's quite amazing."

"Maybe I'll see you again," Olive says. "I come up here pretty often. I get lonely with Clarence gone all day. We don't have any children yet."

"Well." Agnes smiles. "I wish you luck."

"Thanks, we need it, I guess. We've been married three years. I can't wait," Olive said. "They keep you busy—children."

"I'm sure they do."

Agnes turns to go, but Olive isn't quite done. "I'll bet you don't know this used to be a cemetery," she says. Her hooded eyes implore Agnes to stay longer. "This park. They moved all the bones over to that big cemetery out on East Genesee."

"Did they. I didn't know that."

"Oh yes." Olive shakes her head dolefully—or maybe her eyes are naturally doleful. If she were better looking,

Agnes thinks, she could be a tragic heroine, like Eleanora Duse. "All kinds of changes in this city over the years," she goes on, as if imparting bad news.

"I suppose." Agnes clucks at Reggie, who never needs clucking at, he walks by her side as docile as a pony. "Well, it was good to meet you, Olive." She and Reggie set off down the hill.

"Stop over sometime," Olive calls after her. "Six-five-six Highland, big old gray house, second floor. Come for coffee. I'm usually there. Just ring the top bell."

She thinks about Olive Webster as she walks home. Olive talks too much, what she says isn't particularly interesting, and she isn't very pretty—at best, you might call her *handsome* or, when she smiles, *attractive*—but she got Clarence the motorman to marry her. Agnes thinks: *Why her and not me?*

It's a petty thought. And she knows the answer perfectly well.

It's all about money. Jesse's salary at the *Post-Standard* is $25 a week. He has worked it out: In two years, if all goes well, and they are not extravagant, and there are no emergencies, he will have put away enough for half of his law school tuition. His father has agreed to pay the other half. Law school will mean three years without his having an income, though he will probably be able to work summers. Meanwhile, she will work. They will manage. Then, when he graduates from law school, they can marry.

When she arrived—two years ago—she assumed they would be married right away. Wasn't that why she had come to Syracuse?

They talked about it on her second day there, when she was struggling to write her letter home. Mama and Papa wouldn't want just an apology and the assurance that she was well and happy; they would want an explanation and a wedding date.

She was sprawled with her pencil and paper in the big chair, in her petticoat and shift, and Jesse was stretched out on the floor, studying for a French test. He was finishing his junior year. He would work at the newspaper during the summer and on weekends after that. After he graduated, he would be a full-time reporter: the position was guaranteed. Agnes would have to find a job—her income would be crucial.

All this was clear to her. What wasn't clear was when they would be married, and when she asked him, Jesse closed his book and sat up, leaning against the foot of the bed. He didn't think they should marry until they had more financial stability, he said. And until he had made his mind up about what he wanted to do after graduation, which would be either to go on to law school, or simply to devote himself heart and soul to being the best newspaper reporter in the world and perhaps go on to a major metropolitan newspaper like the *New York Times* or the *San Francisco Chronicle*. He smiled at the thought and reached over to take hold of her ankle. "What do you think, Ag? What a life we can have in New York or California!"

The more he talked, the brighter became the glimmer of truth: that what he had really wanted was to have her with him but not to get married at all. And yet she knew he loved her, so she asked him what seemed to her a logical question: What were they waiting for? Married or not, she would work. Their financial stability—had he really used those words?—would not change. Their expenses would be the same. Marriage didn't cost anything as long as they had a ready supply of Jimmy hats. What would be different if they went to City Hall and got a license?

He leapt up then and kissed her. "Why rock the boat? You know I love you, Agnes. I'll never love anyone but you. But let's just let things settle down. There's no hurry."

She wrote home, saying they hoped to be married soon, they were putting money away. It was all about money, something her family could surely sympathize with. She apologized for sneaking away, she hoped she hadn't worried them, she thought it would be easier that way. It occurred to her more than once, as she labored over the letter, that she had been crazy and wrong to simply disappear, to go off to she knew not what because Jesse had said he needed her.

Now and then she raises the question, usually after they've gone out to dinner and drunk some wine. Jesse never has a good explanation, and gradually she realizes he never will. *We're fine as we are,* he always says. Or he makes a joke that isn't really a joke: Why not ask her rich cousin for the tuition money? Then they could get married right away.

She has promised herself she'll stop talking about it—the conversations never go well—but the talk in the park with Olive Webster has unsettled her. The casual way Olive can say "my husband," the absolute normalness of it and, behind it, the idea that, if two people love each other, they get married. It's as simple as that. Isn't it?

And so she brings it up again on a Sunday morning in June. Sunday is a day off for both of them, and they are lying late in bed. Agnes has never gotten used to the heaven of a real bed, their heads on one pillow, their bodies together under the sheet, the blue morning sky and the web of new green leaves out the tall windows, just as Jesse had described it.

She has rehearsed her speech. She tells Jesse she has thought about it carefully, and none of his reasons for putting off marriage make any sense, and she wants to know the truth: what is really stopping them?

"I traveled all this way to be with you," she says, "because I assumed we'd get married."

She has never put it this way before, as a reproach, but now she can't help herself. So many months and miles away from her family, she realizes she has made a sacrifice.

"It was not a small thing, Jesse. I left everything behind. Everyone. You are all the world to me. Is it that you don't love me enough? That's what I need to know. Otherwise, I can get a train ticket and go back home."

He doesn't answer right away, and in that little pause his skin feels less warm against hers, the sun comes through the windows less brightly. She turns over on her side.

He pulls her back to him, and tucks her head under his chin. Under the covers, he strokes her bare back. "You know I love you."

"No, I don't."

"Well, I do."

She wants to say: *Prove it.* She also doesn't want to be difficult. She wants to give him a chance. She doesn't really want to get back on the train. And so she doesn't answer.

They lie there in silence for a while. It gets to be a long while. Reggie is snoring on the rug beside the bed.

Outside, a motorcar sputters, a bell tolls. Miss Markert, who has the room across from them, clatters down the stairs on her way to church. Agnes thinks: *We will lie here forever, without saying another word. We'll lie here until we starve to death. Reggie will stay alive by eating our dead bodies.*

The bells of one church stop and another one starts up, and she can't stand it any longer. She pushes him away and says, "Jesse! Can't you just answer me? Tell me the truth. You don't want to marry me. Back home we talked about it all the time. Once we're married, we'll do this. We'll get married, and then we'll do that. What has changed?"

"Oh God." He pushes a pillow behind his back and sits up. "All right. It's my parents. My father. He says he'll help with my fees at the law school."

"Jesse, I know all this."

"But only if I don't get married."

She absorbs this before she speaks. "To me, you mean."

There's another split second before he answers, but it tells her a lot. "To anyone!" he says, with vehemence.

"Why? What's wrong with getting married?"

"He says I should wait until I'm done with schooling."

But why? She wants to ask again. *What difference would it make?* But she doesn't, and Jesse keeps talking. "He's already angry enough that I'm not planning to come home and take over the business. He wants to retire. I haven't told you everything that's been going on. Before you even got here, he came out here twice to try to talk me out of law school. Once he brought Mother—the heavy artillery. They kept at me. It was pretty relentless. The glassworks has supported the family in style all these years. The glassworks is sending me to college. The world is always going to need glass bottles. Mother said, 'I remember when you were born, the first thing Father said was: A son! He can take over the business!'"

"I don't see you running a glassworks."

"Nor do I. But I'm told I'm an ungrateful son not to want to do it. My parents aren't easy-going like yours, Agnes. My parents are—" He stops, shrugs, doesn't finish his sentence until he's smoothed her hair some more and run his hand along her cheek to her neck and then her shoulder. "Difficult," he says, and scooches down next to her again.

Jesse has never talked much about his parents, but she knows some things about the Zorns, who snubbed her at the opera house and never invited her for a meal. Jesse has told her that punishment at their house meant his father's belt, and that Jesse and his sister had to raise their hands at the supper table if they wanted to speak, and that the barn cat's kittens were always drowned. She knows that this rush of new information is meant to distract her from the marriage question.

"I suppose it's natural they'd want you to take over the business."

"The trouble is, Father sees my not wanting to run the Findlay Bottle and Glassworks as a rejection of everything he stands for. And—you know—maybe it is! Maybe that's what I should have told him."

"Tell me what you actually did say."

"That it's a fine business. Who could imagine a better one? What better way to serve humanity than to provide them with bottles for their ketchup and their beer? But— and I've told him this at least two dozen times—that is not what I want to do with my life. I didn't go into my reasons."

"Which are?"

"That I'm not a businessman, for Pete's sake! I can't spend my life sitting behind a desk in Findlay, Ohio, checking over orders and invoices and requisitions and quality control reports. Making deals, buying and selling, figuring out how badly I can pay my employees to keep them working for me without making a dent in my profits. It's hateful to me. But that's what fascinates my father, that's what gets him up in the morning."

"He and Cousin Clay would get along beautifully."

"Your cousin at least seems willing to atone for his sins by spreading some of his cash around. Father isn't much of a philanthropist, especially when it comes to his son."

"And so the bottles will only pour out half of what you need for law school."

"And I've had to fight for that half! Damn it, Agnes. I worked all through college. I don't want to work my way through law school. This way, if he chips in, it will be two more years at the *Post Standard*. If he doesn't, what—five?"

"Five is too many. I cannot keep this up for five years." She thinks about it. "And so, if you and I put off getting married, we can actually get married sooner than if we got married now and your father refused to pay."

He laughs. "The logic of that is over my head. But I suppose that by giving him what he wants I'm actually thwarting him."

"He's hoping you'll change your mind about me. Or that I'll dump you and marry somebody else."

"I will not change my mind."

"I will not dump you and marry somebody else. I don't know anybody else." This makes him laugh again.

The thought comes to her: *We could get married secretly*. She's not keen on it—exchanging one lie for another— but she tucks it away at the back of her mind. And tells herself that, if Jesse suggests it, she'll do it—and then she half expects him to.

Instead, he says, "But, Agnes—seriously—tell me why you can't ask your cousin Frick for the money. It just might tickle his philanthropic fancy to put your beau through law school. A promising young chap like Jesse Lyman Zorn."

She pulls back. He has asked her to do this before, and his persistence makes her angry. "You know I can't."

"So you keep saying. But why?"

"He's not my cousin, for one thing. He's Papa's cousin. I've never met him. He scarcely knows who I am!"

"What harm in trying?"

"It could make him angry. He could blame Papa. He could stop sending them money, Jesse. I can't chance it!"

"All right. Calm down, Ag. It was just an idea." After another pause, he says, "As it was, I had to play my trump card just to get Father to agree on giving me half."

"And what might your 'trump card' be?"

"I promised I'd return to North Baltimore to prac- tice law."

She looks up at him quickly. "Oh?"

He shrugs. "We'll see."

Agnes encounters Olive Webster again at the park, twice. In an odd way, the two of them have become friends, and so the third time they run into each other, Agnes walks home with Olive and stays for a cup of coffee. It's her day off, and she has no good reason not to accept the invitation. Besides, she's curious. Olive is so odd—a mix of silliness and sorrow that Agnes isn't sure how to take. She hasn't gone to school past the sixth grade and doesn't know anything, it seems, but she has a bone-deep streak of cleverness that intrigues Agnes. She is curious to see where she lives.

Highland Street is still unpaved; the dust clings to their skirts as they walk, Reggie trotting before them with his tail up. Olive talks about a dog her brother used to have that they had to give away to live on a farm because he bit four people. She tells Agnes that her father got frostbite so bad when he was ice-fishing on the lake in Oswego that he lost three toes, and that her mother had five miscarriages before Olive was born so maybe trouble having babies ran in the family. She says that Clarence's mother down in Georgia died after having her last one, number ten, Clarence's brother Aylmer, who was born with a club foot and is also a little simple.

Agnes is about to ask her if anything good has ever happened to anybody in her family, when they arrive at the big gray house and Olive says, "Oh, I can't wait to show you my apartment."

They climb to the second floor. The place is stuffy and dusty, and, though nearly empty of furniture, manages to be untidy, with dirty dishes piled up and an unmade bed through a half-open door, a heap of clothes next to an ironing board. The kitchen table is ancient, scored with the marks of knives, bare wood with patches of blue paint. Olive wipes away the crumbs with a grimy rag she keeps by the sink.

But there's a vase of flowers and a funny set of calico-cat salt-and-pepper shakers. Checkered curtains at the windows, matching cushions on the chairs.

Olive looks around, beaming. "Don't you just love it?"

Agnes says she does, and she means it: there's a hopefulness about the place, and the pockets of messiness remind her of her mother, of home.

They sit at the table. The stove is in the living room, and Olive has a pot of coffee on, but the stove has gone cold, and Agnes doesn't want to wait until Olive hauls the ashes and stokes it up, so she tells her not to bother. It's too hot for coffee anyway. Reggie flops down like a dead dog, his pink tongue hanging out.

"Clarence would like that dog," Olive says. "He likes dogs a lot. I think he wants a dog about as much as I want a baby, which means he'll probably come home with one someday. He especially likes hunting dogs. That's what they always had in Georgia. I can't wait until you meet him. He's tall, Clarence is. I needed to find a tall man because I'm five foot nine. What are you? Five foot three?"

"Five," Agnes says, adding an inch.

"Everybody looks short to me. But Clarence is over six foot. He's a good-looking man. I was lucky to get him." Olive tells her how, after their wedding, they took the train to Georgia so she could meet his family. His father and his brother are farmers. "I've never seen anything like it," Olive says. "They all live together, in the tiniest place—no more than a shed! With horses poking their heads through the windows, and sometimes the pigs would get into the kitchen. And the flies!" She was prepared to stay for a week, but they ended up spending nearly a year there, living over in Macon with Clarence's sister Pearl, who at least has a real house, with a spare room, though they had to share it with Pearl's husband's two small children and also Aylmer, the brother with the club foot. The kids were a handful, and now Pearl and her husband have two more of their own besides. "No trouble having babies in the Webster family!" Olive says. She stops talking to take a breath, then adds that, handfuls or not, children are a blessing from God and she can't wait until she has one of her own. "How about you?"

"Babies?" Agnes can't believe how nosy Olive is. "All in good time," she says. "Not quite ready, maybe."

Olive shrugs. "Sometimes these things just happen."

"Sometimes they do."

"Not always, though." Olive's sunken eyes get sad again, and she rattles on about various people she knows, their children or lack of them, the children's good or bad behavior. Reggie has gone to sleep on the floor, and Agnes thinks she's in danger of doing the same thing in her chair. *Notice everything,* she says to herself. The embroidered "God Bless Our Home" sampler on the wall next to a picture of Jesus with his fiery heart glowing through his snow-white tunic, and what must be a wedding portrait of Olive and Clarence, propped on the mantel. Trying to get a look at it from across the room, Agnes notices that her eyesight isn't as good as it used to be, and wonders how much a pair of spectacles might cost and if she would ever allow herself to be seen in them, and does your eyesight get worse if you don't wear spectacles, or might it get better if the eyes have to keep working harder to see?

After a half-hour—there's a loud-ticking clock on the wall—she takes pity on Reggie, who is panting in his sleep, and says they have to leave. "I have a lot to do anyway," she adds. Even a tiny lie like that gives her a qualm: in truth, she has nothing to do but go home, strip down to her petticoat, and sit in front of the window reading and hoping for a breeze. She could linger all afternoon at Olive's apartment if she wanted to. Agnes asked her once if she liked to read, and she said she didn't have time for such nonsense. Agnes wonders what she does all day.

"When does your husband get home?" Olive asks. She seems to love specific questions that demand specific answers: What time this, how much that, how far away something else. Agnes tells her seven o'clock, and Olive wants to know if she cooks supper for him, and Agnes says they live in a rooming house and usually eat supper with Mrs. Anderson and the other tenants. Olive asks if there's a piano there, and Agnes says yes, and—to her complete surprise—Olive says she wishes she had a piano, she loves to play, she's never had a lesson, but she can play almost anything by ear.

Agnes knows Mrs. Anderson wouldn't mind if she invited Olive over to play, but she doesn't do it. It's easy to get too much of Olive's chatter and her wistful-ness—I wish I had this, if only I had that—and hard to believe she can be any kind of a piano-player. Agnes has a brief, bitter memory of Rudy sitting at the keyboard, singing about marble halls and love that never changes. He went back to Ireland, and he wrote Agnes a letter, which Mama forwarded: he's living with his brother and his wife in Kilkenny, he has a good job, he's engaged to "a wonderful girl," they are looking for a house of their own. The letter ended: "I wish you well, but I will never get over it, Aggie, what you did. I will keep that pain with me until I die."

Olive says, "A piano would help pass the time."

Agnes is at the door. "Yes, it probably would."

"Come back again soon," Olive calls after her. "Whenever you like. I'm usually here."

She doesn't go home, though. She walks to the library, keeping on the shady side of the street and letting Reggie have a drink at the fountain on Montgomery Street. She has Uncle Clem's last letter in her bag, with a list of books he recommends. "Read *The Jungle* by Upton Sinclair," he says, even though she may not like it. There's a book of short stories by a new writer named Willa Cather. He tells her not to waste her time with H. G. Wells. And not to forget Stevenson—he has a feeling she has never read *The Strange Case of Dr. Jekyll and Mr. Hyde*, and it's time she did.

As usual, he never mentions Jesse's name. He has never said so, never even hinted at it, but Agnes knows her uncle well enough to be aware that he doesn't like Jesse, though she doesn't know why. Jesse is a scholar, he has ambitions. Uncle Clem had once surprised her by bursting out bitterly about the hard luck and bad choices that had left him poor—"degradingly poor, offensively poor, miserably poor, beastly poor," he said, quoting Dickens and added, "Don't ever let it happen to you, Aggie." How can her uncle—who thought Rudy, a lowly bookkeeper in a small-town general store, was a good catch—not approve of her being the wife of a lawyer?

She ties Reggie to a post outside the library. Inside, it's cool and silent, with the subtle, almost sweet smell she loves but can never define. Old paper? The wax they use on the floors? She hurries because of the dog, finds the Stevenson book, and checks it out at the desk. The librarian hands her the book with a smile and says, "It will terrify you. And you will love being terrified."

Agnes's best friend in Syracuse is Trevor Carmody, the dining room manager and maître d'. At the time she was hired, Agnes had never heard of a maître d', didn't know what a soufflé was, had never seen an oyster, and barely knew that there were other wines than red, white, and sherry. Mr. Carmody has lived in Paris and speaks French, but he calls himself a "true blue Englishman." He's the son of London pub-owners and grew up in the kitchen and behind the counter; by the age of three, he says, he knew the proper way to mix a black-and-tan and never to store cheese in the ice box.

He trains Agnes patiently. After he calls her a country bumpkin three or four times, she realizes it's a joke, and when he tells her, approvingly, "You're a born waitress," she doesn't wince. You have to be talented at something, and what else is she good for? She's about as likely as Reggie is to go to the university and study Latin or litera-ture. Mr. Carmody makes waiting on tables seem like a noble calling. "One can eat, or one can dine," he says. "At the Yates Hotel one dines. I am glad to see you appre-ciate the difference, Agnes." She does, but only because he has instructed her in it.

Agnes and Mr. Carmody sometimes eat supper together after the dining room closes, not in the kitchen with the other help but at their own table at the back, often with a glass of French wine from Trevor's stash. Sometimes his special friend, an actor named Desmond Durant, joins them after a performance. Mr. Durant lives in New York City, but he tours with two different theatrical companies and shows up in Syracuse every few months, when he's in a show at Keith's or the Empire. Agnes and Jesse go to the theater as often as they can, sitting in the cheap seats, and, before Agnes meets Mr. Desmond Durant, she has seen him as the Baron in *The Merry Widow* and as Dick Deadeye in *H.M.S. Pinafore*. In person, he is a stout, handsome man, half a foot shorter than Mr. Carmody and, offstage, bald as an egg, with an impish gap-toothed smile. Together they look comical, like a vaudeville act.

"We have been devoted to each other for twenty-seven years," Mr. Carmody says. When he says Mr. Durant's name—he calls him Desmond—he smiles. He can't help it. It's a revelation to Agnes that two men can feel about each other the way she and Jesse do.

Mr. Carmody has round blue eyes behind round metal spectacles, pink cheeks, thin gray hair parted in the middle, and beautifully manicured fingernails. He is like an elegant, smartly dressed Uncle Clem—he even reads novels, though only English ones. "I'll always miss the dear old place," he says. "But I can never go back." He does not elaborate.

Oddly, the job at the Yates is much as Agnes described it to Sally before it even existed: she earns five dollars a week plus tips and wears a black uniform, a white apron, and a frilled cap. The hotel takes twenty cents out of her earnings every week to pay for the uniform, an arrangement that Trevor says he makes only with employees he likes. There are two other waitresses and three waiters—nice enough, but Agnes keeps to herself because her private life is so irregular. Telling lies about Dorrie was a game she'd devised because it was necessary. But it troubles her, every time, to answer to "Mrs. Zorn," which is what their landlady calls her, also the postman and the grocer and the other lodgers. Jesse's friends Bill and Harvey, who sometimes come over to play cards on Friday nights, joke about Jesse being tied to his wife's apron strings, while she sits smiling and blushing and seething.

But by the time summer comes, Agnes has confessed to Mr. Carmody that she Jesse are not really husband and wife, at which Trevor flapped his hand in the air and said, "Please, my dear. Don't trouble me with such trivialities. Or yourself either. The world is a wide and wonderful place, and there is room for us all."

On a hot August day Agnes realizes she has missed her period. This occurs to her in Schiller Park, where she and Reggie have taken their walk. She's earlier than usual—if she forgoes her second cup of coffee, she can get outside before the day heats up, and the chances of running into Olive Webster in the park are diminished.

She's sitting on the bench she thinks of as hers, hoping to find a bit of a breeze at the top of the hill. The tall towers of a church rise up below her in the distance between the ruffled tops of the trees—masses of green leaves that look wilted and hazy in the heat. When she woke that morning she was surprised by a bout of nausea. She lay still, and it came to nothing, but now she counts, and knows she's late. She covers her mouth with her hand and, behind it, makes whimpering noises that surprise her, and she stops. She breathes in and out shakily. Maybe I'm wrong, she thinks, maybe I'm just late because I've been tired, or because it's so hot, or—the thought fades away as she's thinking it. She knows the symptoms by now, and she has them all.

I've got to go, she thinks. *I've got to get home.* It seems suddenly urgent, as if there's something she must do. She calls Reggie to her and fastens his leash, but then she just sits there while the sun beats down on her head until she starts to feel faint. She stands up. She and Reggie start down the hill and, when they've almost reached the street, she turns her head into the bushes and vomits.

"Well," he says. "Your timing is again impeccable."

"My timing."

"Sorry." He rubs his hand over his face. "*The* timing."

"What's not impeccable are Jimmy hats. One of them has obviously been pecked."

"Agnes—"

"Jesse—"

"Come here. Sit down."

She hesitates, but finally she sits beside him on the edge of the bed. He's hunched forward, his hands clasped between his knees. She lays her head on his shoulder. "Now what?"

She waits for him to say: *It will work out. Everything will be fine, you wait and see.* Instead, he says, "I will not give up what I want, Agnes. I need to be free to live my life. I will not give up the chance to make a mark. I want to do something with my life besides—"

He makes an aimless gesture and doesn't bother to go on. She lifts her head from his shoulder. She supposes he means Mrs. Anderson's rooming house. The sagging, tarnished brass bed. His pregnant girlfriend. The glass-works. She understands this, in a vague way, but it makes no sense to her. Maybe it's something men think about: making a mark is something they do alone, single-mind-edly, without any detours. Living their life! For her, every precious minute is life, even if she's just walking the dog or waiting tables. Or lying in bed on a Sunday morning with Jesse.

"I thought we were living our lives together."

"We can't do this, Agnes." His voice is stony. "This is not the time. There are ways. There are people who take care of these things."

She thinks about that. Yes, she knows there are people, and she has no doubt that, here in Syracuse, they can find one. She remembers how she hoped Uncle Clem would help her that way—how many years ago? Almost six. Before Dorrie was a little girl learning how to read, when she was just a problem, an encumbrance, a horror.

When Agnes doesn't reply, he sits up and takes her by the shoulders. His eyes burn into hers. "I can't do it," he says fiercely. "I won't do it."

"I can't not do it," she says. "I won't not do it."

It's Mr. Carmody who arranges both the Foundling Hospital and afterward. Mr. Carmody knows about St. Mary's because Mr. Dumont's sister, Imogene, had a baby there many years ago, and they both remember that the nuns were kind. "All you have to do is convert," Mr. Carmody tells her.

Become a Catholic? She remembers Rudy, and the elaborate Latin Masses, the priest in his fancy clothes and the little boys all in white. And Grandma Lu who, if she knew, would be dismayed.

But her grandmother will not know. She tells no one back home about her condition. She has the vague idea that she can't do it to them again, but she knows that's not the real reason. The real reason is that, if she goes back to Ohio with a child, her life will be over.

She writes only to say that she and Jesse have separated, and she'll be starting a new job on the first of January, cooking for a private hospital. The pay is not as much, she says, but she gets room and board.

"You won't have to be a Catholic for life," Mr. Carmody says. "Unless you want to, of course," he adds politely. She can see that he is no more attracted by this idea than she is. "But for the moment, it would be expedient."

"What happened to Imogene?" she asks him.

He tells her that Imogene died in childbirth and her baby was adopted. "But she wasn't like you, she was always a sickly girl," he assures her. Still, the thought of Imogene Dumont stays with her. At the end of October, she goes to see the director of the hospital, Sister Josephine. It's a fine, sunny day, but Agnes is surprised that the nun suggests a walk around the grounds: whatever she expected of nuns, it was not a companionable walk in the sunshine. Sister Josephine asks her about her family back home, about her job at the Yates. Agnes tells her about winning the Latin prize at her high school. She finds herself wanting Sister Josephine to see that she's not—well, what? The usual kind of girl who becomes pregnant without a husband. She doesn't reveal that this has happened to her before.

Past the vegetable garden, now tidied and barren, they come to a small cemetery, with rows of white crosses, and Agnes wonders if Imogene is in there. The nun sees her looking. "Most of those graves are for the little ones who didn't survive," she says.

"But not all of them," Agnes says.

"No." Sister Josephine crosses herself, and Agnes quickly follows suit. "Not all of them."

Before she leaves, the nun shows Agnes the common room: sewing machines on one side, desks on the other, one with a typewriter. A picture of a saint presides over the fireplace, gazing up toward the heavens, a blonde girl holding in her arms a small white lamb, the cleanest lamb Agnes has ever seen. "St. Agnes," Sister Josephine says. "The patron saint of chastity. She wished to remain a virgin, and she chose martyrdom over the marriage her family was trying to force on her. You're lucky to be named after her."

Agnes says, "I was named after my father's Great-Aunt Agnes Frick."

Sister Josephine smiles. "Agnes is our most beloved saint. I hope you will pray to her often for strength."

She has been hired to help with the cooking and the cleanup—three meals a day, for twenty-four women in various stages of pregnancy—and two dollars will be put away for her every week. Agnes figures out that she will have thirty dollars by the time she leaves, but whether that will be a lot or a little, enough or not nearly enough, she doesn't know: what will happen afterward, where she'll go, what she'll be doing—these are all mysteries she is not ready to think about.

For the moment, she goes on living with Jesse on Willow Street, an awkward arrangement in which they each try to be gone as often as they can. She sees him turning his eyes away from her expanded middle.

They hardly ever talk. One evening, she looks up from her book to find him staring at her. He says, "You are inscrutable to me."

"And yet you say you love me," she replies.

"Maybe it's another Agnes I love," he says.

She has no answer to that.

They eat supper with the other lodgers down in the dining room, and they share the bed. Agnes sleeps so far over on her side that, more than once, in the middle of the night, she catches herself falling off. Sometimes, when they're both asleep, his foot will slide over and touch hers, and she pulls away as if it's on fire. Once, toward dawn, they wake up face to face, and on the same impulse they reach for each other and make love furiously, both of them in tears. They never refer to this incident, and it never happens again.

She is still working at the Yates, though Mr. Carmody has told her regretfully that they can't have pregnant waitresses. She'll be there through December, and at the turn of the new year she'll move to the hospital.

She hasn't given up her walks to the park, with Reggie on his leash, though she knows she'll run into Olive sooner or later—almost wishing for it, to get it over with. When she rounds the bend one morning in the path to see Olive sitting on the bench, she stops dead, and Olive looks at her. "Well, my goodness," she says. "You lucky thing! Why didn't you tell me?"

It's a relief, in the end, to have a woman to talk to—a woman who's not a nun. Agnes tells the truth to Olive's astonished face: she and Jesse are not really married.

"So you've been fibbing all this time," Olive says.

"I suppose I have." Agnes has begun to cry, and she wipes her eyes with the handkerchief she brought with her in case this very thing happened.

"If Clarence and I were living in sin, I'd fib too, I guess," Olive says, but her sad eyes sharpen with disapproval. The unspoken words are: *Not that we would.*

"You can call it what you like," Agnes says. "We are not living in sin. We are just living together. I'm not a Catholic." She can't see any reason to tell Olive she's going to become one. "The whole idea is ridiculous to me, so please don't ever say it again."

Olive slumps back on the bench, her feelings hurt, looking peeved, but then she sits up suddenly, struck by a thought. "Well, you'd better hurry up and have that wedding! I could help you make a dress that would hide your condition. We could make tucks around the waist, and you could have a matching shawl to go over it."

Then Agnes has to tell her everything. They will not be getting married. They're splitting up. She will work in the kitchen at St. Mary's Foundling Hospital for her room and board.

Olive stares at her open-mouthed. Agnes waits for her to ask how she can do that when she's not a Catholic, but instead the first thing Olive says is, "And what will happen to the baby?"

She moves to St. Mary's on the afternoon of New Year's Eve. Mrs. Anderson, surprisingly, doesn't ask questions; maybe she has heard the arguments and understands what is going on. She gives Agnes an old leather suitcase that belonged to the late Mr. Anderson and had been stored in the cellar—it bears his initials in gold, MLA, which are Agnes's backwards. "A good omen," Mrs. Anderson says.

Agnes finds it hard to see it as a good omen. The case smells musty and is green with mildew. She scrubs it with lye soap, which helps only a little, and when she stuffs her clothes inside, it's so heavy she can hardly lift it. But she is grateful to have it, and grateful that she has enough money to hire a cab to take her to the hospital.

It's a Friday. The last she saw of Jesse was that morning when he left for work, saying, "All right, then," turning up his coat collar and pulling on his hat as he went out the door. She had hoped for some kind of a formal farewell. She'd wanted to say, "We did have some fun, though, didn't we?" But she said nothing, just went to the window and watched him go.

All day, as she packs her case and walks the dog and tidies up the room, she waits for him to come back and say a proper goodbye. This makes her sadder than almost anything, that he has no shred of affection left for her.

It's nearly dark by the time she kisses Reggie and bumps the suitcase down the two flights to the street, with the brown cloth bag she brought from North Baltimore slung over one shoulder and her handbag tucked under her arm. She's wearing the hat Jesse bought her, trimmed with red felt roses that have become only a bit bedraggled, and her black coat with a red scarf. The hansom driver stows her suitcase and gives her a courtly bow as he opens the door for her. "You're looking very festive, young lady," he says, and Agnes almost laughs.

It isn't until he slams the door and the cab is bumping down the street and she looks back at the rooming house, where the only lamp lit is in Mrs. Anderson's front window, that she understands that Jesse has indeed abandoned her.

Last New Year's Eve, she recalls, they splurged on a champagne dinner with Harvey and his new wife, Nancy, and the four of them had danced until two in the morning. It seems like another world—no, it seems like something she had imagined, or read about in a book.

And where, she wondered, would Jesse be this year, as the world welcomed 1910? She could see him coming home—late, so he'd know she was safely gone—and then what? Would he rejoice in her absence? Put on his gray waistcoat and his blue-striped tie and take someone else out for champagne? Or would he shed a tear? Would he shed even one tear? She had no idea.

On the first of February, after four sessions of instruction with Father Damian Keefe, the chaplain, who also hears her confession, Agnes is baptized a Catholic.

She now goes to Mass every morning, along with the others, in the cold chapel attached to the back of the hospital. Mass and Holy Communion are required for all girls who are not actually in confinement, though they are excused for two weeks after their babies are born.

Agnes doesn't believe a word of what she's been taught—miraculous tales of virgins and saints, and a god who reminds her of Jesse's father—but it's far more colorful than the pale Lutheranism of her grandmother, and she's surprised by how much she likes the ceremony of the Mass. The priest, in his richly embroidered outfits, raising his arms and bowing his head, is like a magician, turning water into wine while he intones Latin words that Agnes follows in the missal the nuns give her. When she went to church with Rudy, it was all a mystery to her; the missal makes it comprehensible, and the Latin is soothing. She memorizes the Pater Noster, and as she cuts up potatoes and picks the meat from a chicken, she mumbles *Et dimitte nobis debita nostra sicut et nos dimittimus debitoribus nostris*—fast, like *Peter Piper picks a peck*, then slowly, savoring the rhythm.

Dimitte nobis debita nostra, she realizes, is what the Church is all about. Father Keefe preaches every Sunday about repentance for sin—the girls at St. Mary's are, officially, sinners—but he occasionally varies his text, and Agnes is impressed by a sermon counseling forgiveness. Jesse has disappeared from her life as thoroughly as if he has died: she knows he's still alive only because, sneaking a look at the *Post-Standard*, she finds his byline above stories that put her to sleep: a politician on the take, a merger between two law firms, the legal wrangling over construction of a gypsum plant south of the city.

Agnes works hard at forgiving him, and sometimes feels she's almost there.

The winter months pass with agonizing slowness. She spends most of her days in the kitchen, where at least it's warm, the baby kicking against the big white apron tied around her middle. Sister Elberta, the cook, is a jolly woman who sings hymns while she works. She's a specialist in stretching ingredients to feed the multitudes, and the food is ample but tasteless—salt is considered bad for pregnant women, pepper is unheard of. Agnes stirs the morning oatmeal and cuts up root vegetables for the soups and stews. She would love to make bread, but a local baker donates the bread—long, plain day-old loaves eaten without butter. There are certain conventions: when Agnes clears the table after a stew night, each bowl has a neat heap of gristle piled beside it, and everyone breaks the bread into the watery soup, which improves both, or into their glasses of milk. Milk is plentiful.

When the stews are being dished out, Agnes always thinks of *Oliver Twist*, the last Dickens novel she read before she left home. Not a soul in the place would understand what she was talking about if she mentioned it. She misses Jesse at those moments almost more than she does when she's lying alone in her bed.

Lent begins, in mid-February. The meals become officially meatless, and the girls are encouraged to deeper repentances. They are denied bread two days a week, but, except for Good Friday, they are not required to fast, because of their condition, though it's obvious that the nuns do—Sister Elberta faints in the kitchen on the afternoon of St. Patrick's Day, her winged headdress knocked awry so you can see her chopped gray hair.

All the girls, however unwieldy their bulk, get down on their knees in the evenings and are led in saying the rosary by Sister Josephine. At Mass, Father Keefe's reds and greens are replaced with vestments of deep purple, and the same color is used to cover the statues of St. Joseph and St. Ann that flank the main altar, an effect that Agnes finds more spooky than solemn. Every sermon during Lent is about penance. A cruel religion, Agnes thinks, not for the first time, with its endless repentances for a long-ago death by crucifixion, and the sin label stuck to life's normal pleasures and people's trivial lapses of good sense. But she feels sorry for the nuns, who take it all so seriously, and even for Father Keefe, who looks wan from fasting and seems so unhappy.

Because she is employed there, Agnes is allowed certain privileges, like pouring herself a second cup of coffee in the mornings and walking with one of the sisters to the library for books. She isn't allowed to visit Olive or Mr. Carmody, but the nuns allow her to receive an occasional guest in the small sitting room off the kitchen, where sometimes there's even a fire in the fireplace.

Mr. Carmody brings small delicacies from the hotel: butter cookies, two popovers wrapped in a napkin, a roll filled with goose liver paté, gherkins on the side. He has had to hire a replacement for her at the Yates.

"That means I can't go back," she says, with the fatalism she's learning. She has almost stopped crying over the

little disasters that keep coming at her. She thinks sometimes of the magician she and Jesse saw at the Empire,
who threw knives at a box that had a girl inside.

"If someone should quit, you know I would take you
on immediately."

Agnes shakes her head. "I should probably go somewhere else. Get away from Syracuse." She imagines
running into Jesse on the street, when he's out walking
Reggie. Or having him come into whatever restaurant
she's working at, with his new girlfriend, the one who
doesn't keep having babies.

Mr. Carmody takes her hand and rubs the back of it
with his thumb. This is what almost makes her cry. Any
kind of physical contact. "Would you go back home,
Agnes, do you think?"

Ohio seems so far away, farther than she would ever
be able to explain. She used to think of Doris constantly;
now she can forget her for days at a time. She just
shakes her head.

"And Jesse—I hate to pry, my dear, forgive me, but—
you're sure that Jesse is quite gone? I mean, he seemed
so—it's hard to believe that—"

She takes pity on him and breaks in. "Quite gone,
Mr. Carmody. Gone with the wind. As gone as it's possible for someone to be."

Until Lent came, she hadn't entirely believed this. In
spite of herself, she retained a shred of hope that Jesse
would show up at the hospital to claim her. Repent.
Beg forgiveness. Make an honest woman of her. But
forty days of the purple-covered statues and the plain-
tive hymns, the Stations of the Cross and the suffering
of Jesus, the crown of thorns and the dripping blood—it
wore her optimism down to a sliver. On Easter Sunday—

when suffering turned to joy because Christ has risen, the chapel fragrant with lilies and Father Keefe resplendent in white and gold—as the girls filed up to the altar to receive Communion, Agnes stayed stubbornly in her seat with her backache and her huge belly and the certainty that she and her baby were alone in the world.

"I'm so sorry, my dear," Mr. Carmody says, and after a pause asks, "So—you'll start over, then. Someplace entirely new?"

The girl in the box emerges from the forest of knives without a scratch, and everyone applauds. "I don't know," she says. "Maybe."

Olive visits too, with a present: a white linen handkerchief embroidered in red with Agnes's initial. "I did it myself," Olive says. "Merry Christmas slightly belated."

The A is very fancy, decorated with French knots and garlanded in deep green. Agnes traces it with her finger. "The Scarlet Letter."

"Yes," Olive says. "I thought it was cheerful."

"Thank you, Olive, it's beautiful. You shouldn't have done it."

"Yes, I should. You're my friend, Agnes. Don't forget that."

Olive is fascinated by her friend's predicament, and especially by Jesse's abandonment. "I'm sorry I never got to meet him. I wonder what he could have been thinking, just to say goodbye like that to his girlfriend and his own baby. I wonder what kind of person does that." Agnes lets Olive rattle on. It's comforting, in a way, to hear her say bad things about Jesse. "It seems so heartless. Doesn't it?"

"I don't know."

"Well, I do," Olive says. "Selfish, I would say. He sounds like the kind of person who only looks out for himself. I wonder what made you take up with him."

He was like a lamp lit in a dark room. "I didn't know he was selfish when I took up with him."

"Really!" Olive's eyebrows shoot up.

Agnes admires Olive's broad, unlined forehead, and her ability to take a long and tangled tale and stuff it into a nutshell. "Really, Olive. I just—" She gestures helplessly with one hand; the other has squeezed Olive's handkerchief into a ball. "Loved him," she says, with a catch in her voice. She smooths the handkerchief so she can dry her eyes.

"Well." Olive looks at her with pity. "He must know how to turn on the charm, I'll say that for him. Then again, I hate to say this, but when you give something away it doesn't mean that much."

It takes Agnes a few seconds to understand what she's talking about. "It wasn't like that." Her voice is unsteady. *What if it was? What if that's all it was?* And yet that was so much, so much . . .

"Well, I'm sorry. All I mean is that something was wrong somewhere."

"Olive? Could we stop talking about this?"

"Oh, all right. It's none of my business anyway."

Olive quiets down, and they sit in silence, looking at the skimpy, dying fire. Agnes is wearing the blue paisley shawl Jesse gave her, and she pulls it tighter around her bulk. Olive and Mr. Carmody, Agnes realizes, are her only friends. For a moment she is flooded with the desire to just say goodbye to it all and go home, where people love her and where her Dorrie is learning her letters and her sums. *She's a bright little thing*, Uncle Clem wrote. *Reminds us all of her mother.* In her Christmas letter, Mama said that they're worried about Clement, who has a cough that won't go away. *We hear him up there in the night, Ag, going on and on, and he looks like a skeleton.*

Olive heaves a deep sigh and clasps her hands at her chest. "The thing I really came to talk about," she says, "is your baby."

The baby is born on the third of April, a week after Easter Sunday and ten days before Agnes turns twenty-two. She goes into labor just after midnight, and the baby arrives before dawn, an easier birth than Doris's. The nuns are kind, but she misses her mother.

She hoped for a boy this time—one of those enviable creatures who always find a way to be free, to make their mark—but it's another bald, puny girl like Doris. Agnes names her Anna. Anna cries more than Dorrie did, and she's so small and helpless Agnes sometimes cries along with her.

A cluster of babies arrives in late March and early April. Agnes is in a ward with three others, among them Patsy Flynn, a girl she's become friendly with, who was raped by her brother. Her baby boy died soon after birth, and until the nuns take Patsy away her sobbing mingles with the wails of the babies who have lived.

For the first week it seems that Anna cries more than she does anything else. She never sleeps for very long, and she has trouble nursing: in the middle of trying to suck, she starts to scream instead. Sister Marie-Angèle, the French nurse who birthed her, is pessimistic. "See how she stretches out her legs," she says. "How she arches her little back." She reaches out a hand. "The cold feet, Agnès." She pronounces it the way Jesse used to: Ahn-yez. "I do not know," she says, shaking her head. Father Keefe comes in with a vial of holy water and baptizes the baby.

The days go by, colored by nothing but Anna's wails. She is not the loudest, but she goes on the longest. Agnes finds herself murmuring, *Please, please let her be all right,* not sure whom she's pleading with—maybe the Catholic god, borrowed for the purpose. Agnes thinks that if her baby dies, she will die herself.

She is not recovering quickly, as she did with Doris. Of course, she is not surrounded by mother, grand-mother, sisters—only sisters who are nuns, who leave her alone for hours at a time. She's in a ward with two other women and their babies. She's still sore, her breasts ache, and sleeping is almost impossible—if her own baby's screaming doesn't waken her, someone else's does. She spends the days slipping in and out of a doze, almost too weak to get out of bed, and she hasn't even enough energy to read—which is just as well, there's nothing to read anyway, and no one to talk to. *My brain will rot away,* she thinks, and she can almost feel it happening: huge sections of her memory are gone—Latin poems, verb conjugations, the names of the characters in *Our Mutual Friend,* Keats's Grecian urn ode, which she recited flaw-lessly on Prize Day senior year and won a medal for.

> *What mad pursuit? What struggle to escape?*
> *What something? What wild ecstasy?*

Her world has come to this: a narrow metal bed, a crying baby, and the unsettling thought that, if she had married Rudy Killian, she'd be kneading bread in her warm kitchen in North Baltimore, with an adoring husband, money in the bank, a couple of fat, healthy children, and the library full of books right down the street.

And then, the day before Agnes's birthday, Anna settles down and sleeps for four blessed hours. When she awakes she's hungry, but with a normal hunger that can be satisfied. Sister Marie-Angèle comes by and clasps her hands, "Oh, the bon dieu," she says, crossing herself. "Just look at this little one. She was starving, la pauvre!"

Agnes lies back on the pillow with the baby placidly sucking at her breast—Agnes has slept too while Anna was quiet. She nestles her cheek against the fuzz on Anna's pink scalp, and feels the belief returning to her that, in spite of everything, the world is a good place. She also realizes that, since Anna was born, she has scarcely given Jesse a thought, and that a day will come when she won't think of him at all. *What pipes and timbrels? What wild ecstasy?*

What indeed?

She and the baby continue to thrive, and, once Agnes is back on her feet, they go out into the air. The weather is warm and dry. Anna is blue-eyed, contented—a light weight in her arms. Agnes carries her into the cemetery behind the chapel, where the white crosses poke out of the greening grass: she counts thirty-two of them. A fresh cross for Patsy's baby boy is stuck into a square of bare earth, but most are in need of paint. One fine day, she decides, she will ask for the job of whitewashing them. "At least we're not here," she says to Anna. "There's always that"—and, at the sound of her mother's voice, the baby turns toward her breast. Her cheeks are pinker in her ivory face, she's getting fatter, but everything about her is tiny and delicate.

"She doesn't take after you," Sister Josephine says. "Maybe the nose."

"She looks more like her father," Agnes replies, not because Anna does (though she may have Jesse's small chin), but to see if the nun will turn away in disapproval. Once it's established that a father will not acknowledge his child, will not marry its mother, and will not pay for its upkeep, he might as well not exist. Anna's birth certificate has a blank space where her father's name should be, as if she's one of the miracles of the Catholic Church.

Sister Josephine purses her lips and says, "Does she now?"

By the middle of May, Agnes is back in the kitchen, the baby beside her in a basket as she works. Some days she's grateful for the refuge the nuns have given her—they will keep her on in the kitchen until July—but on other days she wants only to be gone, away from their strict eyes, the terrible food, the houseful of miserable pregnant girls, the confessional every Saturday morning where she tries to think of a sin or two for Father Keefe.

Where? Anywhere. It's a feeling she remembers from North Baltimore, when she would walk out to the edge of town, past the barrel factory and the limestone quarry and the last red barn, until the world fell away to nothing but low hills in the distance and a long, straight dusty road in front of her. Like Tiberius Humphrey in Uncle Clem's book, she had a longing to set out on it, almost not caring where it took her.

She feels the same way now—anywhere! Anywhere but Syracuse, New York, where Jesse Lyman Zorn lives his carefree life and never thinks about her or his child. She sometimes wonders if he's washed his memory clean of them. Soon after she left, she realized she left her silver bracelet behind. When he found it, did he remember her tiny wrist, the way he would encircle it with his finger and thumb? Has he forgotten the storeroom, the rock, the smell of the tall grass in the field out near Findlay? Her red bloomers, the blue shawl he said matched her eyes? She wonders if Reggie misses her: her anger at Jesse protects her; it's the thought of Reggie now that makes her cry.

Mr. Carmody and Mr. Dumont come together to visit her. The three of them sit on benches in the garden adjoining the cemetery. The lettuces are coming up, and the tomato plants have just been put in. Agnes has white-washed the crosses in the cemetery and banged them into the ground so that they stand up straight, and she and Patsy Flynn have weeded the worst parts, so that the crosses stand out plainly, white against the patchy green. In the garden, hat in hand, Mr. Dumont stands looking at them before he sits down next to Agnes. The baby is between them in her basket, asleep.

"You'd think they'd paint their names on them, wouldn't you?" asks Mr. Carmody. "Or the dates they died. Something."

Mr. Dumont just waves his hand. "What does it matter, really, Trevor? Who comes to this place? Who would care?"

Agnes says, "What's important is that you remember your sister, Mr. Dumont."

"That's true, my dear. As long as someone remembers them, they're not really dead." He smiles at her. "Or so I think."

She almost tells them about Patsy's baby, but decides the moment is sad enough.

Mr. Carmody has brought his box camera with him. He wants to take a photograph of her, and so she sits with Anna in her lap while he takes two of them. Then he joins them on the bench and Agnes, with a laugh, wipes away the drool on the baby's chin and sets her on Mr. Carmody's lap. "I feel quite grandfatherly," Mr. Carmody says, propping the baby up while Mr. Dumont takes a shot of the three of them, but his relief is obvious when Agnes takes the baby back.

"Someday someone may look at this photograph and think that's exactly who you are," Mr. Dumont says. "A strange thought, Trevor."

Strange indeed, Agnes thinks: a day when she'll be gone, and Anna too, and who will own this image? What will they think of the setting, a sunny garden with a cemetery in the background? And will Mr. Carmody in his suit and tie be taken for the father of the smiling young woman sitting beside him?

"I'll see that you get copies of these, Agnes, if they turn out well," he says. And then he asks, "Are you quite well again? Quite recovered?"

"I'm almost myself again," she assures him, and adds with a laugh, "Whatever that is."

He reaches over and squeezes her hand. "You are always yourself, Agnes, dear. Your lovable self. And I wish I could say we have an opening at the hotel for a waitress, but alas, we do not. I can't make myself like this Florence person that we've hired, but, try though I might, I can't find a reason to fire her."

Agnes doesn't mind that her old job is gone—she didn't want it back—but knowing for sure makes her feel, suddenly, alone. She pulls Anna close, for comfort, and kisses her head.

"I suppose I'll find something."

She hasn't been able to solve the riddle of how to care for a baby and at the same time work to support her: her mind goes down one path and finds it blocked, tries another and ends up where she started. She has avoided thinking about Olive Webster's proposal. It's painful, but it's like a blister on her foot—don't walk on it, it won't hurt. She touches Anna's hand with a finger, and the baby curls her pink fist around it.

I will not lose her, she thinks.

Mr. Dumont clears his throat and says, "Agnes? There's something I've thought of, and I wonder if it might interest you. If you'd like to hear it." He waits for her to nod, and when she does he goes on. "I have another sister—Frances—the eldest. Frances and her husband—his name is Stanley Clury—they are the proprietors of a hotel in the town of Norwood, New York, which is quite far north. Near Canada, in fact." He looks at her inquiringly.

She shakes her head. "I don't know it."

"Right—and why should you? Well, now and then I'm cast in a production at the opera house there. They only have one. But the town is on the river, and three railroad lines stop there, so it's quite bustling, really—sawmills, a paper mill, that sort of thing. I believe there's a broom handle factory."

"Agnes would find that exciting," says Mr. Carmody.

"Oh, Trevor. Norwood isn't Syracuse."

"And Syracuse is not London. One accepts certain things."

They're all silent for a moment. Agnes wonders if *accepting things* is the same as *giving up*. She says, "And so— the hotel, Mr. Dumont?"

"Yes." Mr. Dumont continues. "It's called the American House, and it's not far from the depot. I always stay there, of course. It has an excellent dining room—not the quality of the Yates, but for a burg like Norwood it's not bad at all."

"They do some lovely dishes," Mr. Carmody puts in. "All American cooking, of course. But appetizing! I'm not a fan of baked beans, which is one of their specialties, but the corn fritters are excellent. And have you ever had a hot dog, Agnes? Delicious!"

She and Jesse sampled them at the New York State Fair the year before. She tries to imagine Mr. Carmody eating a hot dog. "What wine would you recommend with hot dogs, Mr. C.?"

He laughs. "A German lager, my darling! What could be better? I wish the good nuns served them to visitors! For all their admirable virtues, they're a bit thin on hospitality, I fear."

Across the wooden fence, Agnes can see Sister Felicity's flying headdress bobbing up and down as she hangs up laundry. No doubt listening to every word.

"And Trevor—you liked the chicken pot pie," Mr. Dumont reminds him.

"I did, Desmond. Very much. Frances has a nimble hand with a pie crust. And the sour cherry tarte! I wouldn't mind having her recipe for that. I've tried to wrest it away from her," he tells Agnes. "But Frances claims that all depends upon the cherries from an orchard across the river in the town of Saint-Barbe. Which makes me wonder if it's a French recipe. Perhaps you can find out, my dear."

"Me," Agnes says. "Tell me where I come in."

"Of course!" Mr. Dumont reaches across the basket to give her hand three brisk pats. "This conversation is supposed to be about you, Agnes! The point is, my sister has an opening for a waitress. And perhaps I was presumptuous, but I told her about you. And she's willing to give you a trial, on Trevor's recommendation."

"I told her how sorry I was to lose you. A born waitress! And how you brightened up the dining room at the Yates."

"The thing is," Mr. Dumont says, "I'll be going up to Norwood in July—not for a performance, just to visit my sister and Stanley. A very nice fellow, and a practical one. He not only owns the hotel but has a half-interest in the general store as well. We could ride the train together, Agnes, which would be a great pleasure for me, and I'd see you settled in. If the idea appeals to you at all."

She's silent for a minute, sorting it out in her mind. As she sees it, she has three choices. She can stay in Syracuse, she can return to Ohio, or she can do something else—and the only something else that has turned up is this hotel in Norwood, New York. Another small town, a North Baltimore kind of place. Still—anywhere!

Then something occurs to her. "I would bring the baby with me, of course."

There is an uncomfortable silence.

She signs the papers on the eighteenth of July. The agreement is that she will have six months, until January eighteenth, to reclaim the baby: after that, the adoption will become final, and Anna will leave St. Mary's and become the daughter of Olive and Clarence Webster.

She meets Clarence for the first time at the lawyer's office. Clarence is handsome, tall, lugubrious, with an imposing nose. He has a deep voice and a slow Southern accent, but he hardly says a word, the foil to gabby Olive. This is why he married her, Agnes thinks: so he won't have to talk. She does it all for him.

Olive has a new hat, with a sweeping feather, and a narrow skirt that makes her look taller than ever. She has brought a dress she made for the baby. It's pink with an embroidered yoke: flowers and leaves, and much too big for little Anna. "She'll grow into it fast enough," Olive says, with a smile that's already proprietary.

The baby sits on Agnes's lap. At three months, except for a wispy, light-brown curl at the nape of her neck, she is nearly bald—a sunny and curious baby, with a solemn stare that turns suddenly into a wide-eyed smile. She is smiling in Mr. Carmody's tiny photograph of her, which is in the locket Agnes wears around her neck—displacing Jesse, whose image she had tossed impulsively into the kitchen coal stove one afternoon in February.

Once the formalities are over, they sit in silence for half a minute: the Websters, Mr. Fogarty the lawyer, Sister Josephine, Agnes with the baby. The nun clears her throat. "Well, Agnes."

She keeps her arms tight around Anna, shaking her head. She thinks, *I won't give her up, I won't do it,* before she stands up and puts her on Sister Josephine's lap. She cannot hand her to Olive.

"She will be well cared for," the nun says.

Agnes says, "I will be back before six months," and then she crosses the room and goes out into the lawyer's wood-paneled reception room, past his secretary's desk—almost running—out into the hall and down the spiral staircase to South Salina Street, where Mr. Dumont is waiting with the taxi cab.

PART IV

THE TRIAL

NORWOOD, NEW YORK
1910–11

There is no truth,
A lawyer told me once,
Just evidence.
~ Linda Pastan, "Warm Front"

My mother wasn't adopted by the Goodsons until January 1911, when she was nine months old, probably because out-of-wedlock babies—the children of depraved and immoral parents—were widely suspected to be "defective." By the time little Geraldine was declared fit to leave the foundling hospital and be turned over to a pair of upstanding citizens,[1] her mother no longer lived in Syracuse.

Inez had decamped to Norwood, a village 150 miles north.

Her migrations—North Baltimore to Syracuse, Syracuse to Norwood, and back to Ohio—would have been slow and sooty. But train travel had the virtue of being cheap, and the trains went everywhere. Like North Baltimore, Norwood existed because tracks were laid through it in the 1850s. For only a few dollars, the Rome, Watertown, & Ogdensburg Railroad (ultimately folded into the New York Central line) could have taken a passenger from Syracuse to Norwood in the course of a long afternoon.

---

[1] Early adoption statutes required that the adoptive parents be found "suitable," but the requirement was more form than substance.

Automobiles had recently stopped being exotic, dangerous machines. Roads were still unpaved, maps and road signs were few, and it would have been an all-day trip, but, alternatively, Inez may have hitched a ride up to Norwood in somebody's Tin Lizzie.

No matter how she got there, the Norwood episode is another major mystery: turning it into fiction, I have virtually nothing to anchor it to reality, and I'm as free as if I were making it all up out of my head. I've been unable to discover why she chose Norwood for her next adventure, or exactly when she arrived there—just that it was sometime between April and November 1910. That's when she met a blue-eyed, black-haired young man named Frank Donahue and began sleeping with him.

Inez found a job waiting tables at the American House Hotel on Depot Street, across the street from Timothy Donahue's livery stable. Tim and his twin brother, Michael, opened the stable in 1896, and,

according to a newspaper account, it was "very successful," and "known to every traveling man." The Donahues had a deal with the American House, providing a jitney for guests from the train depot around the corner.

Railway depot, Norwood, New York

Frank Donahue was Tim's son, and seems to have been a problem child. On a small scale of local achievement, Frank's family did well, but Frank himself is notable only for his failure to. Maybe his troubles began with the death of his mother when he was eight; various other Donahue siblings died very young. Maternal deprivation? Survivor guilt? Spoiled rotten by a doting father? Rejected by a grieving one? Whatever the case, he was often unemployed, but in 1910, according to the census, he was twenty years old and working at his father's stable.

On March 4, 1911, Inez and Frank were married at the Catholic church in Norwood, St. Andrew's. (Inez mailed a postcard of the church to her parents in North Baltimore, without a message—someone else has scrawled on it, "One Inez had sent home.") I have a copy of the marriage certificate. There were two witnesses, solid citizens both. Inez was twenty-two, would be twenty-three in April. Frank's father signed the certificate, giving him permission to marry, even though the legal age was eighteen and Frank was almost twenty-one. (There is no convincing explanation for this: another perplexity in the brief Willick/Donahue liaison.)

The marriage did not go well; they split up after two weeks, and, in May, Frank went to court to sue for annulment.

Writing history is not easy.

> *Historical documents are shot through with lies—*
> *the pattern is as old as the human love of*
> *deception and the human appetite for stories.*

I came across those words in an article about Civil War photographs by David Bromwich in the *New York Review of Books* when I took a break from poring over the transcript of the annulment trial. The thought stayed with me, and the deeper I got into the Frank-Inez debacle the truer it seemed. Lies and stories: there's a shaky border between them, as I know only too well. Digging into the saga of Inez, I've found myself wanting more scandalous details, coming up with lurid scenarios and trying to prove them, spending hours hunched over the computer trying to tie Emery Balliet (my half great-uncle) to the Marquis de Lafayette or to find proof that Henry Clay Frick (my first cousin three times removed) financed Inez's trip to Syracuse.

The annulment trial took place in November 1911. Because Inez did not attend, her side of the story is missing. She failed to respond to a summons given to her on May 22—or, as my daughter, Katherine, puts it, with a lawyer's caution, "allegedly" given to her. A summons doesn't have to be signed by the person it's served on, and the only proof of delivery is the server's word. In this case, the server, Sheriff Hyland, swore in an affidavit on May 23 that he'd served it. He couldn't repeat his testimony at the trial six months later because, rather inconveniently, he had died in August,[2] but Tim Donahue—not exactly an impartial witness—swore he saw Hyland hand it to Inez.

Frank Donahue testified that Inez Willick tricked him into marriage. On March 2 she'd had him arrested for "bastardy" before Hollis H. Bailey, a highly respectable local Justice of the Peace;[3] under oath, she claimed Frank had made her pregnant on the oddly specific date of December 14, 1910.[4]

---

[2] Inconveniently and mysteriously: he was "suddenly stricken" in a hotel in Ogdensburg after seeming in perfect health just hours before. Part of me wants to believe the Donahues murdered him because he refused to perjure himself about serving the summons, but that's probably just the "human appetite for stories" surfacing again.

[3] Bailey was only a justice of the peace, but was always known around town as "Judge" Bailey. A lifelong Norwood resident, he was esteemed not only as a Civil War veteran—the town was full of them—but as a decorated hero and a survivor of the infamous Confederate prison at Andersonville.

[4] The original record of this proceeding has not turned up; all I have is Frank's statement.

According to Frank at the trial, Inez had demanded that he either marry her or give her a thousand dollars. He had no money, so he agreed to the marriage, and two days later the wedding took place at St. Andrew's.

Some of Frank's testimony sounds coached, and as if he had trouble remembering his lines:

Q. What was she doing when you got acquainted with her?

A. Waiting on table at the American House Hotel at Norwood.

Q. Did she invite you to her room?

A. She did.

Q. You visited her in her room, did you, at different times?

A. Yes, sir.

Q. What caused you to quit living with her?

A. I seen a picture of a child she carried in her bosom.

Q. Any other reason?

A. Then I heard while I was away one night that another party went to her room and stayed there before I came back.

With his lawyer's encouragement, Frank testified that Inez claimed to be "pure" until she met him,[5] and he had no reason to believe she was not ten weeks pregnant with his child when he married her on March 4. He then gives two very odd explanations for why he stopped cohabiting with her after only two weeks: the picture of a child and

---

[5] I wonder if she tried to sell him the Brooklyn Bridge too.

an alleged visit from "another party."[6] Or so he heard. Nothing about the pregnancy or lack of one.

Frank Donahue was either an extremely naïve young man, or there are more behind-the-scenes shenanigans to this tale than I've been able to discover. Inez, of course, wasn't present to give her side, but she was much discussed. According to other testimony (studded with leading questions by Frank's lawyer), Inez had met at the hotel with Sheriff Hyland, the summons server (also a Civil War vet and almost as worthy a town elder as Bailey), and his friend Charles Caldwell (ditto), sheriff of the nearby town of Canton, and confessed to them that not only had she deliberately fabricated her pregnancy, but she had previously given birth to an actual "bastard child" in Syracuse, at the Foundling Hospital. That would have been Mom.[7]

Again, Hyland's testimony at the trial would be helpful. As, of course, would that of Inez (why would she admit her perjury to these characters? did they get her drunk?), not to mention a bit of cross-examination by her lawyer. But all we have is dim-bulb Frank and the three pillars of the community: Donahue, Caldwell, and Bailey. And the lawyer, Willis J. Fletcher, a very prominent Norwood attorney. Only the best for poor old Frank.

Additionally—and unsurprisingly, given that this is an episode in the life of the elusive Inez—a crucial page of the trial transcript is missing.

The annulment was granted on November 4. At that time, according to Timothy's testimony, Inez was

---

6   "Party" sounds like blatant lawyer-talk, not like something Frank might have said naturally.

7   Maddeningly, in Caldwell's testimony he claims she told him the name of the baby's father but he "doesn't remember it."

still working at the hotel opposite the livery stable, where he and Frank saw her often and had in fact "conversed" with her. (About what??!!) And yes, they could see that she was not pregnant. They must have felt pretty silly.

Or maybe they felt pretty smart. Maybe they went over to the hotel to have a drink with Inez and toast their cleverness. The story is so full of holes that I wonder if Inez and Frank simply decided their brief, ridiculous marriage had been a mistake and wanted to end it, but divorce was expensive, complicated, and a public disgrace: the plaintiff had to prove adultery[8] and, in a small town, the newspaper would have covered the case thoroughly. And, of course, the Catholic Church forbids divorce anyway; Frank would have been excommunicated.

An annulment, however, could be granted in New York State if consent to the marriage "was obtained by force, duress, or fraud."

Frank's testimony leaks improbabilities: his credulous belief in the pregnancy, Inez's marriage-or-money ultimatum and "Judge" Bailey's apparent acceptance of it, and Frank's acquiescence to a pointlessly hasty marriage.

The photograph in the bosom makes me wonder too. Was it a detail added to Frank's testimony as part of an attempt "to lend artistic verisimilitude to an otherwise bald and unconvincing narrative"?[9] Such objects were not uncommon—often they were mourning pieces. (And perhaps that was what the picture of her abandoned daughter meant to Inez.) I have to wonder who took a picture of Inez's bastard baby in 1910, a picture small enough to carry "in her bosom"—presumably in a

---

[8] This was true in New York State until 1966.
[9] *The Mikado.*

locket.[10] You could buy a Kodak Brownie box camera for a dollar. Did Inez own one? Was there a nun-photographer at St. Mary's who took photos of the infants as an act of benevolence—or a reminder of sin?

I've decided that Frank's testimony about the photograph was true. There's no good reason for him to lie about such a thing. Its place "in her bosom" suggests to me that Inez didn't relinquish her daughter willingly, no matter how many papers she signed agreeing to the adoption.

Then there's the legal angle. In a nearly identical fraud case from the early 1910s,[11] a man whose wife had pretended she was pregnant to force him to marry her was unable to get an annulment. Nor is a "bastardy" accusation usually about forcing a marriage; it was included in the Poor Laws so that impoverished women could get child support for a bastard child, and it was usually initiated by a public official, not by a waitress who claimed on no evidence at all to be ten weeks pregnant.

The chances seem overwhelming that she was indeed pregnant and had a miscarriage, or an abortion. And also that she deeply regretted marrying Frank.

Whatever the truth, after the fiasco of their marriage was over, Inez and Frank seem to have gone their separate ways.

Frank did not come to a good end. He enlisted in the Army in 1918 and was discharged when the war ended. His unit, the 312th infantry, saw action in the battle of Saint-Mihiel, where Frank was gassed. The effects of mustard gas included blindness, vomiting, difficulty

---

[10] In Inez's box-office girl photo, she wears a locket around her neck.
[11] Tait vs. Tait

breathing, and painful blisters caused by chemical burns both internal and external. It can also, long-term, cause pneumonia and pulmonary edema.[12]

After being discharged, Frank returned home to Tim's house. His discharge papers say he had a job at the paper factory in Norwood, but it's doubtful he could work much at all. By 1925, the census lists him as an "invalid," and on September 4, 1929, he was admitted to a home for disabled veterans; he was suffering from pulmonary tuberculosis (a result of the gas attack), tertiary syphilis (the symptoms are so horrible I don't even want to write about them), tertiary locomotor ataxia (ditto), and gonorrhea. Unsurprisingly, he died three weeks later.

During my long career as a novelist, I've reached dead ends in my work, when my characters boxed me into a corner and would not show me the way out. I usually take one of two possible routes: go back and rewrite so that they avoid the dead end, or find a way for them to deal with it and find their way out of the narrative mess. In my third novel, I supplied my heroine with a gun and let her take it from there, but mostly I go for a less melodramatic solution, just keep pecking away until something occurs to me. Then my people push their way out, turn that corner, and trot down the road I've paved for them.

But here I am, ensnared by Inez and Frank, the battling newlyweds. What on earth to do with them? Inez is not some concocted character. She's an actual person, a young woman at the age I was when I was graduating

---

[12] Hemingway's Harold Krebs, in "Soldier's Home," who had been at Mihiel, can't forget how he was "badly, sickeningly frightened all the time." Sargent's enormous (7½' x 20') painting "Gassed" is an eloquent picture of the hellish results of a mustard gas attack: a line of nine blinded soldiers making their way toward a dressing station through a field of dead and wounded.

from college and hoping to make my way in the world, though not having any notion of how to do it. Inez seems to have been similarly adrift. Everything I know about her only contributes to the obscurity, and the more I try to find plausible explanations for the events of her life, the smaller the box I'm trapped in.

What I really wanted to do was drive out to Ohio, immerse myself in the look and feel of Inez's home town, see what she saw. Poke around in the historical society.[13] Walk the Slippery Elm trail, which spans the distance from North Baltimore to Bowling Green—part of the great rails-to-trails network, and apparently a particularly pleasant and well-maintained stretch. Maybe, walking my dog down Broadway and South Second Street, or visiting the Willick graves, or having lunch at the Whistle Stop Inn on the site of the old train station, I'd make contact with Inez's spirit, and, in a dream that night at the canine-friendly EconoLodge in Findlay (closest hotel), she'd appear to me and explain everything.

In the end, this dubious scenario didn't really justify an eleven-hour slog.

Then I decided I needed to go to Norwood, where potentially the most interesting but definitely most opaque piece of Inez's life was rooted. Norwood is a lot closer—exactly half as far as North Baltimore. I imagined an autumn jaunt: a glorious red-and-gold drive from Amherst, up through Vermont and the Adirondacks to a quaint town on the Raquette River, just south of the Canadian border. (Norwood started life as Raquetteville.) There is a Norwood Historical Museum. The American

---

[13] Sometimes, on a particularly frustrating research day, what I wanted to do was just stay home in Amherst reading Scandinavian murder mysteries and eating ice cream.

House Hotel where Inez worked still stands, converted into shops. What became of the train station and Tim Donahue's livery stable I didn't know, but I wanted to. I had a vague idea that I might find the missing page of the trial testimony or a record of the bastardy proceedings. And there was always the possibility of the information-sharing ghost.

First, though, I made a few phone calls. I talked to Tony Nocerino at the historical museum. He searched the archives for something, anything, about either Inez or Frank. My secret hope had been a roster from the old hotel, listing Inez as a waitress, giving her address, her salary. Maybe a group photo of the wait staff, Inez in a perky uniform. But Tony's searches came up empty.

And then there was a flicker of hope! I noticed that one of the museum trustees was a man named—my heart leapt—Tim Donahue. Tony gave me his phone number. But he turned out to be no relation at all to the Donahues I was seeking. "I've seen the big gravestone in the cemetery for Timothy S. Donahue," he told me. "We've had a bunch of Timothys in our family down through the generations, and my grandfather was Timothy S. I can't believe he's no relation, but he isn't."

I began to imagine a conspiracy theory. Was this Tim Donahue, with his tale of multiple Timothys, part of the cover-up? Had the telltale missing page of the trial transcript gone missing on purpose? If Inez had anticipated a descendant a hundred years down the road poking into the details of her life, she did a good job of burying them. A witness protection program could hardly have done it better.

I crossed Norwood off my travel plans. The appeal of these excursions was probably all about procrastination anyway.

PART V

PARENTS

Like a small bird sealed off from daylight—
That was my childhood.
                    ~Louise Gluck, "Fugue"

CORA

Meanwhile, back in Syracuse, while her mother and Frank Donahue were going through their marital drama, Geraldine Anna was still at the Foundling Hospital. On January 18, 1912, three weeks before Inez and Frank legally split, the adoption became final, and the baby was living with the Goodsons.

It wasn't until November 29, 1914, that Cora and Horace had Geraldine baptized, a very un-Catholic delay: if she had died during those four-and-a-half years, my mother would have been in danger of going to hell—or was it limbo?[1] Her formidable adoptive grandmother, Nana Woodruff, would have been praying hard for the baby's soul, and the deferral makes me wonder how faithful a Catholic Cora was. The issue would not have bothered Horace, who was born and died a Lutheran. (It surprises me that the nuns released baby Geraldine into a "mixed marriage": could that be an argument for Horace being the father?)[2]

On the other hand, it's hard to believe the baby wasn't baptized at St. Mary's soon after she was born. So was the 1914 baptism a repeat ceremony? Nobody needs to be baptized twice: you can be cleansed of Original Sin only once. Maybe Cora considered her four-year-old daughter so sinful she needed a double dose.

---

[1] In 2007, the Catholic Church repudiated limbo—which is where morally upright but unbaptized souls used to be placed in storage until they could be released at the Last Judgment.

[2] No.

The only photograph I have from my mother's early years doesn't exactly portray a contented Madonna and  child. Cora and Geraldine sit on the grass in a park, my mother's little legs sticking straight out, Cora's crossed yoga-fashion under her long skirt. Cora is somber, even sullen, with alarming dark circles under her eyes; she leans away from her daughter, her body language saying *grumpy nanny* rather than *doting mum*. Geraldine looks wizened and anxious, nothing like the pretty young woman she became. Even that early, perhaps, it was not a happy mother-daughter relationship.

Cora Goodson and Geraldine, 1913

But my mother stayed close to Cora all her life. I called her Nonny. On the Sundays when we weren't visiting my Burns grandparents, Mom and Dad and I would visit Nonny, bringing the cheap chocolate creams from Woolworth's that she doted on. As a widow, she lived alone in a steamy apartment on the second floor over a store at 611 North Salina Street, the main drag of Syracuse ("Salt City"). The stairway going up smelled pungently of food—no particular food, just decades of cooked meals that lingered in the air like fog. Nonny preferred living on a busy street where she could sit at the window and watch the world go by. That was pretty much what she did in her old age. Maybe that's what she had always done.

I brought a book with me on those Sunday afternoons, though I was ordered by my parents not to read it: "It won't kill you to be polite." I wasn't so sure. The visit lasted only an hour or so, but the head-banging boredom of it seemed like a long afternoon in jail. Nonny would sometimes offer me a soda, but never a chocolate; when we handed them over she'd hustle them into the kitchen, then return to the living room, where the chair backs and tabletops were decorated with her embroidered doilies and "God Bless Our Home" hung on the wall. I used to sit there staring at her hairnet and her clunky old-lady shoes and her stoutness (so unlike my mother's slim elegance), fixating on those cheap chocolates, which I didn't even like, wishing I could sneak into the kitchen and eat one—anything to break the monotony. I occasionally allowed myself the fantasy of slipping out the back window to the fire escape and the parking lot below. Not that I was an adventurous child: once I got down there I'd probably sit on the cement and read my Nancy Drew book.

Nonny had one rather endearing quality: she had never had lessons, but she could play songs on the piano by ear—melody in the right hand, simple chord accompaniments in the left—and she sang as she played. Her tiny place on Salina Street didn't come supplied with one, but most houses had a piano in those days. Very likely, there was an old upright in the succession of grubby places the Goodsons rented when my mother was a child. Maybe that's how Cora, who wasn't much of a homemaker and didn't spend quality time with her children, entertained herself—and maybe entertained them as well.

She didn't come often to our house—someone would have had to fetch her and take her home—but when she did she would head straight for the piano. The only tunes I remember are "A Bicycle Built for Two," complete with oom-pah-pah accompaniment, and "The Battle Hymn of the Republic." I can't remember if her voice was good and on pitch—I think perhaps it was—but I do remember she was loud and completely without self-consciousness, her foot heavy on the sostenuto pedal. When I was young and just beginning piano lessons myself, I loved to hear her play, but as I got older I was mortally embarrassed. I suspect that she could be heard halfway down the block.[3]

Geraldine—as an adult she was always called Jerry, her nickname of choice—forgave her adopted mother for her lamentable childhood, even for unsavory Uncle Johnny and the rats in the cellar. She had only two significant quibbles.

One was that Cora had never learned how to cook. "She could embroider and crochet," my mother would say, with what, for her, approached anger. "Brought up to be a lady—ladies didn't cook. And then she went and married a streetcar conductor who gambled away his paycheck every week." I ventured that Nana Woodruff, Cora's mother, could have been at least partly to blame for her daughter's lack of cooking skills, but my mother adored her Nana, and wouldn't hear of it. "Mom should have had more sense," she would say. "All those children, and she never cooked a fresh vegetable. Not once!"

When I was growing up, my mother used to take me with her to the big farmers market downtown to buy vegetables and fruit and chickens and home-made bread and, in the spring, bunches of daffodils and tall sprays of pussy-willows. The market would get her talking about her upbringing; the family had lived a couple of blocks

---

[3] The grandmother in my novel *Duet*, who is in every other way completely unlike Nonny, shares her noisy music-making, and my heroine shares my cringing embarrassment.

from there, but Cora never set foot in it. Instead, she sent my mother to the neighborhood grocery to lug home canned goods, coffee, bread, and lard. Cora ran a tab; if it went unpaid too long, Geraldine returned home without groceries and was punished (cellar, rats). Eventually the bill would be paid, and the supply of lard and sugar was replenished. Lard sandwiches sprinkled with sugar were a staple at their house, though sometimes there was hardly anything to eat. All the kids were skinny and had bad teeth. "She should have known better," my mother said. She had little sympathy for poverty, too many kids, simple ignorance: "It was inexcusable." And, in fact, I was sure that, given the same set of circumstances, Mom would have embroidered less, cooked more, made sure the kids stayed in school.

The school issue was her real problem with Cora.

What Geraldine wanted to be doing in 1928, when she was eighteen, was not selling hats in a department store but graduating from high school and preparing to go off to college and study classics. She wanted to be a Latin teacher. She confessed this to me, with something close to embarrassment, when she was in her sixties—as if such an ambition, in someone from such a family, was ridiculous. And perhaps it was. She would have been the first in her family to go to college—an honor that, as it turned out, was reserved for me.

My grandmother had no more interest in educating her children than in feeding them decently. If Geraldine objected to being kept out of school to do errands and chores, she was punished. There was no money for schoolbooks—my mother was given them by the nuns, who sometimes were nice about it and sometimes took the opportunity to shame her for her poverty. They gave her clothes too, and often lunch. All this was mortifying to my mother. She still talked about it, even in her extreme old age, with an emphasis on the hideousness of what she was made to wear in the name of charity.

The nuns knew she was bright. In high school, she was one of four from her school chosen to take advanced summer Latin classes at Syracuse University with visiting professor George Lee Phelps.

My mother labeled this "Latin class (first prize) July 1924"—that's Mom in the dark dress[4] in the middle, her boyfriend Ray Bills ("Billsey") behind her on the left, and Prof. Phelps standing, third from right.

Incredibly, her mother allowed her to do this—the nuns must have intervened, and someone must have paid the streetcar fare. She had two more years of Latin. But she turned sixteen in April 1926, toward the

---

[4] I have several pictures of her in this dress. It was either a favorite or—more likely—the only one she owned.

end of junior year; she was allowed to finish out the semester and then she was off to the hat department.

What did Inez think, I wonder, when she saw her daughter working in a store when she should have been in school?

MOM

For years after my father died, I had recurring dreams that he was actually alive but had been away—usually in California, but at least once in Alaska—and had forgotten to tell us he was going. I remember how amused he was that I thought he was dead. How ridiculous! He was so sorry that he'd worried us.

After fifty-odd years, those dreams have pretty much stopped, but soon after my mother's death in January 2001, I began to have similar dreams about her, all variations on this one, copied from my diary:

> My mother and Katherine and I are in her emptied-out apartment, and she is not dead. She's wearing a bathrobe, and she's trying to decide what to wear to a party she's going to. "You got rid of all my jackets," she accuses me. "Where's my red silk jacket?"
>
> I talk to her in the dream the way I never would in real life. "Ma," I say. "Get it through your head. You're not going to a party. You're dead!" I'm getting hysterical. I shout at her. "Dead people don't go to parties!"
>
> She's sitting on the edge of her bed. She looks up at me with a little smile and says, "What do *you* know about it?"

In another dream, I'm describing Katherine's wedding, and she says, indignantly, "Why didn't you tell me about this before?" and I say, "Ma, we thought you were *dead*, for Pete's sake!" She says, "Oh, what nonsense."

In the last few years the dreams have changed. Mom hasn't died, she's living alone somewhere, in an apartment not far from me, and I haven't called her or been to see her in ages—so long that now I'm afraid to go, afraid she's lying there dead, alone. But *still* I don't do it. These are dreams from which I wake up sweating, on the verge of a scream.

The pattern of my mother's life alternates between great happiness and great misery. Her Dickensian childhood gave way to a blissful marriage to my father, which became less blissful when my father's sufferings began, and then he died when they were both in their mid-40s. Some worrisome years followed, while I was off at college and misbehaving in various ways, but eventually I settled down, produced a grandchild, and Mom moved to New Haven to be near us. For twenty years she devoted herself to being a grandmother, and she was good at it.

When she returned to Syracuse in her late eighties, she suddenly began to get old, and sad. She lived surrounded by her family—sisters, nieces, nephews, in-laws—but Katherine and I were the family that mattered, and she missed us. I was living in New York City with my second husband. I visited her regularly, sleeping on the couch in her tiny, cluttered apartment, and, on one memorable Christmas, she and Katherine and I crowded in and cooked together. She took the train down to New York at least twice a year to see me. On her final visit, at Christmastime in 2000, we ate borscht in her favorite Polish restaurant in my Greenpoint, Brooklyn, neighborhood, and as we walked home she was starting to complain about a backache.

Just before New Year's, we took the subway to Penn Station and I put her on Amtrak. Three weeks later she was dead.

In the short saga of my mother's illness and death—it took her just ten cold January days to go from bad back pain to death from unsuspected liver cancer—the worst moment, perhaps, was afterward when, the morning after she died, I was awakened at five o'clock by the sound of Katherine crying.

My mother kept annotated wall calendars all her life, closely written with details of weather, who called, who came over, what the mail brought. Katherine, sleepless, had found the latest one, on which Mom had kept track of the way she was feeling. "Very sick." "Dr. T. didn't call. I feel awful." "I still feel awful. Worse. Back hurts." "Don't feel well. Didn't go to Mass." How afraid she must have been, how alone in spite of the aunts, the neighbors, me on the phone every day from New York. The shaky handwriting. The elusive doctor. But the methodicalness. The understatement. *The need to record.* I have inherited this urge from my mother, which is why I note in my own diary, for example, the fact that my mother died exactly 100 years, to the day, after the death of Queen Victoria. And that in her mail, not long after, was a postcard: IT'S NOT TOO LATE TO RENEW YOUR AARP MEMBERSHIP.

Her funeral was very different from my father's. Dad died young, in a community he'd lived in most of his

life, amid three generations of his large extended family.
The grieving parents, Kitty and Frank, were still alive,
augmented by a slew of siblings, nieces, nephews, cousins,
and, of course, nuns: there was an alarming sea of black
at the funeral. A Solemn High Requiem Mass was sung. I
knew the Gregorian chant by heart,[5] and hearing it sung
for my father made its familiar beauty, which had always
moved me, seem distractingly alien.

For old times' sake, I had wanted my mother's funeral
to be handled by Fergerson's, who had buried my father—
which I'm sure would have also been Mom's choice. But
one of my bossy aunts—apparently the family funeral
expert—reminded me that funerals are for the living and
talked me into a place on the other side of town. The
undertaker there was a friend of the family, and my aunt
said it had good access for old people, plenty of ramps
and few steps. (Later it occurred to me: what funeral
parlor wouldn't?)

The undertaker was sunken-eyed, dour, Dickensian—I'm probably thinking of Uriah Heep and his
clammy hands. But the undertaker didn't offer to shake
my hand, didn't even express sympathy, just hustled right
down to business. I took the chintzy route: the $800
coffin, made of cheesy metal and plug-ugly (but in its
way less hideous and obscene than the polished cherry
ones for $3,000+). He was probably used to all kinds
of cheapskate, ungrateful mourners and didn't bat an
eye. When he heard I lived in New York City he told
me about a funeral there that cost $11,000—"and it was
just some ordinary Joe!"—maybe so that the price up
here in the provinces would seem like a bargain. In the
room where he wrote up the order, in triplicate, calcula-

---

[5] Still do, pretty much.

tor handy, as if I were buying a mattress and box spring, music played on a boom box: *Bali Ha'i, On a Clear Day*, and other Broadway hits, all played v-e-r-y s-l-o-w-l-y on an organ. Forms filled out with the name *Justin X. Ample.* Box of Kleenex. Pamphlets about grieving for your pet. Travel magazines (I suppose so you can figure out ways to spend your inheritance while you wait).

At the wake, in the hideous coffin, lay some nice old woman, attractive and youthful-looking for age ninety, who did not much resemble my mother, though she was wearing Mom's blue dress and her wedding ring. They'd provided her with a slightly beaky nose, for some reason, and plump cheeks. She looked a bit like some actress— maybe Agnes Moorehead? I took one look at her and was unable to look again.

The Latin Requiem was not sung at my mother's funeral; there was just some generic organ music, includ- ing "Amazing Grace," which can make you choke up even when everyone is alive and kicking. Few people attended. Mom had lived for two decades in New Haven, returning to Syracuse only two years before she died. Most of her old friends were gone, and all but two of her siblings. The funeral was attended by my remain- ing aunts, some of my cousins, Mom's friends from her retirement community, a couple of old Syracuse pals of mine. My husband and I, along with my daughter and her then boyfriend/now husband, heathens all, sat in the front row. None of us had a clue as to when to stand up, kneel, sit; an aunt sitting behind me prodded me, none too kindly, when we needed to change position. I didn't give a eulogy, mostly because I just wanted to get out of there, but there was also the fact that I found it difficult to stop crying. Now I see it as a dereliction of duty and wish that I had said something. The resident priest, who hardly knew Mom, did his best with the usual platitudes praising her general excellence, with a few twists about her Christmas trip to New York less than a month before, etc. Feisty old lady stuff.

The ceremony at the grave was mercifully brief: it was a bitterly cold January day, something both my parents' deaths had in common. They died forty-four years and two days apart.

My parents—Jerry and Herb—had eloped to California in April 1933, when they were both twenty-three, and were married en route in Joplin, Missouri, by a Justice of the Peace. (He gave them a silver dollar, which I still have.) Neither had ever been out of Syracuse before. They hitched a ride with their friend Mildred Young, who aimed to drive across the country with her little girl in her "very small" 1928 Austin: Mildred needed a second driver.

In Mom's account of the trip years later, she wrote: "The whole idea was preposterous, but the more we discussed it, the more we began to think it was the perfect solution for all of us." The problem that needed a solution was their parents' opposition to their marriage.

Frank and Kitty Burns were by then rising in the world, with a five-bedroom house, a wood-

My grandmother Kitty and one of my young aunts, 1934

paneled station wagon, and a summer "camp" on Lake Ontario. They were not pleased when my father fell in love with a young woman from the other side of the tracks, who worked the switchboard at a department store[6] and lived with a slatternly mother and a motor-man father, seven ragged siblings, and a cantankerous grandmother in a flat above a grocery. It was the heart of the Depression, a decade during which the Goodsons sank deeper into poverty, while Frank Burns, a canny investor, made most of his money.

Cora and Horace were no friendlier to the idea. Mom's salary at the store was ten dollars a week, and she gave her mother five. Marriage? "She said I'd better get that idea right out of my head."

My parents met at a party thrown by my father. Herb Burns (often called Red)[7] was famous for his parties. His father, Frank, was working at Pepsi's New York office, commuting home to Syracuse on weekends except when Kitty took the train down there to be with him.[8] On weekends when they were both away, my dad would send the younger kids up to bed, tell them to keep their mouths shut, and open the house to his friends. In 1932, Prohibition was in force, and my father and a couple of his buddies had concocted a recipe for bathtub gin—actually made in my grandmother's capacious kitchen sink. I asked my mother what it tasted like. "It was awful," she said. "But nobody cared."

It's hard to square the strait-laced mother I knew[9] with this wild girl who came to a party with one man

---

[6] Mom was promoted from the hat department. She loved the switchboard: you had to stay on your toes, but it was always interesting and the day went by fast.

[7] Dad inherited his mother's flaming hair.

[8] In fact, to keep an eye on him, according to my mother. There were rumors about his secretary.

[9] The only bit of raciness I recall was her habit, if someone said, "It won't be long now," of adding, "...as the rabbi said when he put down the knife."

(Jimmie Fox, whose Christmas card in 1931, which was among my mother's souvenirs, read "To my little star of heaven") and was escorted home in the wee hours by another. It was love at first sight that may have been fueled by the kitchen-sink gin but lasted all his short life and beyond: my mother never got over his early death.

A year later, on April 12, Jerry and Herb were off to California, an adventure they were able to accomplish only by telling their parents a couple of major falsehoods: Mom's friend Mildred was making a quick trip out to Oklahoma, and Mom would use her one-week vacation to go along to help take care of little Sallie and "see the country"; Dad left the house early in the morning "to see about a job" and they picked him up a few blocks away.[10] My mother wrote, with a curt matter-of-factness: "We hated being deceitful, but it had to be done."

It had to be done! It makes me laugh every time I think of it.

In her account, she writes, "We stopped somewhere in Ohio for sandwiches and shared a quart of milk." Looking at the map, I can see that the logical route would have taken them right through Toledo, where Inez was living.

Their on-the-road marriage in Joplin was finally "blessed" by Father McGuinness in Los Angeles in June; from a Catholic point of view, they'd been living in sin for two months.[11] Herb got a job peddling soap door

---

[10] He had dropped off his small bag at Mildred's a few days earlier; my mother noted that it contained "a set of underwear, some sox, an extra shirt, a razor, and his shaving soap."

[11] It still astonishes me that my parents, both staunchly religious, started their life together with a civil ceremony. I suspect that, after many days snuggled together in a cramped back seat, they were desperate to share a bed—and nice girls like Mom held out for marriage.

to door; he also played bridge for money. Jerry learned how to cook eggplant, which she insisted tasted like steak if you put A1 Sauce on it. At the corner store a cigarette cost a penny. Jerry got her hair "done" for free by a woman in their building who was practicing to be a beautician.

But when Herb won big at cards and they had money, they didn't hesitate to blow it. They went skating at the Rollerdrome in Culver City and splurged on real steaks at Bot & Hank's Café ("We Never Close") on Sunset Boulevard. They danced at the Clover Club, had a season pass to the dog races, and amused themselves at the Paradise Beer Garden. When they were feeling poor they sat on a bench on Wilshire Boulevard eating sandwiches and watching the parade of waiting-to-be-discovered young women saunter by.

My mother kept a scrapbook: matchbooks from various nightclubs, half a dozen business cards from employment agencies with notes in Dad's handwriting ("call Bob Whyte!!!"), a ticket stating "You weigh 106 pounds" from the scale in front of the drugstore, and a rather puzzling card from the establishment of Mme. M. Refvjeska, "Designer and Modiste," across the street from their apartment on Shatto Place. (Mom loved clothes, and any visit to Mme. R. must have been wishful: but why did I never ask her about it?)

My parents lasted in California until deep winter, then—jobless, hopeless, without even a winter coat between them—they admitted defeat and persuaded the Burnses to wire them enough money to take the train home.[12] Back in Syracuse, Dad went to work for his uncle

---

[12] Mom saved menus: on the train, sandwiches were fifteen cents, a cup of coffee a dime: "Waiters pass through the cars shortly after meal hours enabling passen-

Ralph, selling butter and eggs. My father's family became reconciled to my mother. In fact, they grew to love her—at least up to a point: despite her early widowhood and general worthiness, none of her wealthy in-laws ever left her a nickel.

In those days the only real sadness in my parents' lives was their failure to have a baby. In the late 1930s, when Frank Burns was a rising star in the fledgling Pepsi-Cola Company, nepotism kicked in, and Dad began doing PR for Pepsi, which meant he and my mother traveled around the East Coast in a company car, staying at nice hotels, Mom shopping and lunching with other Pepsi wives while Dad met with Pepsi executives. By the time I thought to ask my mother what his role was, exactly, she was vague. I get the impression it was mostly schmoozing, at which my father was gifted, and coming up with cool ideas for ad campaigns. One was a cut-out figure of "Pepsi" (who was fat) and "Pete" (who was lean) with holes where their faces went; people stuck their heads through the holes in a "who looks the most like" Pepsi or Pete contest. The prize was a case of the stuff.

Mostly, Mom liked to talk about what fun it was, what wonderful hotels there were in those days—their favorite was a place called Shawsheen Manor, north of Boston—and the time they went out dancing to Glenn Miller's orchestra at the Hotel Pennsylvania in New York.

By 1942, assuming a baby would never come along, they were trying to reconcile themselves to the situation. And then, incredibly, I was born—their only child—in May 1943.

---

gers to obtain this service in their respective car seats. Please report to Dining Car Steward any inattention on part of waiters conducting this service or any deviation from prices shown."

Jerry Burns,
August 1942

I have a photograph of my mother, on the back of which she wrote: "Rochester, NY—Jerry Burns, Lee's back yard at 143 Milburn St.—August 1942." Some years later, she amplified: "P.S. I bought this dress in Filene's Basement, Boston, summer of 1941, for $2.88. A soft jersey. I loved it." That she loved it was clear: the dress, those earrings, and her white "spectator" pumps appear in several photographs in the early '40s.[13]

What fascinates me about this photograph is that, when it was taken, in August 1942, my parents' lives were about to be completely, unexpectedly transformed. I was born in May 1943; my mother must have been just barely pregnant. She could not have known it yet, had no idea that her baby daughter is present in the photograph, a polka-dot of an embryo, the answer to ten years of prayers.

One of my few remaining Christmas rituals is to head to New York every December for a performance of Handel's *Messiah* with my friend Judith, another member of that enormous but informal club: Non-Religious Admirers of Early Church Music. As I was researching Inez's life, I was reminded that a foundling hospital established in London in 1714—one of the first—was Handel's favorite charity. He not only bought an organ

---

[13] Something my mother and Inez had in common: both wore glasses, but never in photographs.

for the hospital chapel and composed a stirring anthem as a fund-raiser ("Blessed are they that considereth the poor") but staged many performances there of his *Messiah*, raising thousands of pounds for orphans and fallen women.

Since 2007, Handel's sublime oratorio has reminded me of my first grandchild, who was being born in California while I was in New York listening to "For unto us a child is born . . ." at Avery Fisher Hall. Now when I hear it I'll think of my mother, the foundling, and my grandmother, the fallen woman.

Herb and Jerry Burns, Christmas 1935

Christmases were strange and difficult in the years after my father died, but Mom and I carried on the family ritual of picking out the perfect tree, screwing it into a holder, spreading a star-specked felt cloth around it, and hauling out the big box of ornaments, most of which she and Dad had bought back in the '30s—beautiful and delicate, made in Germany and Czechoslovakia. Eggnog, Christmas cookies, and Bing Crosby's Christmas album were non-negotiable. Sometimes we invited people over—an aunt or two, a couple of my friends, my mother's friends from work. I don't remember whether these rituals were held in 1957, the first Christmas after my father died. I do know that Christmas morning itself was a bit thin. There were just my mother and me. Dad and I had had a tradition of going downtown to the Addis Company every year—even the previous one, a month before he died—to fill one of their elegant silver gift boxes with luxurious toiletries my mother loved but would never buy for herself: bubble bath, fancy soap, hand lotion, her favorite perfume, matching powder in a round box with a fluffy puff. Then Dad and I would wrap her gifts with ingenious and elaborate bows that he taught me to make with instructions from a booklet he got free at the stationery store.

For the first Christmas without him, I tried to duplicate these rituals. I didn't have much money—can't even remember now where I got any money at all—but I bought a few things: a box of powder with a puff, probably cologne rather than perfume. I know I did the wrapping. I'm sure my mother opened her gifts with a brave, grateful smile. We might have talked a little—a very little—about how sad it was to have Christmas without Daddy. We attended Mass and sang carols. My grandmother, Kitty, had died in October, so we might have roasted our own turkey, then gone "up home" to see my grandfather and exchange gifts with my maiden aunts, who tended to give me gaudy rosaries or ugly nightgowns. That night, Mom and I probably cried ourselves to sleep, but separately and silently, because that was how we did things.

Lately, I've thought a lot about that lonely 1957 Christmas, Mom and me gamely singing carols and eating turkey. That year, Inez herself, age sixty-nine, would have been a widow of eleven years, settled in Springfield, Ohio, not far from Doris and her husband and son (age twenty).

Damn it, we were less than a seven-hour drive away. We could have met Inez halfway and had Christmas dinner with her and Doris in Erie, or Buffalo. Or invited them to Syracuse. Or—well, the usual things families do. But not only were we not a family, but my mother, still sunk deep in shame, hadn't yet told me that Inez existed.

DAD

One of my favorite photographs of my father shows him with a rather large fish he has just caught. It dates from the days when he was healthy and strong, his red hair was untouched by silver, and he could spend long hours out fishing with the guys. The photo was taken at his parents' summer place in 1936; no one who was there then is still alive. Frank and Kitty are long gone, the "guys" are all dead, and so is my mother, and all my aunts, and whoever took the photo and whoever ate the fish. My father stands there more alone than we can easily imagine.

Dad and a 32" wall eyed pike, Lake Ontario, 1936

I like to see him like this instead of as the father I recall from his last couple of years. What I best remember are the long summers, when my mother was at work and my father and I were home all day. I hated being stuck at home taking care of him, but I hated even more leaving him alone while I went out to play with my friends. Nobody ever told me I had to, but I knew that when he got coughing or had one of his headaches, it helped to have someone around to make ice water or wring out cold washcloths to lay across his forehead. I'd leave for a while, heading home every hour or so to see if he was okay. Then go out again. Sometimes it was just easier to stay inside and read and make sure Dad had the fan pointed at him properly.

My father had been taking flying lessons, and did his best to continue them even when he was much too ill. He never accumulated enough hours to get his pilot's license. I have his logbook; his tiny, meticulous printing records the date and duration of every flight. When I was seven, he let me sit beside him in the cockpit as we taxied around the airfield. "Someday I'll take you up on a real flight," he said, and I remember his excitement at the idea. But his life was full of "somedays" that never came to pass.

Toward the end, Dad became slightly eccentric, maybe the result of years of waiting to die. He spent a fair amount of time making precise drawings of a sunroom addition he wanted to add to the back of our house (a pipe dream) and the transformation of our unfinished attic into a bedroom and study for me with a heart-stirring wall of built-in bookshelves (slightly more realistic). He designed several versions of a garage with an elaborate workbench area across the back. He'd hunch over the kitchen table with a ruler and a pad of graph paper while I sat across from him and put in my two cents. Yes, a walk-in closet would be great. No, I don't think Mom would like to sit in the sunroom unless there were some kind of curtains she could pull if it was hot. At some point, I realized Dad was dreaming on paper, drawing pictures of the way he wanted to live if the world had been kinder to our family.

He also became devoted to a mixed-race Peruvian Dominican Brother named Martin de Porres, born in 1579, the son of a Spanish nobleman and a slave woman. Martin had been beatified by Pope Gregory XVI in 1837, and my father wrote regular letters to Rome agitating for his canonization.[14] Why and how he got so attached to Blessed Martin I can't recall; maybe it was just that Martin was an animal nut like my parents and me. There was a charming story about his intervention on behalf of the mice in the monastery, sparing their lives and feeding them himself so they wouldn't plunder the cupboards. (I seem to recall that Martin explained the deal to the mice and they went along with it.)

Dad did most of the cooking—as the oldest child in an enormous family whose parents were often out of town, he'd been taught to cook. Usually, even when he was feeling "punk," as he called it, he'd head for the kitchen around five o'clock and start dinner so it would be ready when my mother got home at quarter to six. He wasn't a fancy or an adventurous cook, except for organ meats: we ate them all: sweetbreads, beef heart, chicken hearts, lamb kidneys, liver of every persuasion—a legacy of the Depression days in California. But Dad knew not to over-cook vegetables,[15] and he could make light, fluffy biscuits (for both chicken and strawberry shortcake). He believed in making things from scratch. When my friends came for sleepovers, he treated us to pancakes for breakfast: drib-bling batter into Nana Woodruff's big cast-iron skillet[16]

---

[14] He named our green parakeet after Martin. The blue parakeet was named Francis, which was both a family name and my father's favorite saint, partly because one of his three nun sisters was a Franciscan. Dad made a large cage, atop which Smokey the cat used to lie, benignly dozing, while the birds pecked at his belly fur. Francis died in childbirth: we had no idea he was female until we found him stiff one morning next to a tiny pure-white egg. Dad and I buried bird and egg together in the garden, in a little box.

[15] Mom—thinking no doubt of the feckless Cora—was a vegetable buff who not only hit the farmers market every Saturday morning, but also had her own back-yard garden.

[16] I still have it.

to form our initials and heating up the Log Cabin maple syrup in an enamel pot he reserved just for that purpose.

I didn't recognize it at the time for what it was, but underneath the jolly "big heart" jokes and the attempts to lead a normal life, my father in his last year or so was severely depressed. He used to head upstairs after dinner—he'd made a desk area for himself in a corner of the attic—and sit there alone, doing nothing, smoking his Camels. At my bedtime, he'd still be there, and my mother would remind me to go up and say goodnight. I did this reluctantly. I could feel the melancholy seeping out of his raw little space as I climbed. I'd say, "Goodnight, Dad," and he'd rouse himself to give me a kiss and a hug and a smile. Then I'd flee back down the stairs. Sometimes I'd lie awake with my cat Smokey, listening to the *Buckaroo Sandman* on my radio, waiting for my favorite song ("The Cat Came Back"), and unable to sleep until Dad came down and got into bed with my mother and I could hear their hushed voices in the room next door.

After my father died, my mother sold our house, and we moved into an apartment. Just before moving day, Smokey disappeared—walked out the door one day and didn't return. I spent all my spare time back in the old neighborhood searching for him, walking the streets and venturing out into the woods behind our house, calling, putting out bowls of food in case he turned up.

But in spite of the song, the cat didn't come back. For a long time, I mourned Smokey more, it seemed, than I mourned my father. But it was all the same thing.

RESILIENCE

The Encyclopedia of Adoption has a section on resilience, i.e., "the capacity of a child to adapt to and sometimes even thrive despite difficult and sometimes extremely harsh early environments." Characteristics of resilient people include "good social skills, feelings of empathy, a sense of humor, problem-solving abilities, personal attractiveness to others, positive peer relationships, academic success, and membership in a faith group"—as well as "the ability to focus on the positive side of life rather than ruminating on past problems."

That profile is a picture of my lovable, kind, droll, practical, earnest, devoutly religious mother. Relinquished by her own mother, treated badly by her adoptive mother, abused by her uncle, dirt-poor growing up, a widow at forty-six—despite it all, Mom was famous for her good humor, her even disposition, and her refusal to spend much time in that wonderfully descriptive cliché location "down in the dumps." She objected strenuously to the word *depressed*: if anyone used it in her presence, she muttered, "What a lot of nonsense."[17] If anyone had accused her of *being in denial*, she might have responded, "And what's wrong with that?"

Mom was never much of a complainer. Mostly, we lived on her salary from General Electric (in 1952, it was $54.35 a week), and so there was never much money. She was quickly promoted off the assembly line and into the office, where her boss was an imposing woman called

---

[17] She would be outraged to know that I applied it to my father.

Mary Connors. (This is not her real name; hers is just as innocuous but nonetheless still suggests *ogress* to me.) Mary was a more subtle equivalent of my grandmother: she didn't lock Mom in the cellar with rats, but she overworked her, browbeat her, and on a slow day would talk endlessly about her own miseries. She relied completely on my mother, but was stingy about recommendations for raises. Mom expressed her indignation to Dad and me and possibly to her carpool buddies,[18] but never to anyone else: she just grinned and bore it, got her work done, and no doubt prayed for Mary Connors's soul. She worked for her for twenty-two hard years.

Because of Dad's illness and our relative poverty, my family's life was a bit askew when I was a kid, but there was a lot of laughter at our house too, and company. For two stressed people, my parents were pretty laid back. Aunts and uncles and friends always seemed to be dropping in on us. It was something people did in those days—go out for a drive and stop in to visit someone— but it may have helped that my father was an invalid and we were usually home. My parents were always ready to make a pot of coffee and sit down to chat. They also let me invite my friends over whenever I wanted: sleepovers, jitterbug parties, elaborate birthdays, impromptu picnics on the back lawn.[19] Even after my father died, it wasn't unusual for Mom to come home after a long day at work to find the house full of kids dancing to loud music and drinking up all the Pepsi. (I probably played the "lonely only child" card on a regular basis.)

---

[18] One of whom was a nice man named Adam Oot, which I thought was the funniest name I'd ever heard except for my father's friend Harry Joynt.

[19] Somebody made a recording labeled "Hot Dog Roast July 1956" in which my thirteen-year-old girlfriends and I have a lively discussion as to whether Elvis is more handsome or more cute.

When my mother was about the age I am now—long-widowed, an expert grandmother, recording secretary at her senior center, singer in her church choir—she lived for a time in a little house on a pond just outside New Haven. She had been born not only with the resilience gene, but with a kind of built-in contentment that was at its height during her years in Woodbridge. What she liked best, especially if my daughter or I went with her, was to take the old rowboat out on the pond and fish for small sardine-like fish (sprats?) that swam there in abundance. The guy next door would debone them, and Mom would save them up in the freezer until there were enough to dip in flour and fry in oil and eat with a squeeze of lemon.

Mom, Woodbridge, Connecticut, 1977

She loved to fish. Going out in a boat on a summer day and fishing—even for these small fry—reminded her of my father, who was a master angler, complete with rod, reel, and hip boots. My mother's injunctions to me were modest and earthbound, usually along the lines of "Don't forget your gloves" and "Turn that light on, do you want to go blind?" But one day early in the Inez quest, when Mom and I were out in the rowboat, she looked at me and said, "Always be grateful that you know who you are."

I hadn't been, but her words stayed with me, and after that I was. People "are" much more than their ancestry, but there's comfort, and also a kind of logic—a sense of belonging to the world and having a place in it—in knowing you have your father's smile or your mother's eye color. My mother never had those certainties, and, in spite of her natural gaiety and optimism, she felt their absence all her life.

Maybe it was to make up for that, that she craved abundance. When she died, the three rooms she lived in were crammed with the accumulations that must have added up to some kind of comfort: at least 200 pairs of earrings;[20] seventy-five handbags (summer, winter, leather, straw, cloth, large, small, red, beige, navy blue, black, white, including the one we had just given her for Christmas because she said she needed a new brown one); forty-five pairs of shoes; six five-pound cans of coffee; service for at least sixteen of the rose-patterned china she collected; two fat ceramic brown-robed friars made by Hummel that I recalled from my childhood, one a sugar bowl, one a cream pitcher; a milk glass hen and a carnival glass candy dish and some McCoy pottery vases and my Goodson grandmother's embroidered linens and my Burns grandmother's cranberry-glass slipper with a sprig of philodendron rooting in it and Nana Woodruff's skillet and my neatly ironed First Communion dress (1950)[21] and a well-used electric mixer and a never-used electric mixer and hundreds of recipes on index cards and a never-used microwave oven with boxes of cereal stored in it and a collection of canvas bags including one (filled with small empty jewelry boxes) from the Brooklyn Botanical Garden that Mom bought when we went there in 1999 and a cupboard dedicated to the storage of plastic bags, some labeled with notes like "Good sturdy bag—SAVE!" And that was only the tip of the iceberg.

---

[20] And a little box of singles with the note: WHERE ARE THE MATES TO THESE?
[21] My granddaughters now wear it to play dress-up.

The standard explanations for such hoarding are childhood poverty and/or living through the Great Depression. Both can be applied to my mother. But in addition there was not knowing who she was—all she knew of her mother was that she wore glasses and had given her up. Of her father she knew nothing. That was a large void to be filled.

PART VI

INEZ'S GRANDDAUGHTER

Autobiography is an exercise in self-forgiveness.
~Janet Malcolm, "Thoughts on
Autobiography from an
Abandoned Autobiography"

When I was nine or ten, the book I checked out of the library more than any other was *Nancy Keeps House* by Helene Laird, published in 1947.

The year my mother died, I tracked down a copy from a bookseller in California, and as soon as I opened its light pink cover, it was as if half a century hadn't passed: the illustrations, the dog, the general craziness—they were as familiar to me as my feet. I found that I nearly had it memorized.

This Nancy was a far cry from Nancy Drew, girl detective; this was Nancy Leland, girl housekeeper. The book's premise is that Mother is expecting a baby and will be in the hospital for two weeks. (Those were the days, eh?) Nancy will have to take care of the house, and of Father, and Mother sets about teaching her how to do it. "I think it'll be fun," Mother says. "You know when I married your father I knew as little as you do about housework, but in less than six months I was doing all right, wasn't I, Henry?" (Henry gives his wife a "proud and foolish and loving look" and agrees that she was.)

Each chapter covers an aspect of housekeeping: planning menus, marketing, changing the beds, doing the laundry. While Father is at—where else?—the office,

Mother, a slender dynamo, is home keeping house. It's a nice, big, airy house. Mother loves taking care of it, and she passes the joy of housework on to her willing pupil. It's not drudgery, Nancy learns: and it does indeed look like "fun" to do the wash, which involves putting the clothes through the wringer, mixing up the starch, hanging everything outside on the clothesline, and then ironing it all, even Father's pajamas (though Mother says gaily that you can be a *little* less fussy with things like pajamas). Every chapter ends with the wonderfully organized, coherent notes that model-child Nancy jots down about doing the chores.

The fact that Mother must be getting larger and larger as the story progresses is never mentioned, and when baby Henry Jr. comes home he's bottle-fed: no breasts in Nancyville!

In my *recherche du temps perdu* via *Nancy Keeps House*, I learned again one of the big lessons: you really, really can't go home again. The line drawings in the text are delightful, and I'll always be grateful to Nancy's mother for tacking a poem up over

Nancy keeping house

the sink that she can memorize while she's washing dishes (I still do that). I remember Doris the dog as a great eccentric, and indeed he (yes, ha ha, it's a running joke) is the most colorful figure in the book. But the characters, though lovable, are saccharinely idealized, their attempts to be wild 'n' wacky fall flat, and the relentless emphasis on the rapture of domesticity is hard for my cynical, liberated, lazy adult self to swallow.

But the appeal of the book when I was ten had nothing to do with its literary quality. What I adored was its orderly normalness: Nancy's mother even had a table in the (nice big cool clean) basement covered with white oilcloth, where she sprinkled clothes before they were ironed.[1] My own mother did indeed strive for such domestic heaven—she loved housework as much as the Nancy people did and would have killed for a clothes-sprinkling table—but it was never achieved: we had no money, our house had no basement, and it was Mother and not Father who went to "the office" every day. I yearned for the serenity and predictability of Nancy's house, and I read her housekeeping notes with uncritical approval: 1. Sprinkle the clothes, 2. Heat the iron, 3. Do the flat things first. . . . Yes. Absolutely.

I envied Nancy's stability: Mother didn't die in childbirth, Father wasn't sick, baby brother is perfect. The worst thing that happened to the Lelands was that Nancy wanted a sister and she got a brother. Needless to say, she coped.

Nancy no doubt became a stable, happy, secure adolescent and young adult.

Then there was me.

In the summer of 1966, I was twenty-three and single and pregnant.

I was working in Boston for a Massachusetts state representative who ran a small—very small—advertising and market research business on the side. The work was

---

[1] Note to anyone born after 1950: to achieve the proper dampness, cotton clothes (i.e. most everything you owned) had to be sprinkled with water from a bottle—in our house, an old ketchup bottle—with a perforated top from the hardware store, then rolled into balls, covered with a damp towel and allowed to sit for an hour or two (but not too long in summer, lest they mildew). Then you could iron them.

light, his clients were few. It seemed a kind of toy business, so that he could have an office and a desk and a secretary, just because they were cool. He was always in a good mood.

I was his only employee, his "Gal Friday."[2] The office was two rooms in a building above Ken's Delicatessen at Copley Square. On my lunch hour I'd meet friends at a sandwich joint on Boylston, or sit in the garden of Trinity Church and read T.S. Eliot, or window-shop at Peck & Peck and Bonwit Teller and the posh shops on Newbury Street. My job was to go through the local paper of the small city my boss represented and, on my classy blue Selectric typewriter, in a variety of creative fonts, type out condolence notes, wedding felicitations, birthday greetings, congratulations on winning the bowling trophy—whatever I could devise that would make contact with a constituent: the personal touch was what reelection was all about. I worked hard at making the notes well-written, individualized, and error-free. My boss liked to find a neat stack arranged on his desk at the end of the day, ready for his flamboyant signature. I would mail them after work on my way to the MTA stop near the library.

What my boss did at the state house was a mystery and didn't seem to take much of his time. I accompanied him there every once in a while, and was introduced to Tip O'Neill (rumpled, warm) and Peter Ustinov (suave, funny, though what he was doing there I can't imagine). Back at Copley Square, my boss either went into his big front room with his gorgeous Latina girlfriend and

---

[2]   As an admirer of *Robinson Crusoe*—in which the original Friday is a cannibal who worships a god called Benamuckee until Crusoe steps in— I did not find the term offensive. I also loved the old film *His Girl Friday*, though, believe me, my boss was no Cary Grant. (But then I was no Rosalind Russell.)

shut the door, or he dictated letters to me, after which he would—literally—chase me around the desk, as if we were in a *New Yorker* cartoon. The whole setup was not unamusing, gave me plenty of time to work on my novel, and paid $60 a week. I shared an apartment with my college roomie, Sara; my portion of the rent was $50 a month. (The first rule for sensible budgeting in those days was that your rent should equal no more than one week's salary: I considered myself loaded.) My two-pack-a-day cigarette habit cost me about $4 a week. On Sundays Sara and I cooked up a huge batch of chicken-rice-and-frozen-peas (known as Chicken Shit) and ate it for dinner for the rest of the week. For special occasions, I knew how to make Chicken Kiev and Chicken Caccia-tore. I once made Chicken Cacciatore for my boyfriend, who commented politely, "I like the chicken, but not the cacciatore," as he scraped off the sauce.

I remember the moment I knew for certain I was pregnant, the sick fatalistic sinking into the swamp of its reality, the dull clang of how-could-I-be-such-an-idiot pounding in my head. I thought about an abortion. Abortions were not easy to come by. An exotic college friend (she was from Greenwich Village, her parents were painters, she'd been to Europe many times) had had two abortions—she'd gone to Puerto Rico both times, an expense I was not, to put it mildly, prepared for. Nor was anyone else I knew. Everyone was poor. The idea was that we were all going to be famous writers or scholars or artists or musicians someday, so what we did for a living in our early twenties hardly mattered. My friends had office jobs that were less colorful and no better paying than mine. My boyfriend was going to graduate school at night and doing I forget what awful minimum-wage thing during the day.

Kitty Burns, 1966

But it wasn't only the expense that made me decide against an abortion. By 1966, I hadn't been a Catholic for a long time, but you don't have to be religious to want to let the appalling but astonishing creature inside you see the light of day. Maybe you just need to be some kind of egotist: this is *my* baby, this baby has to live, the world will be a better place because of this baby. There was a story that went around among Catholics in those days: Beethoven was the youngest of twelve children: imagine the horror if his mother had said "Enough!" and had an abortion instead of Ludwig. In truth, the van Beethovens only seven children, and Ludwig was one of the eldest. But biographical accuracy wasn't the point of the story: the point was that any fetus could be a genius who could change the world. In some dark, illogical recess of my brain I bought into a version of this. The other problem was that I already loved the fetus, the baby, the unfathomable child I had conceived. It was furiously real to me even before it began to kick. But with that first kick, that curiously intimate and strange assault on your innards that's a baby's first real declaration of life—well, that did it.

In the end, desperate and increasingly pregnant, I couldn't figure out where else to turn, and so, like a lost lamb seeking the fold, I turned to Catholic Charities. I found them in the Yellow Pages. (Under *Mothers, Unwed?*) They had a cheerless office downtown where a woman with a crucifix hanging from a chain around her wrinkly neck and a name I recall as Mrs. O'Shaughnessy grilled me about my relationship with my "friend," asked if I was planning to continue having (grimace of distaste) sexual relations after the birth, and was I prepared to use (pause before uttering the horrid words) *birth control* this time? I told her we were already using birth control—usually. But maybe not that one time.

She didn't want to hear about it. Slowly, laboriously, as if she was doing the devil's work, she took down my information and that of my "friend": ethnic background, medical history, educational level, blah blah. With something that dimly resembled a smile, she assured me cruelly that a healthy white baby would be very adoptable. I made myself not cry.[3]

I wasn't doing well. Shame, self-loathing, and a book of poetry were my constant companions. After I worked on my boss's reelection campaign (unsuccessful—just: he lost by something like fourteen votes), I quit my job because I couldn't bear to go to work. I couldn't bear to leave the apartment. I couldn't bear to see people. I couldn't bear to be seen. I used to take my expanding stomach out in the early mornings for long, cold, dreary walks before anyone else was on the streets. I had to force myself to get on the MTA and go downtown to the

---

[3] In the wonderful movie *Philomena*, Judi Dench is a pious elderly woman looking for the son she gave up for adoption fifty years before, who was sold for £1000 to an American couple by the nuns at the Irish foundling hospital where she had taken refuge. Her punishment for her sin was to lose her child. The very un-religious reporter who's aiding her search wonders if God gave humans the sexual urge, then condemns them as sinners for indulging it, as "a weird game he invented to alleviate the awful boredom of being omnipotent."

unemployment office to collect my weekly check, but it was pretty much all I had to live on, and so I did.

A friend took me out one weekend for a prime rib, which I wolfed down and then puked up outside the restaurant. I had a pair of slacks with an elastic waist, a men's shirt size Large, and two hideous maternity dresses, one of which I made myself out of itchy purplish wool that I bought on sale. I spent a lot of time alone, reading. I became deeply enamored of Byron and Keats, and continued my long affair with T.S. Eliot. ("Prufrock," "La Figlia Che Piange," and the end of "The Wasteland" used to just about rip my heart out.) I was also devoted to my cat, Hector, a manipulative genius who would knock things off various surfaces during the wee hours until I hauled myself out of bed and fed him.

Sara made sure we had some kind of dinner every night. We stopped cooking stuff like Chicken Caccia-tore and sometimes left the chicken out of the Chicken Shit. Catholic Charities wouldn't arrange an adoption unless you were regularly seeing an obstetrician, so my boyfriend saved up money and paid for the doctor and the hospital. He gave me the money in installments, in cash, and I kept it in a drawer in my bedroom. We talked mostly about politics and books, but now and then we talked about marriage, though not with much enthusi-asm: my getting pregnant made us realize we didn't love each other enough for that.

My appalled, grieved, angry mother came to Boston for Christmas. At some level I hoped she would suggest that I come home with the baby and live with her until I got on my feet (whatever that might entail), but, from the beginning, Mom pushed hard for marriage: "Get married, and after a couple of years, get divorced," she said, as if this were both logical and simple; in the desperation of her crusade against my producing a bastard, she overlooked the fact that the Catholic Church did not condone divorce and would excommunicate me pronto, consigning me to eternal hellfire.

But to lay on this baby the stigma of illegitimacy was a more immediate and tangible disaster.[4] I tried to convince her that the stigma no longer existed. That wasn't quite true in 1966, and I probably wasn't very nice about it, but how could I know she was speaking from the heart? Or that my own grandmother was a woman who, by the time she was my age, had given birth to not one but two bastards?

I did think about the pain my mother, who had had such trouble conceiving even one child, must have felt at the idea of casting one away. But we didn't talk about this, because we didn't talk about most things. Over Christmas dinner, I tried to distract her attention by making her laugh, something I could usually count on, and eventually she did laugh, though I'll bet she cried all the way home to Syracuse on the train.

The baby was born on a dank, cloudy day in March. I took a taxi to Beth Israel, and when the contractions got really bad they put me under. *Like a patient etherized upon a table.* When I came to, they brought the baby in. I'd never seen a newborn before. He didn't seem very pretty—though, looking back, I can see that he was just a regular baby, with the usual squashed hairless head and no chin, muddy blue eyes, a red forceps mark on one cheek. I named him after his father and took a pill to dry up my milk. Every day they brought the baby in at

---

[4] Edna Gladney, a Texas advocate for children, wrote in 1933, "There is no such thing as an illegitimate child. There are only illegitimate parents."

feeding time, and I gave him a bottle. I whispered in his ear, "Remember me. I'm your mother." He closed his eyes and drank. I thought he smiled for a minute, but the woman in the next bed said it was probably gas.

When I told the nice nurses that I wouldn't be taking the baby home, I was giving him up for adoption, one of them took my hand and said, with tears in her eyes, "I hope we'll see you back here soon, with a good man by your side." On the fourth day, I signed a paper and the baby was removed, along with the white blanket I'd bought for him, and I went home on the MTA on another dank, cloudy day.

I ask myself now: how could I do it? The answer is easy: I did it like a zombie. I did it the way a robot would do it—or, most likely, the way Inez had done it. I hardly let myself think about it. I didn't see much choice. I could marry someone I didn't love; we'd be planning our divorce as we bought the crib and the diapers. Or I could keep that baby and raise him by myself, a prospect so ludicrous that, though I thought about it plenty, I never even proposed it to anyone—and certainly no one proposed it to me.

With good reason. Like birth control pills, the word *dysfunctional* hadn't been invented yet. I was merely a jobless, clueless, witless young woman, not really good at anything but reading books. In those days, unwed mothers were as scarce as hens' teeth and just about as socially acceptable. At times I've reproached myself for having no guts, no imagination, but at the time I felt just barely smart enough to be sure I'd make a hash out of being a mother.

I sent my son out into the world, and he prospered. Soon after I turned fifty, I hired someone to find out what had become of him. He lives in a small New England town not all that far from my small New England town. He has an Irish last name and a nice first name, though not the one I gave him. For many years, I sent him a card on his birthday, supplemented by an occasional letter: "I do not wish to intrude on your life" (not sure this was true), "just want you to know that I am here if you'd ever like to meet" (true but terrifying), "and that I deeply regret that I found it necessary to give you up when you were born" (definitely true). I sent him my website. I wrote to him with news about my writing career, so he would see how respectable I am, not some pathetic old lady trying to extort money from him. Whenever I moved I wrote him a note so that I would be findable if he ever decided he wanted to find me.

He never has. He's as enigmatic as he was in the hospital at two days old. I used to try to think of ways to force the issue, like enclosing an s.a.s.e. in one of my letters. A friend suggested I send him a check for his birthday, to see if he might cash it, or return it. Long ago, someone I know who lived not far from him hunted up his picture in the yearbook at the local high school, was able to copy it, and mailed it to me. I kept it in my handbag, and the bag was stolen in 1997 at a restaurant in St. Mark's Place. I recall his fresh young face: the chinless baby turned into a handsome lad with a winning smile that reminded me of my father's.

My son is now in his forties. The Internet tells me he has a pretty wife and two kids—I try not to think of them as my daughter-in-law and grandchildren. He has a successful business, and a house nicer than any house I've ever owned.

I read recently about an exhibit of the artifacts mothers left behind when they gave up their babies at a foundling hospital in England in the 1700s—perhaps at Handel's pet charity. An ivory carving, a button, a ring. Maybe my son still has the blanket I wrapped him in when he left, and clings to it as the only remnant of a lost mother he has no wish to see but occasionally might think about. Or maybe his adoptive parents dumped it in the trash and took him home in a blanket of their own. Maybe they never told him he was adopted. Maybe the first letter I sent him was a wrenching surprise. Maybe they told him it wasn't true. Maybe he thinks there's a very disturbed woman out there who's convinced she's his mother, poor thing.

Once, when I was living in Brooklyn, I went to the meeting of a support group for "birth mothers." I really dislike that term, though I can't articulate why. I know you can't call us *real mothers* because, of course, their real mothers are the ones who raised them. Maybe *original mother, first mother. Lost mother? Abandoner? Fuckup?*

The fact that the name for this condition bothers me is probably part of the reason I did not do well at this meeting. We had to pick a word from a wall of cards that described how we were feeling: ANGRY, SAD, RESENT-FUL, BEREFT, DESPERATE. I felt mostly RIDICU-LOUS, but that wasn't among the choices. I chose SAD. When it was my turn, I told my story. I didn't cry, just talked fast to get it over with, then sat there staring at my shoes. Nobody commented. We passed to the woman next to me. She was in tears—loud, violent tears. She had made contact with her daughter, but it hadn't gone well, they were now re-estranged, this had gone on for twenty years, she cried herself to sleep every night, sometimes she thought of suicide. People cried along with her, held her in their arms. Another woman said the inability to find her son had wrecked her life, she was unable to function, she had been divorced twice, she had no desire to have any other children, all she thought about was this baby boy. Weeping, hugs.

The prevailing feeling at the meeting—among twelve or fifteen women—was that giving up a child had grievous, disastrous, destructive effects on your life. The weeping women were stalled: until they found/ made contact with/re-established contact with/ stopped resenting the adoptive parents of/had a better relationship with their lost child, they couldn't go on. They were grieving: grieving was what they did, what defined them.

I sneaked away before the coffee hour. The truth is that I couldn't wait to get out of there. Yes, I mourn my son. Yes, I would give a very great deal to bounce his children on my knee, to talk to him about my father, my mother, his father, my daughter, my books, his business, the best way to grow peas in New England, his kids' school. I would like to tell him the family stories I've written about here.

I suspect it was something like that for Inez. She had Doris, just as I have Katherine. But Inez obviously needed to see her lost daughter, and somehow she finagled that view from the mezzanine—just as I have half a hankering to drive by my son's house and get a glimpse of him. Inez may have returned to Toledo with a feeling more of satisfaction than of grief, a sense that a book she'd been reading, then mislaid, had finally been found and the last chapter read, and now she could get on with her real life. If that's how she felt, I understand it.

Losing my son hasn't blighted my life. But I sometimes wish I could see him—just a glimpse—and wave.

Not long ago, I had lunch with two women I didn't know well—both writers, both my age—and, as we talked about our work and its relation to our lives, we realized that all three of us had gotten "in trouble" when we were young. Each of our experiences is different: one married the baby's father, the other recently reunited with the son she surrendered, and I gave up a child who wants no contact with me.

But what moved me about our conversation—aside from what an old, sad, commonplace story it is—and made it possible for me to write myself into this memoir, was the ease we all felt with our forty-year-old mistakes, and the sense we shared that time has passed, life has gone on, we've survived, and so have our children. The past is enormous, and it's getting bigger every day—a tangled jumble of events and people and feelings. When you look back on the things that went wrong in it, the hardest person to forgive is yourself. Until the three of us sat there at lunch, talking over our youthful follies, I hadn't realized that, at some point in these many years, I'd managed to do it.

The winter of 2014 continued cold and snowy, like the 1936 winter Inez described in a letter to her sister: "So much snow and ice and cold, one nearly freezes—be glad you're in California." I spent long days indoors, wrestling with my family's history—the murky bits, the painful bits, the fictionalized bits. The book was not going well. Something had been bothering me since I got the packet of photographs from Duke, and I couldn't put my finger on what it was.

Whenever the temperatures got up into the 20s (after a month or so of a New England winter, that's all one asks), I'd take Freddie out for a walk. I think better when I'm walking, and sometimes the cold air clears my head.

It was on one of those walks that I figured out the source of my uneasiness. When I left the house with the dog, the weather had been bearable, but it began to snow, a wind came up, and by the time Fred and I were struggling up the last hill the weather was pitiless. It made me think of Syracuse, and Norwood, and the mystery of why Inez had traded in one foul-winter location for another, and that's when the question came to me:

Why did Inez give my mother up for adoption?

The answer can't be simple.

I have no way of knowing how she felt about producing a bastard child at sixteen, but we can probably safely assume that, when she discovered the pickle she was in, her emotions were not primarily joy and gratitude. It's even more difficult to imagine her feelings when it happened again six years later.

She chose to have the baby, she agreed to its adoption, and then she left town. But, bruised and battered as she must have been, why didn't she return to North Baltimore with her daughter?

The photographs suggest that the Willicks were a close and loving family. They never seem really prosperous, but, unlike my mother's adoptive family, they don't seem destitute. Inez was nearly twenty-two, not a teenager; she had always worked, and could have supported her baby. Maggie and Jacob were raising Doris—so, presumably, were not closed to the idea of taking in a child Inez gave birth to. Inez knew first-hand the joys of keeping your child instead of relinquishing it to strangers: she and Doris were close all their lives. And she kept a photo of baby Geraldine "in her bosom," according to the Norwood trial transcript. It's not a stretch to conclude that she gave her up with reluctance. Much is unknown, but I simply don't believe that her parents—though they may have been upset, mortified, even furious with her—would not have welcomed Inez and her baby girl into the family. Inez's decision is one of the puzzles of her life that I've been unable to solve.

But, as I wondered about it, I became aware of something else that was gnawing at me. It had never occurred to me before, but once it did, I knew that it was the most disturbing part of the whole narrative of Inez and Geraldine and, finally, of myself.

After many years, I've been able to accept my decision to give up my son, but that acceptance hinges on my acknowledging not only what an immature, mixed-up young woman I was, but also on what a small support system I could call on. My family consisted of one person—my mother—whose only proposed solution to the problem was a shotgun wedding to remove the "stigma of illegitimacy."

But my mother, in fact, had no direct experience of that stigma. She wasn't raised by a single mother, wasn't taunted by schoolmates or siblings. No one knew she was a bastard child. She herself didn't find it out until she was an adult, and for many years she told no one except my father.

Of course, such things can seem wrong even without personal experience of them. But I think that, at the bottom of the general disapproval, what really bothered my mother—soaked as she was in religion and orthodox morality—was the cause of the illegitimacy: sex outside of marriage.

She herself lived a life of sexual rectitude. It is doubtless an accurate assumption that my father was the only man she ever went to bed with. She was a good daughter of the Church, and also highly conventional. It would have been unthinkable for her to sit down with me during that fraught Christmas in Boston and plan a way to cope with my pregnancy. She was unable to suggest I come home as a single mother (the term wasn't even in use yet) to raise the child under the eyes of my Catholic relatives—the nun aunts, my Pepsi grandfather, the hordes of chaste and churchgoing cousins—not because of the stigma of illegitimacy but because of the stigma of having people know her daughter—like Mom's own mother—was a wanton and a sinner.

She and I came from different generations, and, like many people her age, my mother was dismayed by the social changes of the '60s. She could not have understood that what I felt wasn't chagrin at being caught having sex before marriage, or even having sex with someone I had no real intention of marrying. Those were not among the urgent concerns of the time. Aside from the pain of having to break the news to my mother and hide it from my relatives, my feelings were more angry than anything else—partly at the workings of fate, but mostly at myself for being so stupid and careless.

I can't blame my mother for my failure to keep my child and raise him. I was willful and self-destructive; my mother was the victim of the oppressive narrowness[5] of

---

[5]   This eloquently economical phrase is George Eliot's, from chapter two of *The Mill on the Floss*, describing the environment in which her heroine is raised.

her own background and beliefs. And it was a long time ago—there are probably ingredients in this stew that I can't make my memory stretch back to. But I can call up the feeling of abandonment. I was a wretchedly immature twenty-three-year-old. I wanted my mother to make everything all right. And she wouldn't.

Now, almost half a century later, I study the pictures of Inez. I reread her letter, with its loving, sensitive voice. And, even though I'm writing myself out of the picture, it's hard not to wish—or almost wish—that my mother had been raised in North Baltimore by the Willicks instead of in Syracuse by the Goodsons. How much easier her life would have been if she had grown up surrounded by the love of a single mother and an extended family rather than oppressed by the negligence of two parents and the inhumanity of her religious upbringing.

But I can't squeeze any sense out of it. Why didn't Inez just take the kid, get on a train, and go home? Instead, she went to Norwood, got pregnant again by the first jerk who came along, and married him.

PART VII

LEAVETAKING

June 1913
Syracuse, New York

"I will miss your sour cherry tart," she says to Frances. "And I will miss your jokes in the kitchen."

What they mean is that they will miss each other.

Tim Devlin pulls up in the jitney bus and stows her luggage by the front seat—the sturdy old brown bag from North Baltimore and a handsome travel satchel trimmed in leather, a gift from the staff at her goodbye party. Mrs. Anderson's suitcase from Syracuse is now in the Norwood dump.

She hands Tim her nickel, but he waves it away. "I don't want your money, Agnes."

She shrugs and turns to Frances. "I hope everything will go well for you," she says. "Always."

"You take care of yourself, my girl."

"I will try."

"Maybe you'll find somebody to take care of you instead."

Agnes makes a face. "I'm better off taking care of myself."

Frances laughs. Tim climbs into the driver's seat and stares impassively out the windshield.

"No other passengers, Tim?"

"The chariot is all for yourself this morning."

"Well, then." Suddenly Agnes is flustered. "I guess I'm really going, Frances."

"It appears so," Frances says and takes her hand. "Though Stanley and I wish you weren't."

"Tell Stanley . . ."

Frances nods, smiling. "I will."

"And don't forget about Betty and the coat."

"I will not."

"I hope it will fit her."

Frances says. "Don't worry about a thing. Just write to us. Hear?"

"I will, I will."

Tim says, "If you want to make that train."

The two women embrace, Agnes climbs in. She turns around to wave. The bus pulls away, and she sits looking at the back of her ex-father-in-law's head.

"Will you be glad to see the end of us, then, Agnes?" he asks.

She thinks for a minute before she answers. She has been in Norwood for nearly three years, and she tries to come up with some regretful thing to say to Tim Devlin. But finally, all she can do is be honest: "I suppose I will, Tim," and then they turn the corner and pull up at the depot.

Her seatmate slams the window shut. "Still can't get used to the filth," he says. "Although I've traveled all the way across the country and back on these things. How about you? You ride the railroad much?"

"This is only my third time."

"Is that a fact."

He's a smiling man about her age, overweight and already balding, and she knows he wants to while away the time with conversation. She is tempted to ask him some questions about riding the train across the country; her sister Helen and her husband are planning to move with their family—four children now—out to California, where Roger has been offered a ministry. In her last letter, Helen said they're debating the merits of buying an automobile and driving out West versus going by rail.

But instead Agnes smiles vaguely and turns her head toward the window. They will be in Syracuse in just over three hours.

She wishes she could sleep; she'd lain awake the night before long past midnight. But she keeps thinking about Tim's question. She's twenty-five: three years is a whole eighth of her life—or a ninth? A lot, anyway. It would be a sad thing, to remember those years as nothing but a waste. Or not even a waste: more like a descent into hell, she thinks. And then chides herself: *Do not be melodramatic*.

And the hell was only the first year. Things settled down after a while. She makes a list of the good things. Her co-workers, Betty and Alice and Richard. Old Mrs. Devlin, who was so unexpectedly kind to her that day in the post office when she opened the letter about Grandma Lu and Uncle Clem, dead within two months of each other. And Mr. Dumont, when he came to town in *The Mikado* and took her and Betty out to dinner in Potsdam. The beautiful walk out Spring Street to the river and over the bridge. Mrs. Carver at the library.

And, at the top of the list, Frances and her husband, Stanley. Frances is like a sister to her now, and Stanley— she had been half in love with Stan Clury almost from the day she met him. "How lucky you are," she told Frances late one evening when they were having a whiskey together after the dining room closed. "If I ever find a man like Stanley, I'll wish for nothing more." By which she meant someone as good-hearted as Rudy Killian and as handsome and smart as Jesse Zorn, but a better man than either of them.

"Give it time," Frances said. "There are plenty of men in this world, and my Stan can't be the only one who's not a cad."

"Or a nincompoop."

"Or a bounder."

"Or a complete chowderhead."

They got laughing so hard they couldn't stop. Remembering it now, Agnes smiles out the window. *Jesse Zorn and Mike Devlin*, she thinks. Two extremes on some scale or other. *And me in the middle.*

In more than three years, she has never heard a word from Jesse. By now he'd be in law school, or out in the world making his mark, or married to a girl so rich he could pay his own way without a second thought. Agnes still can't remember him without pain, though knowing Stan Clury has helped ease it. She is warmed by the fact that she had felt something for him, even though he was unavailable, another woman's husband. At least that part of her is not dead.

As for Michael Devlin—well, there was a cad and a nincompoop rolled into one! She'd fallen into his arms because he had a pretty face and because he wanted her and because her unhappiness terrified her: her loneliness without baby Anna, without Jesse, without the comfort of Mr. Carmody and Mr. Dumont. Even without the nuns and the hospital—she'd become used to it there, working in the garden, singing the Catholic hymns in the kitchen with Sister Elberta.

But there was Mike with his shock of black hair and his weak, ingratiating face, claiming it was love at first sight when he spotted her in her white apron at the hotel, with her curls escaping from under her cap. *You were like a goddess,* he said. He'd come in with his father for dinner and gaped dumbly at Agnes while she waited on them. She was reminded of Rudy, though Mike hadn't the wit to make her laugh. It was his father who'd done all the talking, turning on the Irish charm as he did with any woman he met, Mike shining in the glow of it.

She'd married Mike because she was in the family way—as Frances had put it when Agnes confided her story, "Your fecundity is almost uncanny"—but also because of his father's money. That is the hard truth. She had hoped to have enough to somehow ransom Anna—a mad idea, no doubt, but now she has her own money, a wad of bills tucked down in her purse, and the idea continues to lodge at the back of her mind as she rides the train to Syracuse.

She dozes off and is jolted awake by the conductor announcing they've arrived: "SAIR-acuse." Her wrist-watch tells her it's just past noon. She gets off with the jostling crowd and is immediately overwhelmed. After her years in Norwood, she's forgotten what a city is like, and the station seems enormous, with its people and carts and noise, a bell dinging somewhere, a sign made out of electric bulbs reading: TICKETS.

Her heart is pounding. She sinks down on a bench in the vaulted waiting room. It's been a long time since breakfast; she knows she'd better stop somewhere for a sandwich. During her health troubles of two years ago, her usual energy and stamina deserted her, and they've been slow coming back.

But she doesn't dare sit for long. She feels a sense of urgency that may or may not be justified: she has no idea whether they're more likely to be home now or later. She hurries to the ladies' restroom, where, seeing herself in a mirror over the marble sink, she washes her sooty face, shakes out her skirts and tucks in her blouse, which is no longer crisp and white. She tidies her hair as well as she can and pins on her hat. A woman beside her is putting on lipstick, and Agnes rummages in her bag for hers: she is still nervous about applying it—"Just a little," Frances told her when she gave her a tube for Christmas. "Don't make your mouth look like a slab of raw beef"—but she brushes on a light coat of carmine. It does brighten her appearance. Has Olive Webster taken to wearing lipstick, she wonders, and at the thought of confronting Olive she feels almost faint. She touches the locket around her neck. *Stay calm.* A cup of coffee will help.

She retrieves her travel case from the baggage claim and leaves it in one of the dime lockers in the station. She finds her way to the café, where she orders an egg salad sandwich and coffee. The overnight train to Toledo doesn't leave until 5:00. She consults her watch again. She has plenty of time. She knows she needs to relax. She forces herself to eat slowly, and she accepts a second cup of coffee when the waitress offers it.

When she emerges from the station onto Montgomery Street, she feels better. It's a warm afternoon, and she takes off her hat. The sun feels good beating down on her head. She realizes she should have reapplied the lipstick. But no matter. Who will care how she looks?

She walks north, and pins her hat on again when she turns the corner at James Street, named after the grandfather of Henry James, which Mr. Carmody called "the Fifth Avenue of Syracuse." She can't think of Henry James without remembering *Portrait of a Lady*, which Betty had checked out of the tiny Norwood library for Agnes to read during the month she spent in bed. Her fury at Isabel Archer's inability to leave her faithless, sadistic husband had been wonderfully distracting.

Every woman she passes is fashionably dressed, every man is elegant. Agnes has a fleeting urge to cash in her ticket and stay in Syracuse—just settle down, finally, in a nice city. How beautiful it is, the grand houses and the elm trees and the wide paved street. Mr. Carmody would help her find work. Until then, she could live on the money she's saved. Find an apartment, a little place to call her own.

She leaves the mansions behind, turns left on Highland Street to the corner of Willow, where she comes to her senses. She will not be stopping in Syracuse.

She's not tempted to walk by Mrs. Anderson's rooming house. She keeps going on Highland—it's paved now, with cobblestones, and she counts six automobiles parked before she gets to number six-five-six. She looks at her watch: the walk has taken her less than half an hour. She looks up at the windows: the Websters' apartment is in front, on the left, second floor. She was there only once, but she remembers it so well: the unmade bed, the Jesus on the wall, the wedding photograph. She pulls her eyeglasses out of her bag and puts them on.

From the street, she can deduce nothing. She's not even sure they still live there, although, with her glasses on, she thinks she recognizes the checkered curtains. She imagines her Anna living up there with Olive and Clarence, drinking milk from a bottle, learning to walk and talk—the baby who is now three years old. She is unable to properly imagine this, remembering Anna's sparse hair and the one little curl. She crosses the cobblestones, walks up the steps and goes in. There's a smell of cooking in the narrow hallway. She climbs the stairs to the second-floor landing and knocks.

The door swings open, and it's Olive, in a flowered house dress with the sleeves rolled up. "Hello," Agnes says. "I was passing through town and thought I'd stop by." She has rehearsed this, but, even though what she says is true, it sounds unconvincing.

Olive just stares. Her hair is untidy. The circles under her eyes look slightly darker. Agnes ventures a smile. "How are you, Olive?" she asks, which sounds even worse.

Olive blinks and says, "Well, of all the people I expected to see when I opened this door, you are the last."

"And yet here I am," Agnes says. "Do you think I could come in for a few minutes?"

They sit at the kitchen table, as they had before. There are no flowers this time, but Agnes recognizes the salt-and-pepper shakers, shaped like cats. The sink is heaped with dirty dishes.

"You wear eyeglasses now," Olive says.

"I don't need them when I read, only for distances."

"Clarence had to get them too. He got them cheap through the railway company. I think I told you he's a motorman on the trolley."

"Yes, you did tell me. How is he?"

"He's fine." Olive purses and unpurses her lips, looking at Agnes's blouse, her wristwatch, her hat. "So you've been up there in Norwood all this time."

"Yes. But now I'm on my way back to Ohio."

"Well, it must have been pretty cold and snowy up north there. Probably a lot like Oswego, where I come from."

Agnes nods. "The winters in Norwood were very hard."

Olive is different in some way Agnes can't put her finger on. A few years older, but not just that. Less sure of herself. Tired, maybe. "Why are you in town?" she asks.

"I just wondered how Anna is." Agnes can hardly get the words out. She can see no sign of a baby.

"Well. I suppose you would, wouldn't you?"

"She's here?"

"Where else would she be?" Olive seems genuinely amused. "She's having her nap. She's three years old now."

"I know that."

There's another silence, uncomfortably long. Agnes is afraid that, at any minute, she may begin to cry. It's harder than she'd expected to sit in this kitchen, to watch Olive's hard brown eyes watching her.

"Well, all right!" Olive seems suddenly to make up her mind to something. "I'll get her. I want you to see her before you go back to Ohio. How big she's gotten. What a good girl she is."

"Oh, don't wake her up," Agnes protests, but Olive is halfway to the bedroom. Once she's alone, Agnes takes the opportunity to breathe deeply, breathe away the sob that had been rising in her chest. *She's all right, she's here, she's just down for her nap.* What had she thought? She takes off her hat and realizes that her hands are trembling.

In a minute Olive returns, carrying a little girl, who yawns and rubs her eyes and starts to cry a little.

"Shush now," Olive says. "There's a lady here who wants to meet you." The child hides her head in Olive's shoulder. "She's a nice lady," Olive says. "She won't hurt you." She settles Anna on her lap so that she's facing Agnes. "See? Isn't she a nice lady?"

Agnes looks into Anna's blue eyes. *My daughter,* she thinks, but it's like something from a dream, an idea she can't quite grasp. "Hello there, Anna. My name is Agnes."

Anna says, faintly, "Hello."

Olive bounces her on her knees. "Speak up, child. You can talk louder than that."

Anna says "Hello" more loudly and continues to look at Agnes in a way that reminds her of her sister Helen, the same unblinking stare.

"I've come to visit you," Agnes says. "I came on the railroad, from a long way away."

"Tell the lady what a good little girl you are. Say: I'm a good girl! Show her what a good talker you are."

Anna frowns, and Agnes smiles. "You don't have to tell me, Anna. I can see what a good girl you are."

Anna has the same tentative smile she had when she was an infant. The smile and the steady gaze. She's tiny like Doris. She has Jesse's light brown hair, cut like his in bangs. Agnes wants to touch her—to put her hand for a second on her head. The warmth there as she used to lay her cheek against it is her most potent memory. She remembers when the nuns thought Anna would die, and the day she slept, woke, and began to nurse, as if she'd waked from a dream that told her she must live.

"It looks like a nice day out there," Olive says into the lengthening silence. "Not too hot. Maybe we could go to the park."

Agnes says, "What a lovely idea." Anna's face brightens.

Olive takes Anna with her into the bedroom while she changes her clothes. Agnes sits at the table, then gets up and walks to the mantel. Among a scattering of knick-knacks and a heap of embroidery floss, the wedding portrait is still there: handsome Clarence sitting stiffly in a fancy chair, Olive in a lacy gown, tightly corseted, standing to one side, her hand on his shoulder. Olive wears her usual shadowed, discontented look. Agnes has no picture from her own wedding—and just as well, she thinks: that freezing March afternoon when she was so sick and so desperate, even then feeling the baby dying within her. That baby had never felt right. A boy, Frances told her when she asked. Badly deformed.

If she could be hypnotized and make those first months of 1911 disappear out of her life, she'd do it, beginning with Mike Devlin and ending with the letter about Uncle Clem coughing himself to death in his cold attic.

Olive emerges with her hair put up neatly, wearing a shirtwaist with a pin at the neck and a striped skirt. She has put on a touch of lipstick. She's carrying a box camera in one hand; Anna holds the other. "Maybe you could take our picture at the park. I don't have a photo of us two together."

Agnes says she would be glad to take their picture. Olive puts a hat on Anna and ties it under her chin. The hat is too big, and her little face peers out from under the brim. Agnes takes the camera while Olive carries Anna down the stairs, panting a little when they reach the street. During the walk to Schiller Park, Olive holds Anna's hand with her right, and Agnes walks on her left. The child has to skip to keep up, and once nearly stumbles. "Maybe she could walk between us?" Agnes asks. "If I held her other hand . . ."

"She's all right." Olive says curtly, but she slows down a little. "Tell me about that Norwood place. What did you do up there?"

I got pregnant, but I lost the baby. I got married, but I got rid of the husband. I was very sick, but I got better. I fell in love, but he was already taken.

"I was a waitress at a hotel," she says.

"You must like being a waitress. I could never do it, I don't have the strength for that line of work. Clarence says I might be anemic. He thinks I should go to see the doctor. But we don't have money for things like that. I try to rest a lot, but it's not easy with a little one in the house. Always needing something." She gives Agnes another appraising look. "I'll bet you had trouble with the men. That's what I wouldn't like about it, all those strangers when you wait on tables. Did they give you a hard time? Or maybe you didn't mind that."

"They didn't give me a hard time."

"The other thing I'd worry about is germs, picking up those dirty plates and things."

"I didn't have to do that. We had a busboy."

"A what? Well, I never heard of that before! You mean you'd give them their food, and then somebody else took away the dirty dishes? I suppose that makes sense, but of course they'd have to get paid to do it. Must have been a fancy place, to lay out that kind of money. Did you make a good wage, if you don't mind me asking?"

"Good enough."

"Well, I should hope so."

When they get to the park entrance, Olive says she doesn't think Anna can walk all the way up to what she calls "our bench." Agnes says she wouldn't mind carrying her, but Olive ignores the offer. She surprises Agnes by sitting down on the grass, folding her legs under her skirt, and pulling Anna down beside her. "This is fine."

"Shall I take the photo?" Agnes asks. "Before we forget."

"Go ahead." Olive pulls Anna's skirt over her knees. "Smile and look at the lady," she says. Agnes notices that she hasn't yet called Anna by her name. Also that Anna has said nothing since "Hello."

Agnes ventures, "Maybe we could take it without the hat?"

"Too much sun is bad for children. She's very delicate." She pushes the hat up a little. Then she reaches her arm behind the child, as if to steady her. Agnes takes off her glasses, peers through the viewfinder, puts them on again. Olive says, "You just look through the hole and then push that lever down on the side. Make sure to hold it steady."

"I know how. I've done it before."

"Well, you seemed confused." Olive is irritable. Maybe her own generosity is burdensome to her: a walk to the park, the long minutes she's allowed Agnes with Anna.

Agnes looks over the top of the Brownie. "Anna? Can you give me a nice smile?"

The smile returns. By the time Agnes centers the two of them in the viewfinder and pushes the release lever, it has faded again, but the child's expression is alert and winsome. It's Olive she wants to say "Smile" to: her face is impassive, almost angry, and doesn't change.

Agnes snaps pictures until Olive says, "That's enough, I don't want to use up all the film."

Agnes sits down with them on the grass. Anna's attention is caught by a flowerbed in the near distance— bright reds and pinks against the green grass—but her gaze keeps returning to Agnes, the lady who came to see her on the railroad. Does she know what a railroad is? Agnes wants to speak to the child, get her to talk, but she can't think what to say. She's suffering from the wrenching need to pick her up and hold her, touch her tiny hand—anything. Instead, she asks, "How are things, Olive? How have these years been for you? Is it—" She spreads her hands helplessly. The situation is so odd, but it may be all she will ever have, and she needs to squeeze something from it. "Everything you hoped?"

"I'm not sure you should ask me that," Olive says. Of course she is right. It's none of Agnes's business. But that's not what Olive means. "You were going to come back in six months. Not that I wanted you to. But I wondered why you changed your mind."

"I didn't change my mind!" Agnes crosses her hands over her heart and breathes deeply, as Frances taught her to during those bad months. *Breathe, breathe, it will help you stay calm.* "I meant to come back," she says after a minute, keeping her voice low and even. "But I was not well in January. I wasn't able to come. I wrote to the lawyer in March."

"Fogarty."

"Yes. Mr. Fogarty. I told him I'd been ill, and asked him if it was too late, could I still come to Syracuse and—"

She breaks off, and Olive finishes for her: "And take her away from us."

"I suppose that was the idea. He didn't answer my letter." She doesn't say that she wrote four letters, and that he answered none of them.

"I'm not surprised," Olive says. "He had no business answering a letter like that."

The little girl picks up a twig and waves it in the air, hits it against the grass. Was she listening? Was she bored? Was she happy?

"She's not always good like this," Olive says. "She keeps me busy, believe me."

"That's what you wanted. To be kept busy."

"That's right." Olive gives her a sharp look. "You have a good memory."

Agnes says, "She's a darling child."

Watching Anna with her twig—does she have toys, does anyone ever make her laugh, is she loved, is she sung to—Agnes wants her daughter back more than she's ever wanted anything. Now, after half an hour with her, Anna is so recognizably her child, so thoroughly the baby she handed over to a nun in the lawyer's office, it seems the child must feel it too, and know Agnes is her mother. She imagines snatching her up and running off with her, and Anna relaxing in her arms, smiling up at her, patting her cheek, saying "Mama."

Agnes tries to think of the right words to say, the best way to offer Olive the money she's brought with her, and suddenly she knows she can't say it, she can't tempt her, because she's afraid Olive will take it. The horror of that is not something she can be responsible for. She sits there staring down at Anna's little boots, her gray stockings, the twig she's trying to poke into the hard earth. Agnes is conscious that she's learned something about herself, but half-wishes she hadn't.

Olive speaks suddenly to the child. "You like those pretty flowers over there, don't you? There's some pink ones. See? You like pink." Anna smiles and claps her hands. "Maybe the nice lady could walk you over there and look at them with you. Maybe if you're good she'd let you pick one."

Anna looks at Agnes and says, "Flowers!"

"Well." Agnes gets to her feet and smooths her skirt. "I wish I had time, but I'd better get going if I expect to catch my train." She picks up her bag and hooks it over her shoulder. "Thanks for this pleasant afternoon, Olive. I wish you well."

Before she can change her mind, she turns and strides to the park gates, walking fast, knowing Olive's puzzled eyes are on her. Out on the street, she slows down and, when she gets to the corner, she stands in the shade for a minute or two, watching a wagon go by, pulled by a horse wearing a straw hat. Two women pass, talking about a pair of new shoes. From the next street, she hears the clang of the trolley car.

Breathe, breathe. There's no hurry, the Toledo train won't leave for nearly three hours. She'll find a table in the café and have another cup of coffee and maybe a slice of cake. Thank goodness she's brought a book with her.

EPILOGUE

This book isn't about getting to a destination,
it's about taking a journey.
~Uncle Clem

During that same Christmas season that my mother begged me to marry a man I didn't love, Inez was dying. Age seventy-eight, she took a bad fall, passed out, was hospitalized, and died soon after.

However, as with so much of her life, the truth is not clear. There are conflicting versions of what happened. Several letters between Mary Fay and John—Inez's two remaining siblings, both elderly and far off in California—discuss the event. In one account, John hears from Doris's husband (Doris had died two years earlier, age sixty) that Inez is in the hospital: "She has no broken bones, but she is badly bruised, especially in the face." In a niece's version, she falls, is taken to the hospital in an "emergency car," and is dead on arrival. Her death certificate gives the official cause as an aortic aneurism, compounded by arteriosclerosis. She was buried in North Baltimore, Ohio, the town where she was born.

I've pursued this grandmother, with her stubborn Ohio roots and her convoluted love life, about as far as I can go. Admittedly, I haven't consulted a psychic, prayed, or made the pilgrimage to her hometown, but I think I've come to the end of what there is to know.

She's an odd kind of grandmother, unaware that she ever had a granddaughter, but at the end of my quest I feel close to her in a way I didn't anticipate when I began it. I look at her face and see nothing of myself there. She didn't bequeath to me her curly hair or her buxom figure. But I think I've inherited her resilience—passed down through my mother—and a tenacity that kept me plodding along on this journey, begun so many years ago with nothing but a name and a city and the fleeting sight of a woman in glasses looking down from a mezzanine at her daughter.

AFTERWARD

A mong the many joys of writing fiction is the minor but not negligible delight of choosing characters' names. I still rely on a battered paperback called *Name Your Baby*[1] that I acquired in the early '70s. I also use phone books, mastheads of magazines, bibliographies, and an elementary school graduation program I picked up on the street years ago in Brooklyn, with a slew of multicultural handles I wouldn' t dare use, like Nanacaterina Goldstein, Sumo Arefino, and Sofia-Marie Sharing Roggeveen.

I prefer not to name my characters after people I'm close to, or ex-husbands, or old spelling-bee rivals from eighth grade, or anyone who might sue me. I don't give two characters similar names, lest the reader mix them up. Nor do I use names that are hard to pronounce or that look confusing on the page. I don't like names that might be construed as symbolic of anything.

In this book, since so many of the fictional characters are based on their real-life counterparts, my pickiness had to rise to even greater heights. Names had to not only fulfill all the usual criteria but be true to the people they represent, some of whom are my relatives.

Inez, my grandmother, was the easiest: the Anglicized form of her name, Agnes, seemed inevitable. It's also a name I particularly like, and it was a standard baby name in 1888, when Inez/Agnes was born.

---

[1] By a woman with the delightfully improbable name Larcina Rule.

I converted her family name, Willick, into the off-rhyming Miller, which is a family name on both the Frick and the Strawbridge sides, and also the surname of the heroine of my second novel, so I had a soft spot for it.

Then there was Inez's sister Mary Fay. I went to Catholic school with a trove of Mary Pats, Mary Alices, Mary Helens, Mary Kays, Mary Janes. I was born Mary Ann Katherine.[2] I had never heard the name Mary Fay, which seemed an exotic turn on the Mary-plus syndrome, and I would have been glad to use it. But when she turned out to be Cousin Duke's grandmother, I felt she needed some distancing: hence the neutral Sally, which seemed to evoke a sassy little sister. Two other Willick sisters, the twins Maud and Mabel, morphed easily into Helen and Hazel—I know very little about them, so, writing about them, I gave my imagination free rein. As for the boys, I let poor Charlie Willick (the one who drowned as a boy) keep his name.[3] The surviving brothers, Ralph and John, are now Robert and Sam, both names drawn from Willick history. (Few 19th-century family trees lack Roberts and Samuels among their leaves.)

It wasn't easy to transform Maggie Willick into Bessie Miller—but the Maggie/Aggie rhyme was distracting, and when I changed Maggie it seemed only fair to change Jacob too, so he is Gilbert, and his brother Lewis is Clement: Uncle Clem, of whom I'm only slightly less fond than his niece Agnes is.

---

[2] By the time I was a teenager, my name, for some reason, didn't feel right, and when a friend of mine seized on Katherine and dubbed me Kitty—which was also my father's mother's nickname—I ran with it. Kitty Burns was compact and comfortable.

[3] He was Charles Raymond, and usually called Ray, even in the harrowing account of his drowning in the local paper ("He sank for the third time, feebly beating the water with his hands as he disappeared beneath the surface…"). . . . ").

I decided not to rechristen Inez's first daughter, Doris, though in her fictional incarnation she's nearly always called Dorrie (or Agnes's fanciful "Little Dorrit"). Grandma Lucinda Frick Willick has merely lost a couple of syllables: to her grandkids, she's Grandma Lu. Cousin Clay, that off-stage but imposing figure, had to remain himself.

Olive and Clarence Webster struck me as better names for the characters than their real-life ones, Cora and Horace Goodson.

Some of the North Baltimore names are real: Emma Bartz, Edith Mercer, and Louise Adams came from the pages of a history of the town supplied by the estimable North Baltimore Historical Society. Agnes's Latin teacher, Mr. Phelps, shares a name with my mother's high school Latin teacher, a reference Mom would appreciate if she were still around. The names of other North Baltimoreans—Archie Sweet, Virgil Bendix, Mrs. Ober and her pig Swiney, Miss Truitt the librarian— were devised during long walks on the Norwottuck Trail near my house in Amherst.[4] Rudy Killian came alive for me as soon as I christened him. To me, the name of Jesse Lyman Zorn, my fictional grandfather, has the proper period sound, but was probably influenced by the ambiguous Jesse Pinkman, my favorite character on *Breaking Bad*, which I was watching while I was working on this book.[5]

Zorn is a North Baltimore name, but the Zorn glassworks is a fabrication, though there were other glassworks

---

[4] My walks on the rail-trail with the dog are the equivalent of Uncle Clem's "thinking walks" around his back yard (which really were inspired by Darwin).

[5] Junkie and murderer though he is, Jesse Pinkman could teach Jesse Zorn a few things about honor and kindness.

in the area. Deter's grocery was an actual establishment, along with Hoffman's drugstore, the opera house that burned down in 1911, and Ellis's, site of Agnes's first waitressing job.

As for Agnes herself—lively, book-loving, reckless, odd, romantic—she's the grandmother I hope I had. I've modeled her to some degree on my mother, though perhaps on the gutsier, more broad-minded woman Mom might have been had she been raised differently. But I've given her my mother's optimism and brightness of spirit. The indifference to religion, the desire to get out of the town she was born in, and of course the bookishness—those come directly from me. Because why should I not have gotten them from her?

My fictional grandfather, Jesse Lyman Zorn, was created from a mix of wishful thinking (he's handsome, smart, ambitious) and the plain and unhappy truth (he fathered two children and revealed his true caddishness). I wish he had been less irresponsible, more mature, less selfish. But then the history of Agnes and her baby would have been very different, and it would be somebody else's story—not Inez's.

Still, I wanted my grandmother to have some happiness in her life, and I couldn't leave out love, however imperfect, however doomed.

ACKNOWLEDGEMENTS

For help with research, I wish to thank Tim Donahue and Tony Nocerino in Norwood; Paula Dean, Tom Boltz, and Millie Broka in Ohio; and especially Margaret Dube, whose genealogical investigations and insights were vital.

Thanks to the librarians at the Onondaga County Historical Society, to the curators at the Frick Museum, and to Don Crossett for escorting me around Syracuse and pointing me in various useful directions.

The Encyclopedia of Adoption, by Christine A. Adamec and Laurie C. Miller (Facts on File, 2006) was full of useful information, as was *Henry Clay Frick: An Intimate Portrait* by Martha Frick Symington Sanger (Abbeville Press, 1999), who very kindly answered some questions.

I'm immensely grateful to my Amherst writer friends: Susan Snively's sensitivity to words helped me navigate through many a swamp of overwriting; Dixie Brown and Mickey Rathbun provided close, thoughtful, and patient readings of the manuscript, and bountiful good advice. Then there are my perennials: thanks to Jane Schwartz and Pat O'Donnell; to Karen Kleinerman, who designed the family trees and the map; to Carl Rubino, who helped with the Latin (any errata are due solely to my own overconfidence and haste); and to my indispensable daughter, Katherine Florey, who across 3,000 miles held my hand through much of the research and writing of this book.

My thanks also to Jean Stone for copy editing and to Linda Roghaar for just about everything else.

And a special thank-you to my newly found cousin, Duke Hingley, for the photographs of the Willicks and much more.

NOTES

A lice Munro's statement on page 3, which so perfectly encapsulates my search for my grandmother, was quoted endlessly when Munro was awarded the Nobel Prize in Literature in 2013. It was also cited in an essay by Jonathan Franzen in his 2012 book of essays, *Farther Away*, as being from "one of her rare interviews." But nowhere is the source given.

The Linda Pastan poem, "Warm Front," quoted on page 199, is from her book *A Fraction of Darkness* (1985).

The article by David Bromwich quoted on page 201 appeared in the August 15, 2013, issue *New York Review of Books*.

Louise Gluck's poem "Fugue," quoted on page 211, is from her book *Averno* (2006).

Janet Malcolm's essay "Thoughts on Autobiography from an Abandoned Autobiography," from which I have quoted on page 245, has been collected in her book *Forty-One False Starts* (2013).

The illustration on page 246 from *Nancy Keeps House*, first published in 1947 by World Publishing Co., is by an illustrator known only as Sari. I have been unable to find out anything about her. I regret that I was unable to get permission to reproduce her work and would be grateful to hear from Sari or her descendants.

INDEX

Photo by Turi MacCombie

K itty Burns Florey is a native of Syracuse. She has lived in Boston, Brooklyn, and New Haven, and is now happily settled in Amherst, Massachusetts. She is the author of eleven novels, many essays and short stories, and two works of nonfiction: *Sister Bernadette's Barking Dog: The Quirky History and Lost Art of Diagramming Sentences* and *Script and Scribble: The Rise and Fall of Hand-writing*. Her most recent book is a historical novel, *The Writing Master*.